OUTRAGE, THE FINAL STRAW

Signe A. Dayhoff, PhD

Outrage, The Final Straw
By Signe A. Dayhoff, PhD

Copyright © 2020 by Signe A. Dayhoff, PhD
Published by Effectiveness-Plus Publications LLC
80 Paseo de San Antonio
Placitas, New Mexico 87043-8735

Cover Illustration by eduardlang@fiverr.com
Cover by http://www.bookclaw.com

ISBN: 978-0-9985324-3-1

DEDICATION

This book is dedicated to animal lovers everywhere who continue to help protect animals in every way possible despite their outrage, despair, and ongoing frustration at the overwhelming instances of organizational, institutional, and individual animal abuse. As animal advocates, you sign petitions; call and write to legislators, corporations, and universities; walk or run for animals; make donations; volunteer at homeless animal shelters and adoption clinics; participate in rescuing the abandoned and hurt; and foster and adopt these animals. You are not only heroes for all you do but also are *superheroes*.

This is especially dedicated to those of you who in your darkest moments have wished you could somehow avenge the abuse of these animals, to physically "get even." But, to your credit, you haven't. You still do the moral, ethical, and legal "right" things—instead of what's expedient or darkly satisfying. You do the slow, hard work of education, enlightenment, and inspiration that incrementally helps accomplish all your animal protection goals.

Never forget that the true test of *animal champions*—not necessarily Caped Crusaders or Marvel Superheroes—is whether you can overcome the obstacles created by others, as well as your outrage and vengeful thoughts, in order to achieve each small triumph.

Hopefully there will come a time when humans will look upon animal neglect, abuse, and murder as they now look upon the human neglect, abuse, and murder. With that in mind, I thank you as animal lovers/activists/advocates for all you do and continue to do.

ACKNOWLEDGMENTS

The author wishes to acknowledge the assistance of Dr. Jennifer Smith, DMV, who shared her name, medical expertise, and her Red Irish Setter "Maiti" with this book. And Dr. Barbara Bayer, president of the no-kill, all-volunteer, non-profit Companion Animal Rescue and Medical Assistance (CARMA) in Corrales, New Mexico, for sharing her name and her organization as well with this novel. Both Drs. Smith and Bayer, as professionals and caring, compassionate individuals, are *invaluable* for all they do for animals. Thank you. You're the best!

§ § §

"We need, in a special way, to work twice as hard to help people understand that animals are fellow creatures, that we must protect them and love them as we love ourselves." – Cesar Chavez

"If you really care about animals, then stop trying to figure out how to exploit them 'compassionately'. Just stop exploiting them." – Gary L. Franchione

"One of the most dangerous things that can happen to a child is to kill or torture an animal and not be held responsible for it." – Margaret Mead

"I am in favor of animal rights as well as human rights. That is the way of a whole human being." – Abraham Lincoln

"The idea that some lives matter less is the root of all that is wrong with the world." – Paul Farmer

"The greatness of a nation and its moral progress can be judged by the way its animals are treated." – Mohandas K. Gandhi

PROLOGUE

According to American writer Sigrid Nunez, "Innocence is something we humans pass through and leave behind, unable to return. But animals live and die in that state, and seeing innocence violated in the form of cruelty to a mere duck can seem like the most barbaric act in the world."

When we departed the womb, despite being suddenly adrift in the cold confusion and helplessness of reality, we all began to develop such high expectations for the world around us, from universal love and justice being our due to seeing ourselves as at one with the environment and Nature. In my early childhood's innocence, I believed that most humans embraced and respected animals, that they saw them as being a fabulous array of beings which likewise shared the Earth, its resources, and the right to live unfettered. But time and experience whittled away most of those luminous presumptions, leaving only a tangential, hopeful glimmer behind.

When I first began hearing about animal brutality, in my naïveté I believed it was an aberration, that only a handful of evil people hurt animals or took their lives just because they wanted to. However, when I was five years old and my father took me fishing in Maiden Creek near where we lived in Leesport, Pennsylvania, I saw an earthworm writhing on the hook that had been thrust clear through its body ... twice. I felt bad about the poor creature. And the caught catfish that were flapping their gills, struggling to breathe in a partially-filled steel bucket of water, likewise pained me. There was something wrong with this picture. Perhaps if my father had been fishing to prevent our starvation, I might have understood a little better, that those animals had to be sacrificed so we could live. But this wasn't for our survival. He was doing this for his "fun." Thus, I made the heartrending discovery that it wasn't just those "evil" people who harmed animals. That was a hard truth for me to square with my feelings for my father and what I considered right, just, and acceptable behavior.

Over the decades, with the re-emergence of investigative journalism about more than political corruption and with the advent of the Internet, the broadcasting of ongoing animal brutality at the hands of humans around the world had thoroughly disabused me of that early Henri Rosseau "Peaceable Kingdom"-tinged hope. Increasingly, animals were being demonstrated to be mere objects to be dominated, exploited, and staggeringly abused for financial gain or fun. It was anything but allowing animals, domestic or wild, "to have their right to live their lives naturally." My closely-held ideal of protecting and providing animals the freedom from unnecessary pain caused by humans was under attack by a utilitarian zombie-like apocalypse.

Over the years there has been a swelling incidence of *reported* animal abuse: from factory farms to medical research/medical schools; from "entertainment" (cock- and dog fighting, rodeos, circuses, movies, TV shows, crush films, roadside zoos, killing contests) to "sport" hunting, poaching, and decimating whole species of animals for economic or political reasons; from puppy mills to people taking out their anger, frustrations, and violent tendencies on animals.

Clutching the tattered remnants of my illusory dream, in spite of all that had happened as I grew older, I thought that maybe *I* could help make a difference. As a result, I immersed myself in activities that would provide a direct benefit to animals which were being abused. I contributed to local and national animal humane organizations, helped with dog and cat adoptions, signed petitions, wrote letters to legislators, and participated in local activist and advocacy projects to create awareness, change laws, and foster enforcement of those laws.

When the consequent changes were only miniscule in the big picture, I joined others in the trenches to physically rescue homeless and injured animals. Rescuing provided true gratification by way of making a microscopic but individually significant dent in a world-wide staggering problem. However, too often what had been done to these victims ripped your heart out and stomped on it with metal football cleats. But it wasn't until I unexpectedly encountered several compelling situations that I found my course being altered dramatically.

1

It was ten years ago in the frigid gloominess of winter where the sky was like a ponderous down quilt of slate-gray clouds covering over ninety-five percent of the western Massachusetts sky. The watercolor crystalline blue, cloudless sky with its snow-blinding brilliance of the day before was gone as if it had been only a mirage. With the de-materializing of the sun came a penetrating temperature decline, predicted to be from a sixteen-to-twenty-six-degree Fahrenheit drop and projected to linger. Bare skeletal trees, interspersed with conifers, had glistened as yesterday's sun reflected off their melting ice-tipped twigs. But today they sagged morosely as they re-froze. They looked beyond rigor, even approaching petrification. Regeneration as a harbinger of a verdant spring seemed a total impossibility at this frigid moment.

My name is Kiri Sumner. My mother named me after famed Australian opera singer, Kiri Te Kanawa, who was best known for her joyful and confident interpretations of Mozart and Strauss, to which my mother listened whenever she could. At this time, I was twenty-six years old, on my own, and working on my clinical psychology doctorate at Boston University, which, regrettably, was not the field in which I had started out.

Driving south along the white pine and maple heavily-treed Route 141 from Southampton to the Holyoke Hospital in my dark blue Honda Civic five-door hatchback, I was bundled up with my heater roaring on high so the outdoor temperature change felt of little consequence. The radio blared 1980s nostalgia as I rhythmically tapped the steering wheel to the beat of Gloria Estefan and the Miami Sound Machine doing their 1985 "Conga." Following that was Billy Joel's 1986 song "Modern Woman" which was used the same year in the black comedy, *Ruthless People.* Smiling, for a few moments I was feeling oblivious to the outside world until my car tires slipped. They were occasionally losing some traction as yesterday's road slush had become icier, slicker, and trickier. The real possibility of uncontrolled skidding crossed my mind. It was discomforting but only temporarily as I slowed to a safer thirty-five mph.

Distracted, I had somehow forgotten about whether you should turn the wheels of the car out or into a skid. Envisioning it made it simple. Take your foot off the accelerator and brake. If the front of the car turned in the direction of the rear-end skid, the car would start to make a circle. Whereas if it turned counter to the rear-end's movement, that would interrupt the car's circular momentum. For a front-end skid, straighten the steering wheel. I chided myself, "You're too young to be having a senior moment," but I knew that wasn't it. My rhythmic pummeling the steering wheel resumed as the station next played Steve Winwood's 1986 number-one hit, "Higher Love," with Chaka Khan doing background vocals.

An ice patch suddenly jerked the steering wheel to the right. Given how busy Easthampton Road usually was, I had no expectation of so much ice buildup. However, it was becoming immediately clear that only more care and awareness of the road conditions could prevent an accident. Grudgingly, I knew I needed to eliminate external distractions such as the radio. With an abrupt snap I turned it off.

As much as I knew I needed to focus on driving, I found my thoughts straying wildly. Strangely, today's weather, and my own circumstances, made everything feel eerie, nightmarish, and vaguely reminiscent of an episode from the *Twilight Zone*, entitled "Stopover in a Quiet Town." In this frustration-infused television play, a married couple who were comfortably driving along suddenly find everything going dark. They awaken as if from a deep sleep to find themselves in a strange town, now without their car. Confused, they begin to wander its empty streets but they cannot find another living soul—not a tree, animal, insect, or another human being, only props of them. They finally encounter a train. Believing this will aid their escape from wherever they are, they board it. It moves but to their surprise and chagrin, it only returns them to where they started. Then they hear a frightening sound from the sky. Looking up, they are shocked to discover they have become the miniature toys of a giant, giggling child, ostensibly on another planet.

Adding to my general feeling of dis-ease was that I had been driving for the last twenty minutes and had only infrequently seen another car. Disaster scenarios flitted through my mind. What if my car skidded out of control and I needed help? This seemingly endless stretch of road appeared even more deserted, solitary, and remote in this frozen, forty-watt half-light. Despite the fact I was driving cautiously and had my cell phone with me, anxiety was tickling my spine, keeping me on edge.

Adding to my discomfort, I was resentfully on my way to the hospital in Holyoke where my only sibling was preparing to give birth to her first child. As unfeeling as it no doubt sounded, it didn't matter at all to me. In fact, I was really pissed off that everyone expected me to put on a happy face, rush to the hospital to be present for the big unveiling, and, all the while, pretend I was truly thrilled for my older sister, Gia, and her husband.

After all, their having a baby wasn't the only thing going on in the world or in our lives at that moment. As in the past, whatever was going on in Gia's life superseded everything else. I had to wonder if that was because Gia's name meant "gift from the angels." This had been endlessly annoying, especially when I was younger. The passage of years hadn't altered that very much. My mood was darkening further to match the afternoon's creeping disappearance of light.

What had been dismissed in all this grand celebration was that my nearly life-long companion and confidante had died the day before. My ten-year-old Malamute-mix dog, "Mr. Rogers," had succumbed to pancreatic cancer. But no one seemed to care about it or my pain and unfathomable sense of loss. It seemed to me that his demise was worth at least being acknowledged.

My life had revolved around him since I was a still-shy sixteen. We played and slept together and participated in all manner of outdoor activities. He even came to my softball games and track events, rooting in his own canine way for me. We jogged together, though he was much faster than I was. When I read to him how-to books or about what veterinarians did to help dogs, he'd lay his large furry head peacefully on my lap, looking up at me with adoring, milk-chocolate-colored eyes. I never revealed to him that competitive Westminster Dog Show pure-bred elitists only cared for very dark brown Malamute eyes. They didn't know what they were missing in their superficiality.

Through his last pain-filled days—when buprenorphine was no longer effective—I nursed him, assuring him he would never be alone and that things would be better for him somehow. Now remembering, I set my jaw and willed the hot tears which were threatening to spill onto my cheeks again to stop in their tracks. Yet what required my full attention was that my tires were slipping ever more often, directing my attention to the fact that the road was becoming icier. It didn't matter. As I stared through the bleary windshield, visions of how Mr. Rogers and I met re-emerged.

By the age of sixteen, I had begged, beseeched, and cajoled my parents for eleven years to have a dog. They were unyielding, providing many inadequate excuses which I took to be a reflection of what they thought of me and my abilities. Gawky and somewhat introverted, I mostly kept to myself, reading about animals of every imaginable species which was my favorite subject, and holding confidential "conversations" with my coming-apart-at-the-seams stuffed dog, Harvey, my substitute.

8

Made of tan cotton duck with sewn black string eyes, nose, and mouth, he had been with me since I was six months old. He was my first gift from Uncle Harvey, his namesake. That this inanimate companion had lasted this long was a miracle in itself. It was the only toy that had ever really entertained me as a child and it still retained its endearment.

I'd named it after my mother's brother who understood about my love of animals. In our private talks, he admitted that he too had wanted to be a veterinarian but things hadn't worked out as he'd hoped. He was employed by a pharmaceutical company as a drug rep and hated it mostly because of what pharmaceutical companies' research did to animals, like rabbits' eyes and skin. In his spare time, he volunteered to rescue companion animals and participate in animal-welfare protests. He was a true advocate.

One time he took me with him when he was helping capture a dog that had been abandoned to roam the streets of South Hadley. It had been unsuccessfully seeking adequate food and shelter for at least a couple of years. Uncle Harvey worked with two other people as a team, Tanisha, a high school history teacher, and Tommy, a city garbage collector. They were armed with hamburgers, lassoes, and leashes. Based upon tips from concerned neighbors who thought the dog had been left after a family moved and had been unsuccessful in capturing it but left food and water for it, Uncle Harvey's team discovered their quarry under a faded, dented black Beetle parked at a closed, weed-strewn gas station.

The small creature they sought looked nothing like a dog. Its fur was dirty gray with splotches of black and so badly matted it could hardly walk. It looked to me like a headless miniature sheep. After a half-hour of patiently tossing bits of hamburger and bun under the vehicle, each a little closer to one of the rescuers, they lassoed the frightened dog. Panicking, it fought and tried to bite its rescuers but was too weak to do much damage. As soon as Uncle Harvey could slip a leash over what was likely to be its head, it seemed to give up. I tried not to cry. He stroked it and spoke soothingly to it. Cautiously, it lifted its head to gaze at Uncle Harvey as he gently picked it up.

Once in the rescue van, it cuddled as best it could into his lap. From there it went to the veterinary clinic for shearing, bathing, and a physical examination. The process seemed to take forever. After its beauty salon treatment, it manifested itself as a sweet little Lhasa Apso. Tanisha took it home to foster until it could be adopted. It seemed incomprehensible to me that someone could even consider rejecting this little love.

From my earliest days, whenever he visited, Uncle Harvey had always brought an animal book for me. Early on he read to me, like Kathryn and Byron Jackson's 1942 Little Golden Books' *The Saggy Baggy Elephant* about a baby elephant alone and shamed in the jungle because of his appearance. As he tried to find himself and his place, he ultimately learned to love himself for who he was and how he looked. Uncle Harvey shared all kinds of animal stories and experiences with me. I never thought of these books as "toys."

It was he who also took me to Southwick's Zoo, a three-hundred-acre, privately owned and operated zoological park in Mendon, MA, where we discussed the different animals and I had the thrill of petting deer and baby goats. And to a farm that had pigs, burros, a dwarf horse, chickens, ducks, and sheep, where he asked if I were going to treat zoo and farm animals as well as dogs and cats when I grew up. This was a difficult decision for me to make. It bothered me I couldn't give him an answer then and there even though he assured me there was still plenty of time to make that determination.

Watching the exotic zoo inmates, animals I would never have seen except in books if it weren't for zoos, thrilled me. But at the same time, it was sad to also discover that in so many zoos the animals were caged, living on unnatural concrete floors, unable to roam and do what they normally would do in the wild. It didn't feel right. And sometimes when I saw the big cats and bears of all kinds continuously pace the perimeters of their small enclosures, tears began to run down my face. They looked so bored and frustrated, manifesting what I later learned was labeled "zoochosis," the equivalent of a human's disengagement from reality. Slowly as I became aware of the destiny of many farm animals, their being killed for food, some in truly torturous ways, that didn't seem right because they suffered. Just the thought of it choked me up with anger.

When Uncle Harvey wasn't around, I tended to have little social contact with others except in school. It had taken me a while to engage with school mates, primarily females, and in team sports, where I could shine. I didn't take to teenaged boys because they didn't take to me. In general, strangers made me uncomfortable. And Gia, who was seven years older, wasn't interested in interacting with her "baby" sister, except when she had a boy problem, which she invariably brought to me. In effect, I was a child living mostly alone.

Then things changed one afternoon. It was the day of my sixteenth birthday. Uncle Harvey was visiting to celebrate with me. After our family gathering, he and I were in the living room discussing his latest series of sometimes hair-raising rescues when he suddenly grabbed his chest, gasping for air. As I held him, I quickly lowered him onto the floor to initiate CPR. Between breaths, I managed to shout for my mother to call 911. Despite my efforts, he died there on the colorful L.L. Bean oval braided wool rug before the paramedics arrived. He had suffered a massive heart attack. While my mother was distraught, I was numb and uncomprehending. He was gone ... gone forever. He was the only one to understand me. I was bereft, at sea. But, holding on to him, I was unable to produce the tears which when splashed on him would magically revive him.

While he had always been there for me, I now felt as though he had abandoned me. After the paramedics who had arrived quickly gave up on trying to resuscitate him, I went upstairs to my room. There, seated on the bed, I stoically stared at the bookshelf collection of animal and veterinary books he had given me over the years. As a tear drop broke through my mask of insensibility, I melted into shuddering sobs, artless and unself-conscious like a child. Inconsolable, I hugged the threadbare remains of my stuffed dog Harvey. For nearly sixteen years I had lavished my love and attention physically on it. He was my only real animal companion, the one with whom I shared my secrets. He also represented my connection with Uncle Harvey, who was the only person who seemed to love the *real* me, not his expectations of me, and respect my ideas and plans, as an individual, not just as his niece.

When my mother, who was downstairs making funeral arrangements, came upstairs, she heard me. Hurrying to my room, she wrapped her arms around me. She tried to console me.

"Honey, I know you loved Uncle Harvey. I loved him too but he's gone ... to a better place."

I looked up at my mother with eyebrows raised. Suddenly the exclamation, "A better place? Horse shit!" formed on my tongue as my eyes swam in despair. Instead, I just shook my head and wailed even more pitifully.

"No, no, a 'better place' is here ... with me, with rescuing the animals he loved. He was going to help me become a veterinarian. We were going to work for animals together. He'd rescue them and I'd heal them."

My attitude became gloomy, even at the dinner table. The mac and cheese, made with real Vermont cheddar, which I normally loved and had done so throughout most of my childhood, sat in a cooling lump on my plate with *al dente* steamed broccoli with a touch of lemon juice, which I also liked, all untouched. Swallowing any of it was impossible due to the huge lump in my throat. After dinner, my mother found me hunkered on the floor in the corner of my bedroom, head bowed, gently placing what was left of stuffing-less Harvey into one of her shoeboxes. I planned to bury it in the yard as a memorial. Both Harveys were gone.

Even though I was almost an adult, I felt like a six-year-old who had been orphaned.

For days my body wandered around at school and at home, going through the motions, silent. When I had to speak to friends and teachers, it was in flat, short, mono-syllabic sentences. It extended into almost two weeks. The school counselor called my mother to express her concern. My teachers had spoken with her about me. They stated, "Normally alert and participating, she now seems immobilized and depressed." That evening my mother instigated a conversation with my father about the situation.

As I listened from the downstairs hall, not sure what I hoped to hear, my father expressed his opinion.

"It's just normal grief. It will pass in time. I think she was too attached to Uncle Harvey. She needs more social outlets. She's too much of a loner. Why can't she be more like her sister. Maybe she should have a stronger relationship with Gia. Gia could show her the ropes. You know, how to interact better with boys."

My mother didn't sound so sure. "Yes," she said, "that might work over time but she needs something right now."

"What are you suggesting? Going to a shrink? It's just normal grief. She's not a mental case. She'll get over it, hopefully sooner than later."

"I was thinking more of finding her a real companion to see how that worked."

His response was incredulous. "What do you mean? Hire a companion for her? Come on. Be serious."

"No," my mother sighed, "I mean get her a dog. She's been wanting one since she was a child and we have fought it for years. But she's certainly old enough now to care for it and be responsible for it. It would give her something to sort of replace her time with Uncle Harvey."

A smile crept onto my face as I listened. It was the secret smile you see on a dog's face when it's dreaming about chasing and catching a squirrel. Nothing could replace Uncle Harvey but finally having a furry companion could help a lot. We'd share everything in spirit. I peeked around the corner at my father. Looking both stymied and exasperated, he agreed. Despite their knowing how much I had always cared about animals of all kinds, surprisingly they had done nothing about it until now that I had suffered a significant loss. Only then did they finally accede to my wishes, unlike with Gia.

If Gia had wanted a dog, it was assured that she would have had one in an instant. Not that she would ever have wanted a pet that she would have had to spend time with, care for, and be responsible for. At least I was finally going to be given an animal to love and care for. As a result, they were going to take me to the local animal shelter the next day after school.

2

As we approached the glass front door of the Southampton companion-animal rescue shelter, dogs and cats inside were visible through the large plate glass windows. My solemn expression instantaneously broke into a grin. This was really finally happening. Life might be looking up after all. Perhaps my parents were now showing they understood me and cared about the real me. Maybe they were even acknowledging me as a responsible young-adult.

Bright and friendly, the red-brick-fronted animal shelter building had been a flourishing travel agency which needed more space. When it moved its location down the block, the owners, who were animal lovers, rented the space to the shelter for a low monthly fee, a pittance actually. It was their contribution to the community and its homeless animals.

All around the perimeter of the twenty-by-thirty-foot room were kennels for dogs and puppies with cages for cats and kittens on eighteen-inch by seventy-two-inch aluminum training tables in the center of the room. All the animals had fresh water, filled food dishes, a blanket or bed, and a toy or two. The cats also had small litter trays. I felt as if I had found my destination.

As my parents walked slowly from kennel to kennel, I moved ahead, quickly reviewing each dog. Some ran to their kennel's chain-link-fence door to show their athletic prowess, exuberant personality, and desire for attention. Eyes wide, tongues lolling, prancing, and waggling from shoulders to tail with eagerness, they were ready to make a connection with each potential adopter. Licking any part of the human's anatomy they could reach, they silently shouted, "Take me! I'm the one! Take me!"

I had stopped in front of the kennel of a scruffy-looking, heavily-furred puppy wearing an Elizabethan collar. It had shaved and naked patches of painful-looking raw skin on its lower back, tail region, and rear legs covered with some kind of salve. It stayed on its blanket facing the back wall, hunched over, its head down, eyes closed. That forlorn look was familiar. I'd seen it often in my mirror after Uncle Harvey's death. When I called to the puppy, it appeared reluctant to take the risk of looking at me, much less of leaving the security of its blanket. It was as if it couldn't afford to get its hopes up. I sat cross-legged on the recently-added gray linoleum floor in front of the kennel door in my worn jeans, Dartmouth sweatshirt, and sneakers. There I continued to talk softly but enthusiastically to it.

One of the shelter managers came over to my parents and explained within my hearing.

"The owner of that puppy," pointing to the one with which I was trying to make contact, "handed it over because, he said, 'It whined all the time.' Because of its constant, annoying noise-making which, he claimed, kept his children awake, he had relegated the puppy to a closed, unused bedroom where it whined even more."

"That was totally dumb," my father interrupted.

"Then, when he infrequently let it out of the bedroom into the house, not just when it went outside to eliminate, it began to follow his children around everywhere which concerned him. He said he worried about its nipping at their ankles, even though he never saw any sign of it attempting to do so. Over time, he recalled, the puppy seemed to become obsessed with sucking the end of its own tail and chewing on itself."

"Oh, that poor puppy," my mother added.

"He said the compulsive display made the dog look diseased. He also added that to force the puppy to cease its 'repulsive' behavior he had tried swatting it with a rolled-up newspaper, forcing it to wear a muzzle, and wrapping an Ace bandage around the gnawed leg. Then when nothing worked to stop the increasingly-destructive habit, he brought it here."

My mother said, "How awful and insensitive. He shouldn't have had the puppy in the first place. I hope he treats his children better."

The manager indicated that the skin condition, which had not been previously addressed, had been evaluated by the shelter's vet. "The diagnosis was possibly an allergy or exposure to something toxic but, more likely, a neurodermatitis associated with the puppy's frustration and anxiety."

"Of course, it was anxious. It was just a baby needing love and attention," my mother replied, clucking her tongue.

"The puppy has been given an injection of the corticosteroid Depo-Medrol to address the inflammation, irrespective of its cause, and an antibiotic salve to ward off a secondary bacterial infection. It'll have to wear the E-collar until the wounds start to heal."

My parents nodded.

"There is no evidence the puppy has any other *physical* problems." She left it there.

My mother uttered, "Oh!" as my father shook his head. My parents and I knew what she meant. This puppy was likely to be neurotic and overly needy: a real problem pet. This was a questionable pooch for any teenager to adopt, or, more to the point, for any family to have to deal with.

As they talked, I tuned out my parents' concern. My focus was on communicating with this puppy. Slowly, cautiously it turned its head toward me, the plastic protective collar scraping the floor. It looked up at me, its eyes seeming to reflect what appeared to be a sense of rejection, abandonment, and betrayal. The reluctance in my parents' questions and responses continued to waft in my direction and intrude on my efforts.

My father ended the discussion.

"This dog already has big problems. What would we be getting into? Vet bills and behavior problems? Special training? I think we need to avoid this pooch and seriously check out some others instead. There are lots of happy, normal dogs here."

The manager pointed to a bouncy Jack Russell adolescent which began to do back flips at the attention.

"That's 'Bojangles.' He was found running loose. He's young, healthy, energetic, and has no problems."

My father smiled, nodded, and grunted his approval as they continued down the line of kennels.

I turned my attention back to the ball of thick fur before me.

"Ignore them. It's okay. Come on. Walk over here. You want to. I know you do. I can help. Please come here. Please."

My fingers stretched through the holes between the links as I smiled and gestured to the puppy.

"Come on. We will be friends ... best friends ... friends forever. I promise."

Minutes dragged by as I beckoned to the puppy. It was as if it were carefully processing my words, intent upon considering every auditory nuance, but unsure if it should dare to take the chance. Then it shifted its body slightly toward me. Tentatively, it raised its head, keeping its eyes on me. Perhaps it was summoning the courage to hope that things could be different. In an instant, it began to crawl on its belly toward me, its head still lowered, collar scraping, but looking up through its eyebrows expectantly.

When it arrived at the gate, it turned away from me, its body pressed again the metal links, its head down. I gently stroked its neck and scratched its shoulders, careful to avoid the angry-looking areas on its lower back and legs. The puppy raised its head an inch and looked around at me peripherally.

At that moment I knew. This was my dog. We were on the same channel. We understood each other. We needed each other. Then seeing it was a male, I immediately named him "Mr. Rogers," after Fred Rogers whose comforting, informative television show had delighted me as a child. I determined this puppy would be my constant companion. We'd share, have fun, and grow up together. We would be there for one another for as long as the fates allowed it, which I hoped would be until eternity.

My parents relented but planned to return the puppy in three weeks when they were sure he wasn't working out. What A.A. Milne's Christopher Robin said to Winnie the Pooh I said to Mr. Rogers.

"Promise me you'll always remember that you're braver than you believe and stronger than you seem and smarter than you think."

With my constant, loving attention Mr. Rogers showed amazing progress by the deadline. Quickly he healed and bloomed. He went on to transform himself from a depressed, distressed puppy into a calm, confident, "braver, stronger, and smarter" adult dog ... and my best, most loyal friend.

His transformation reminded me of what Uncle Harvey had done for me and that, in spite of "Mr. Rogers," I still mourned him. Sometimes it seemed that "Mr. Rogers" was really Uncle Harvey reincarnated. In Bankhar, Mongolia, nomadic herders who felt a great sense of pride in their dogs, gave their dogs names. No other animal was so privileged. This was because they believed that dogs and humans shared one spirit. Consequently, dogs could be reincarnated as humans *and* humans could be reincarnated as dogs. I could relate to that.

Reminiscing about Uncle Harvey brought to mind words from Wordsworth's "Ode: Intimations of Immortality from Recollections of Early Childhood."

"Though nothing can bring back the hour,
Of splendour in the grass, of glory of the flower,

We will grieve not, rather find
Strength in what remains behind ..."

And it was Mr. Rogers who remained behind to help me out of my shell. We ran together. When we went for walks, he was always a magnet for strangers to admire him, ask about him, and want to pet and play with him. I began to enjoy sharing him with others and made not only lots of acquaintances but also lots of friends.

Throughout our years together, he developed a number of health issues which were common to Malamutes, from a heart murmur and hypothyroidism to cataracts. Because of potential heart problems, I had to keep his teeth clean which he somehow accepted. Fortunately, he didn't also have a Malamute's hip or elbow dysplasia, diabetes, or hemophilia. For each new or ongoing problem, I dutifully cared for him. This required me to become more aware of his potential symptoms from my veterinary books. But even with my increasing attention to his health, I had somehow not detected his pancreatic cancer before the disease had reached an advanced stage. By then it had spread to other parts of his body.

As a result, guilt ensnared me, like a trawling net dragging along the sea floor, scooping up anything and everything, displacing and harming marine species. Even though Dr. Shelby, Mr. Rogers' veterinarian, had tried to impress upon me that the disease was essentially undetectable until it was too late, I still felt I should have known. Since Mr. Rogers and I shared the psychic link that I'd had with Uncle Harvey, somehow intuition should have made it obvious to me. I couldn't shake the belief that if only I had tried harder, we could have detected it in time and he might still have been with me today.

Because I was always connected to animals and Uncle Harvey's love for them, it was apparent from my earliest days that veterinary science would be my destiny. Dr. Kiri Sumner, DVM. Therefore, I was constantly reading all I could about dogs and cats, their health concerns, and how to deal with them. This likewise had prepared me early on for the probability that Mr. Rogers would develop some of his breed's related health problems. And as he did develop them, however, it never ceased to amaze me that in spite of each one, he took it all in stride. He took his medications and remained affectionate, devoted, loyal, and dignified. Even in spite of his sight-limiting cataracts, he trusted me to help him to stay active, directing him to run, hide in high grass to jump out at me, and play tug of war with whatever he found. That is, until the cancer, with its gnawing, deep-seated pain, took over.

The first sign that something was wrong was when he began losing weight in spite of his good appetite. Because of his heavy coat, detecting it didn't happen quickly. In fact, it was only when I periodically gave him his two-level coat a brushing that I discovered his bony hips. I attributed it to old age since Malamutes live to about ten to twelve years. Consequently, I provided more of his favorite food. But it wasn't long before his appetite slowly decreased as well.

One by one other relevant symptoms revealed themselves: jaundice of his eyes then digestive problems which included abnormal stools and vomiting. When Dr. Shelby palpated his upper abdomen, she discovered a swollen gallbladder and pain which extended to his back. At that point, Mr. Rogers' debilitating, terminal condition was finally confirmed. His time was up. Sadly, I learned that neither surgery nor chemotherapy would help him. It was a fait accompli.

3

Now, as I drew closer to Gia's hospital, thoughts of Mr. Rogers had to be put aside for a moment to think about my sister. I shook my head. No matter what else was going on in my family, it always seemed that Gia was the center of attention. It was Gia's needs, wants, activities, cares, and issues. As a result, it often felt as though I must have been a step-sister, like Cinderella, or adopted. Gia and I were nothing alike in any way. Gia had shoulder-length, wavy chestnut hair she parted in the middle, alluring green-flecked brown eyes with long dark lashes, a slim face, sculpted cheekbones, and narrow chin, topped off with a Myrna Loy retroussé nose. She was the image of our slim, petite, 5'4", mother.

However, unlike our mother who had a naturally high metabolism, Gia was slender through constant dieting and a history of binging and purging, mimicking the near-scarecrow stereotype of what fashion and *Cosmopolitan* magazines suggested was the young feminine ideal of that day. She shared with me that this image was necessary for her to match her outgoing personality and social popularity, especially with boys.

Making myself barf for the sake of "beauty" and "acceptance" was totally inconceivable.

In contrast, I had dark blonde ear-length, straight hair I parted on the right side and combed back behind my ears, dark blue eyes with long but undramatic lashes, a straight nose, and undistinguished cheek bones. At 5'11" I had broad shoulders, long limbs, size ten feet, and a trim frame that remained that way as the result of my running six miles a day, taking karate, lifting weights, and watching my diet. I didn't favor anyone in my family. Not being cute, petite, or a classic beauty like Gia, I showed less interest in a social life in general. Besides, boys had always seemed intimidated by me. In high school a few referred to me as Godzilla, Amazon Girl, or then-Boston Celtics' power forward, Larry Bird.

So, at this moment on this lamentable winter day I was hurrying to my full-term pregnant sister's side, because … Well, it was not that I wasn't happy for her in an abstract way. Gia was getting what she'd wanted for years. She was the social butterfly, acquiring the latest fashion, interested in having lots of boys vying for her attention, partying all the time, and setting her sites on being married well-to-do, in a home featured in *Architectural Digest*, and having two perfect children—a boy and a girl, in that order. I had been there for her, as best I could, whenever she felt she needed to share her angst about some relationship that she thought was not going as she had wanted. Surprisingly, she once mentioned as an aside that I was easy to talk to … and that I truly listened to her. Compliments from her didn't come easily or often, especially to me.

She had repeatedly told me her life plan. I wondered if she had been "testing for gas," to see how it sounded. In the last few years she had begun frequently confiding in me. People in general tended to do that as well. I didn't know why. However, what was distressing was that she showed no interest in reciprocating. Listening to me about my plans, issues, feelings, or problems, which I offered very infrequently for comment, was apparently not on her to-do list.

Of course, I, on the other hand, was more involved with animals, books, and practical things like what to do in emergencies or how to fix things. That occasionally involved studying manuals to help my father in his workshop in the garage, working on the car, and fixing problems around the house—things in which Gia had absolutely no interest. I was practical, mechanically-minded, and coolly objective in decision-making situations. Unlike Gia, I had set my own professional destination in stone: helping animals. Marriage and children didn't even enter into the equation. I had no desire to be social, like Gia, or have to compete with others for attention. It always felt too hollow, trivial, and boring.

However, more and more whenever Gia and I saw one another, which was even less often as she focused on having the consummate house and children, she tended to express to me how sorry she felt for me that my interests and social life were so anemic. It never sounded as though she were actually expressing heartfelt concern. Instead, it usually had the burning-sulfur whiff of sarcasm. I didn't understand why she bothered. We weren't rivals. Yet, not once did I confront her about her hurtful comments. That angered me. I wanted so badly to stand up for myself, but never could quite do it. By my not saying anything, I gave her my permission to continue making her unsolicited, cutting remarks. Being unassertive made me feel weak and one-down. My sister and I would never be close unless something in the mathematical expression drastically changed for the positive.

As I drove, the image of arriving at Gia's private hospital room, crowded with relatives and well-to-do friends, helium message balloons, cards, wine, boxes of luxurious chocolate, and flowers of all kinds made me shudder. Everyone would be chatting happily around me. I would be invisible, an outsider to this Times Square New Year's Eve mob. All I was expected to do was play the "good sister," dutifully greet and kiss my sister, and utter the assumed words of celebration, irrespective of my submerged feelings. And never forget: New life trumps death.

The death of Mr. Rogers had left me depressed, exhausted, and perplexed. We had been alter-egos for a decade. During his last month, I spent all my time with him after my classes, helping him move around when he was in the mood. When he was feeling up to it, I took him to the university with me. He'd sit quietly beside me and sleep. I gave him his pain shots and tasty treats which he soon couldn't taste. He became less interested in taking his medications. I shared with him upbeat VHS animal videos, romantic music, both classical and popular as long as it was soothing, and provided anything and everything that might make him as comfortable as possible in order to help ease him out.

Euthanasia, however, had been ruled out of the question by my father. Even though I was twenty-six, an adult, independent, and living on my own, my father vociferously objected, putting his foot down.

"You cannot, will not, kill that dog."

My mother and I argued with him that it wasn't right or fair to let Mr. Rogers suffer at the end. Amazing myself, I looked him the eye.

"I am the one responsible for his well-being. I promised him I'd always take care of him. And that includes relieving him of his painful life," I stated unequivocally.

My father was as shocked by my calm assertiveness as I was.

It was frustratingly hard to divine my father's attitude and objection. After all, he was an advocate of death with dignity for human beings in general and certainly for himself. Why was there a difference? Was it that Mr. Rogers being a dog couldn't decide for himself or communicate what it was he wanted? I didn't understand my father's reasoning ... and, frankly, I didn't care. Mr. Rogers and decisions about him were my concern alone.

When Mr. Rogers could no longer eat, drink, eliminate, or comfortably cuddle, he looked me sorrowfully in the eyes and told me it was time. He had just begun to softly whimper because his last fentanyl patch, which had followed his series of increasingly ineffective injections, was no longer squelching his pain. That was it. No ifs, ands, or buts.

I informed my mother who offered to help me take him to the vet to say our good-byes.

"I'll tell your father tonight. He really does care."

As far as I was concerned at that moment, it really didn't matter whether he cared or not. The only thing that mattered was that Mr. Rogers was no longer suffering.

During his illness and after he died, I had been astounded by how many people had seemingly misunderstood the depth of the relationship between my dog and me. Perhaps that was because many of them had never had a pet or they valued pets differently, if they valued them at all. Unfortunately, my sister had been one of those I considered deficient in sensitivity to and understanding of my situation. I mean, I knew Gia was engaged in the upcoming birth but didn't understand why she didn't show any sympathy—forget about empathy—about what I felt and was going through.

Gia had never shown any particular interest in the dog. It's not that she disliked him. She would pet him now and then. But other than that, she seemed indifferent to him. He simply wasn't part of her world. She had never had any "pets" and didn't seem to value them or their effect on their human companions. To me that really was her loss.

When she was visiting the day before, right after his death, she demanded, "Will you stop crying. It's really annoying." I tried to share my grief. I talked about my sense of physical and emotional loss, to which she rolled her eyes and waved her hand dismissively as if shooing away a fly. Finally, she shook her head.

"Come on. For heaven's sake, will you shape up? It's not the end of the world. Life goes on. Besides, you're making everyone around you, especially me, depressed."

I just looked at her, unable to respond.

"This isn't good for the baby, or me. Okay, you had it for a long time but it's not as though you can't get another."

I almost said, "I'm sorry," but didn't.

She was on a roll. "The shelters are full of dogs that need homes. If you're such a rabid advocate for adoption, why aren't you simply getting another one to take its place?"

"What?" I managed to utter.

"I mean, for God's sake, it was *just* a dog."

"Just a dog?" Incensed and indignant, I wanted to shout, "How dare you say that! He was my loyal and loving friend." And I thought, "A more loyal and loving companion and a better friend than you have ever been." However, I bit my tongue instead. Something screamed at me inside my skull that it wouldn't be smart to get my sister upset now. If something went wrong tomorrow with the birth or the baby, I'd feel responsible ... and guilty. When I finally cooled down, I just sighed and shook my head. Part of me really had wanted to stay home today to decide what to do with his remains to celebrate *him*, not Gia.

I reflected that few people had been there for me the way Mr. Rogers had been. He never laughed at my mistakes or my occasional boy problems that I would later look back on, cringe with embarrassment, and awkwardly laugh about. He had been there for me when no one else was. When I felt ill, he snuggled to keep me warm and cared for. When I did less well on a test that I was sure I would ace. When David dropped me right before the prom, pretending he had to go to New Hampshire to visit his grandfather, because he had discovered that the most popular girl in class had finally said yes to his original invitation. And, when I scraped the front fender of my parents' Cadillac Brougham V8 Coupe as a result of misjudging the boat-like car's front-end width within the narrow confines of the drive-through at McDonalds. He overlooked my gargantuan height and loved me no matter what.

When I came home from high school, it was Mr. Rogers who raced toward me, nearly knocking me on to my butt to climb my front and give me long, wet doggy kisses and bury his snout in my neck. As soon as we exchanged our greetings, I would snare his electric blue leash and playfully ask if he wanted to go outside. He'd leap about with high springy steps in the foyer then nearly pull me down the three porch stairs as soon as the door opened. Sitting on my lap, he would look into my eyes, cock his head to the right, and listen without judgment to all my thoughts and secrets. We had a special bond that he would never betray. He always showed he knew it was mutual.

Today's drive seemed interminable but, fortunately, it was only another ten miles before I'd reach the hospital. Just then something caught my attention. Ahead on the right side of the road was something dark on the top of the several-foot-deep, snow-plough-created embankment. At first it appeared to be a dark shrub or oddly-shaped black garbage bag. It was moving ever so slightly opposite the direction of the arctic wind which was still lowering the temperature. I couldn't tell if it was alive. But engrossed in reminiscing about Mr. Rogers, I didn't want to stop.

Then something began rapping on my skull, declaring that no matter what I preferred to do I needed to investigate. It was my duty. It's what Uncle Harvey would have done. If it were an animal in need and I didn't act, I would never forgive myself. That was not how a former veterinarian-to-be or a lover of animals was supposed to act. I could feel the push and pull within me. What if it were someone else's Mr. Rogers? It didn't matter specifically what because down deep I knew I would have to check it out and help if necessary. There were no other real options for me.

As I carefully slowed down, the car slid toward the snowbank. Straightening the steering wheel, gently braking, and putting on my flashers, I alighted and climbed the two-and-a half-foot icy wall. Trudging the five feet to the dark shape, I could see it clearly. It was a young adult, dark, double-coated dog in colors of gray, black, and white. It looked like a Keeshond with its wedge-shaped head, lion-like ruff, expressive foxlike face, and small pointed black, velvety ears. It had beautiful "spectacles" from a delicate dark line running from the outer corner of each black rimmed, almond-shaped eye toward the lower corner of each ear. Coupled with markings forming short eyebrows, this gave it a distinctly intelligent, understanding look. The fur on its hind legs feathered out like large, hairy jodhpurs. It also had a tightly curled, plumed tail that lopsidedly arched over its back.

It was hardly moving except for chest rise-and-fall and an occasional deep-throated moan. There were traces of dog prints in the snow, with tracks of dragging a leg to where it stopped. I pulled out my cell phone to call 911 for Animal Control. Damn! The signal level was low and the transmission was less than intermittent, there and gone, out here in the boonies. No houses around. Just fields, beyond the treed enclaves, that seemed to stretch forever in this season's colorless desolation.

The dog's right rear white lower leg appeared to be encased in a few inches of frozen snow to just below its hock. It was likely the result of its jumping onto the snow that had warmed from yesterday's higher temperatures, its body collapsing, and then getting caught in place as the temperature dropped precipitously overnight.

What I didn't know then but later discovered in a lengthy, detailed newspaper article about the authorities having shut down the local puppy mill, was that before finding himself encased in icy snow, this Keeshond had likely spent his entire adolescent life in a puppy mill's cramped, feces-encrusted wire cage. According to the article, he, like other puppies, would have been removed from his mother at such an early and tender age that he had never received proper socialization from her. As a result, as a youngster, his behaviors would have tended to be fearful. He would have been shy, somewhat anxious, and a little aggressive when confronted with the unknown. But upon his achieving near-adulthood, those characteristics would have seemed to fade into the background to a degree, being replaced by a situationally-evolved frustration and depression.

What I knew from my reading about dog breeds was that as a puppy, the Keeshond tends to be very playful, with quick reflexes and strong jumping ability. They are thoughtful, eager to please, and very quick learners. They love children and are excellent family dogs, preferring to be close to their humans whenever possible. Being intuitive and sensitive, they also had

34

been used as comfort dogs with rescue workers at 9/11 Ground Zero. They generally get along with other dogs as well and will enjoy a good chase around the yard.

But this Keeshond, as a puppy-manufacturing dog, would not have experienced any of that. Without access to exercise, fresh air, clean water, proper nutrition, veterinary care, or comforting human touch, he would have spent his days and nights in the dark of an uninsulated barn without adequate protection from the summer heat, winter cold, wind, rain, hail, and snow. Underweight and suffering from his fur matted with feces and overall neglect, he would have served his prime purpose of constantly siring puppies. He would have helped produce brood after brood which were often ill, with congenital problems, or hereditary abnormalities. He would have been physically constrained in a thirty-by-twenty-inch wire contraption which was stowed in the open building with fifty-eight other cages.

As the article detailed, most of the cramped wire cages at this puppy mill were smaller than his because they housed smaller dogs of nearly all breeds, males and females in separate cages except when being bred. Instead of being placed in a horizontal line on platforms or tables, most large cages were located on a floorless surface. Smaller cages were generally stacked vertically, one upon another, in some places precariously balanced two or three cages high. Where the cardboard or short plastic partial-floor inserts where no longer useful, some dogs shared their waste with dogs in lower cages. Because of the Keeshond's weight, which was heavier than most of the smaller dogs even in his state of malnutrition, his cage would have been placed on the ground, where the frigid cold would have directly seeped up from the earth beneath him to challenge his survival.

The metal wire "floors" of these cages would have cut into their paws, between the pads and toes, of all the dogs trapped there because of the inadequate or non-existent flooring. Painful foot problems were common among puppy mill dogs. No one attended to their cuts, scrapes, abscesses, infected eyes, inflamed or missing teeth, parasites (internal and external), broken bones, musculoskeletal disorders, pneumonia, or chronic diarrhea. None would ever have received vaccinations or medical care.

Typically, until the last time she gave birth, his mate would have been kept constantly pregnant, with very little time between litters. As a result of literally endless puppy production, she would have begun to look and act exhausted, depleted. Her puppies, likewise, would have looked less healthy and fewer would have survived. The last several births would have been long and difficult, ultimately loosening, then finally tearing, the ligaments holding her uterus in place. As it became detached, it would have prolapsed, slipping, then protruding from her body, leaving her lying on her side softly moaning in feverish pain.

In order to free up her cage, the puppy mill owner would have roughly grabbed hold of the female's head. She would have cried out, whimpering, a low groan coming from deep in her throat. She would have been unable to struggle to defend herself. Hanging on to her, he would have wrestled with her body to yank her out of the cage. Her legs would have become entangled in the mesh at the sides of it and her wire-cut feet would have caught in the door. The man would have yanked harder as she yowled.

When she was free of her prison, her full body would have come in contact with the frozen ground with another cry. He would then have seized her by the scruff of the neck and begun to drag her dead weight like a sack of garbage. She would have continued to cry out and whimper as her tender rear area bumped along, burned by patches of ice. Not three minutes later, a loud, sharp yelp would have cut thought the crystal cold morning, shattering the quiet, quickly followed by an ominous thud. Her lifeless body would have joined the accumulated other bodies of spent adult dogs and sick, injured, or deformed puppies on a pile of rotting carcasses behind the barn. The authorities had found her body and re-constructed the scenario.

The puppies she had just birthed five weeks ago would now have been without their mother to try to suckle, love, and teach them. On schedule, at six weeks, they too would likely disappear, some shuttled off to unconcerned pet shops if healthy-enough-appearing and not obviously genetically deformed. Those that couldn't make the appearance grade either just magically "disappeared," like their spent mothers, or were sent to medical experimentation labs. But those that looked good enough to be sold to those pet shops too often carried with them a special, unsuspected gift for their adopters. If not with a hidden genetic problem, then they often arrived at their destination with a disease.

Puppies produced by this rural, filthy puppy factory had the cards stacked against them from the very beginning. Many would not survive for long after their

"Welcome home" because of parvovirus, distemper, giardia, kennel cough, heartworm, upper-respiratory infections, and/or parasites. But those that did would likely require significant veterinary attention, sometimes chronic. Either way, these "consumer products" would too often break the hearts of those humans who had added them as beloved members of their families.

As the journalist also discovered, the male Keeshond had disappeared. In puppy manufacturer's ritualized task of hauling a disposable mate away, he had likely neglected to check to see that the fastener on the male's cage was locked down properly. The old, worn latches sometimes slipped. Seeing his mate being harmed, the male would have been agitated. When the owner didn't return, the Keeshond likely would have pushed his shoulder against the door of his cage over and over again. Using his wire-abraded front paw, he would finally have managed to hold the fastener up as he pushed to let the door swing open.

When I read those words later on, I could envision the male just barely able to stand upright in his cage, his limbs unwilling to flex as he needed them to. For at least a year he had been deprived of any real sustained movement. At first, he only would have slowly squeezed through the opening. But the brisk air would have pushed him to move forward then faster, in a direction away from the barn. He would have fought to do so, muscles aching, joints creaking, and injured paws smarting. Even as fatigue overcame him, he would have pushed on.

I could imagine the dog slowly covering a few miles until he reached Rt. 141. Before him there would have been a road that led somewhere, anywhere. He would have walked to where the snow plough-accumulated precipitation at the side of the road stopped and looked around. As he approached the edge over two feet above the road, he would likely have slid off onto the icy road's surface, stunned, shaking his head from side to side to get his bearings. Then having difficulty judging the safety of going ahead, he'd have started to cross with trepidation. With the sky intermittently clear, and the full moon's light reflecting off the snow and occasional clouds, he would have had enough illumination to continue his journey.

However, his being out of the barn for the first time ever, he would not have been prepared to recognize the significance of the pair of lights on the horizon, just above the road surface, coming closer. Not until the lights were nearly upon him would he would have sensed the danger. But his exhaustion would have made him unable to run fast enough to avoid the vehicle. The car would have been barreling toward him, catching his dark body before he could scale the snow drift on the opposite side of the road. Being struck, the impact would have sent his crumpled body flying several feet on to the snowbank where he collapsed, in pain, into the black hole of unconsciousness.

4

After assessing the Keeshond's current situation, I knew what I needed first: a digging tool and hot water, lots of it. But I had neither a pan to hold snow nor a heat source to melt it.

I spoke to the dog as comfortingly as possible.

"It will be okay. You'll be warm and fine soon. Just hang on. I have to look for some tools. Don't worry. I'm not leaving you. I'll be right back. I'll get you out."

After a few head strokes to reassure it, I plodded back to my car to see what I could use to start the ice loosening process on its lower leg. Even a metal ice scraper could help in a pinch but I was looking for sturdier implements.

In the trunk of my Civic was a large red canvas tool bag. Inside, along with replacement windshield wipers, jumper cables, engine oil, a five-gallon plastic bottle of distilled water, and miscellaneous car repair equipment was a hammer and a large, wide-bladed screwdriver. The last time my father couldn't get the hubcap off to change the tire on the Cadillac when at the house he had finally used the hammer and large screwdriver he had available on the work bench shelf. At that time, he decided that a matching pair belonged with my car as well. These two items could at least start the digging process.

After determining the depth of the lower leg in the ice, I squatted down and began carefully chipping away the hard ice at an angle toward the leg about three inches from it. Suddenly a small camper approached on my side of the road. I stood up to wave it to a stop. The driver pulled in behind my car. A young man, in his late twenties with dark brown hair, tawny skin, several days' facial growth, and wearing camouflage, alighted and stood by his vehicle.

"Is everything okay? Are you having a car problem?"

"No. I have a dog here, likely hit by a car. Its back leg is encased in ice."

"I'm not following you."

"Would you have some way to make hot water?"

He looked quizzical.

"Better come on up here and let me show you the situation and what I need."

As he climbed the snow bank, he saw what my body had been blocking. His jaw dropped.

"Oh, now I understand."

"Do you have a blowtorch or something like that?" I explained that the icy snow around the leg had to be melted to release the leg.

"No blowtorch but I think my small camp stove is still with the rest of camping gear in my vehicle. I'm sure I still have some fuel as well. I'll go look."

As I continued to chip, he climbed down the snowy embankment to search around in the back of his camper. After about two minutes, he emerged, his arms waving in the air holding three objects in his hands, shouting.

"Yeah, got them." He closed up the back of his camper and scurried up the snowbank.

"Great! By the way, I'm Kiri."

"I'm Alejandro. But just call me Al. This reminds me of some of the emergencies I experienced in Afghanistan during my third tour of duty."

As he put the extra fuel canister onto the snow, he checked the fuel reserve in the stove, pumped it, struck a wooden match, and started the flame. It was then I noticed he had a prosthetic left arm. That reminded me of the Wounded Warrior Project which had a booth at the local fair where I helped with dog and cat adoptions. We had been working with veteran's groups to adopt dogs to military people who had returned from service in the Middle East with PTSD.

Al methodically settled the stove on the icy snow, filled the small cooking pan with a detachable handle with loose snow. He placed it on the stove, and started the heating process. While creating hot water seemed agonizingly slow, things moved along relatively quickly.

Another car slowed as they passed, a young girl sticking her head out the passenger window. The driver called out from behind her.

"Can we help?"

Before waiting for an answer, she pulled in ahead of my car. It was a slim, brunette woman in her early thirties and a chubby, blonde pre-adolescent girl.

"What's happened? What can we do?" She asked as she scaled the snow bank. The child struggled to climb with her, refusing her mother's offered help but eager to see what was going on. Al passed me the pan of hot water.

"By the way, I'm Miriam and this is my seven-year-old daughter, Bettina."

When the child saw the dog, she scrunched up her face, her cheeks turning pink, as if she were going to cry.

"This dog's right rear foot is stuck in the ice. You know, even though it has a heavy coat, it could be useful if you happen to have a blanket or rug in your car that we could use to help keep it warm. I suspect it's been here all night."

"Yes, we usually keep a wool car blanket in the back. Let me check."

She climbed down, followed by her daughter, searched the car backseat and trunk, and called out.

"I'm sorry. I forgot. I took it into the house to wash."

"That's okay. Thanks anyway."

Bettina pulled on Miriam's jacket to get her attention.

"Mom," she whispered loudly enough for Al and me to hear, "What about the coat we got from Goodwill? We could wrap that around the dog."

Her mother quietly gasped, looking reluctant and conflicted. Then she swallowed hard and took a deep breath.

"Gee, honey," she said, "that's a great idea. I'll just retrieve it."

With the coat in her arms, Miriam climbed the embankment, this time being allowed to help Bettina back up as well.

"Hi. I'm Kiri and this person heating snow is Al."

Miriam handed their new purchase to her daughter and urged her to put it around the dog. Bettina took the heavy, thickly-woven wool, too-large child's coat and placed as best she could over the dog's body.

"Be careful," Miriam warned gently. "Watch out for the hammer and screwdriver. And try not to let the coat get wet as you tuck it under the dog."

Bettina smiled and nodded to her mother while she made sure the collar was under dog's head as well.

Assured the dog was properly covered, Bettina began watching Al closely.

"Are you a soldier?"

"I was," he replied as he handed another pan of steaming water to me,

"You mean you're not anymore? What happened to your arm?"

I inhaled quickly, keeping my head down as I carefully hammered away on the screwdriver.

Miriam gulped. "Bettina," she said, "That's not nice to ask."

"No, ma'm," Al said as he looked at Bettina and smiled, "that's okay. It's just natural curiosity. I don't mind."

He paused to hand me another pan of hot water. As soon as I had poured out the contents of the pan, he scooped up another load of snow.

Al asked me if he could share with us what happened. I nodded, wondering why he was asking permission. As he continued to heat the snow then scoop some more, he told us his story.

"There was a dog in Iraq, in the Gulf War, that saved my life. I love dogs and have always had them. Mostly Chihuahuas. This tan, friendly dog followed me around all the time. He became like my best buddy, keeping me company when we weren't under fire, sleeping with me, sharing my meals. He was able to detect if the enemy was nearby and regularly alerted me to them."

Everyone was listening.

"One day when my unit was under fire, he became very excited and grabbed hold of my clothes with his teeth. I was about to get into our Humvee but he tried to pull me away. He raced a few feet away, looked back, then ran to me, grabbing my pant leg again, and pulling me as hard as he could away. I didn't understand what was going on but I remembered he had protected me before. I began getting out of the vehicle in response to him but didn't do it fast enough."

"What happened?" Bettina asked anxiously.

"What had happened was that the Humvee which had already started to roll had dislodged an IED. When it exploded, it killed my soldier buddy and took my arm with it. If the dog hadn't tried to pull me to safety, I wouldn't be here today."

"What happened to your dog? Is he okay?" Bettina looked apprehensive.

"Yes, he's fine. I had to talk to a lot of people and do a lot of paperwork to get him to be able to come home with me, but here's now. I'm very thankful."

He handed me another pan of hot water.

"That was a great thing to do." Bettina clapped him on the shoulder with a pudgy hand.

An older model black GMC pick-up truck approached, slowed, and pulled up, parking behind the camper.

"What's going on?" called the auburn-bearded driver with a rash of freckles across his nose and cheeks.

Wearing a soiled and worn sheepskin coat with a vintage green John Deere ball cap, he ascended the embankment. Upon seeing the dog, he blanched.

"Oh, no!" he exclaimed. "No!" Screwing up his face which was rapidly glowing bright pink, he turned his back on the scene and blew his nose. "Dammit!"

"Is this your dog?" I asked, fearing the worst, as I took the hot pan from Al.

He half-turned to look again at the dog. As he paused, tears streamed down his face. He shook his head.

"You look so distraught. Is there anything we can do to help you?" I asked,

He started to shake his head but paused, and turned his back to us again.

"Maybe it would help to talk about it?" I offered.

Struggling to hold back his emotion as he turned around, he hesitated.

"This dog ... reminds me ... of ... Mooch ... my Husky-mix dog. I ... lost him ... yesterday. An accident." He stopped to blow his nose.

"Oh, no," Bettina cried.

"How awful," Miriam said.

"You poor thing," I chimed in.

Al added solemnly, "That's so sad."

"It was on a frozen lake ... near the house. He had been my best buddy ... for years ... since he was a pup."

"What happened?" I inquired, still chipping and pouring hot water.

46

"Well," he stopped, pulled out his handkerchief once again to blow his nose, then resumed reticently, "Mooch went out to do his business. I called him for his dinner. He didn't come back. Mooch never turned down a meal." He stopped again as I poured more hot water on the ice. "You don't really want to hear this."

"We do if you want to tell us." I added.

Looking conflicted, he waited. A minute dragged by. Everyone looked at him.

Al said, "Yes. Tell us."

"Well, ... I began to search. Saw him. Center of the lake. Thin ice. He was in the water. Struggling to stay afloat. I had no idea ... how long he's been in it."

Bettina sniffed.

"How frightening." Miriam, shook her head.

Al asked, "What did you do?"

"I found a rope. Couldn't walk on the cracking ice. Had to wriggle myself on my stomach to him. But, not fast enough. Just as I dropped the rope noose around him," he coughed and his voice became reedy, "Mooch went down."

"Oh, no!" everyone gasped.

Bettina started to cry, "But you saved him, didn't you? Please say you saved him."

He paused to blow his nose as tears once again doused his reddened cheeks. He roughly wiped them away.

"No," he cleared his throat, "I wasn't in time."

Everyone shared their sympathy.

"I'm so sorry. That must really hurt."

"And he was your best friend," muttered Bettina, now crying copious tears as her mother tried to comfort her.

"Yeah, he was."

The trucker's emotion was threatening to create a deluge again. Suddenly, he looked deeply embarrassed. After taking a deep breath, he slowly regained his composure. Sniffing and wiping his face on his sleeve, he approached the ice-encased dog.

"Okay," he said, throwing his shoulders back as he cleared his throat and deepened his voice, "so, what happened here?"

Al responded first. "The dog has its foot caught in the ice and we're trying to dislodge it."

Standing taller and puffing out his chest, the trucker declared, to no one in particular, "I know what to do about that." He walked around the dog, rubbing his chin, seemingly making his own evaluation of the situation. Then he said to me, "You're doing it all wrong. A hammer and screwdriver are useless. What you need is a rope. I have one in the truck."

We all looked at him, uncomprehending. "Rope?"

"Of course! To pull the dog out."

Al and Miriam said almost simultaneously, "You can't pull the dog's leg out. Its foot is still incased in some ice."

I continued, "We have to get the ice away from the foot first. That'll be any time now."

"*I* know what I'm talking about. You're doing it all wrong. What you're doing is further endangering this animal. You've certainly heard of gangrene, haven't you?"

I thought, what the hell is he talking about? I knew what I was doing and it was the only thing that was going to work with the least possibility of further injury to the dog. Moreover, I'd experienced this sort of implicit male bravado before. In the past when some male had tried to "put me in my place," I felt cowed and submissive, and usually gave in, saying nothing. But not now! Like when my father refused Mr. Rogers' euthanasia, adrenaline was surging through me. Never had I felt so strong.

"This is what the emergency manuals for animals say to do." It didn't matter what he thought. He didn't know how to save this dog. *I* did. "Look, mister," I paused my digging in order to stand up to literally tower over him, "I don't know what you've done in this situation before but the best way to save *this* dog's leg is to finish melting the ice around it before we try to pull it out."

The trucker's face suffused with magenta. He looked uneasy then awkward and then furious.

"Look, sweetheart," he stammered, "by the time you finish your useless chipping and pouring, the dog will have lost its foot anyway to frostbite. Just pull the leg out!"

The group cried, "No!" in unison. He disappeared momentarily but returned with his rope.

After I had squatted again, he tried to elbow me out of the way.

"Look, I'll show you how it's done."

Employing my weight- and karate training, I remained immovable.

"Hey," said Al, who was beginning to stand from his crouching position, "knock that off."

"No! You can't do that!" Bettina screamed.

Al stated, "You pull the leg out you'd tear the skin off its paw and you'll damage the muscles and bones."

The trucker tried angrily to stand his ground, though it was becoming increasingly clear the odds were against him. He exclaimed with authority, "You're wasting time. By the time you dig the dog's foot out, the dog will be dead of hypothermia anyway."

As calmly as I could, I started to say, "This dog appears to have a two-layer coat so that's some protection ... and he has the wool coat covering him," but stopped. I had more important things to do than waste my breath on him.

The trucker sputtered, rushing full-speed ahead, as if riding a runaway train.

"If you really want to save him, the quickest solution would be to cut off the dog's foot."

Al shouted in alarm, "What? Are you out of your freaking mind?"

Hearing this, Bettina, who was no longer crying, turned to the trucker with her hands balled into fists on her hips, her face dark with outrage. Nearly spitting out the words, she shouted, "You can't cut off the dog's leg. I won't let you."

Al said, turning to the trucker, "You can't really mean that. That's cruel and unnecessary. Things are moving along fine. We're nearly done."

Miriam echoed, "That's an inhumane and disgusting idea. And you just lost your dog. What's the matter with you?"

As I glared at the trucker, his face had already flushed bordering purple. Another tear clung to his lower eyelid. He blustered, glaring at me.

"Who made you God? Have it your own way." His words were getting caught in his throat. "I'm telling you how to save the dog. But if that dog dies, it will be *your* responsibility, *your* fault, *your* blame, *your* guilt." His shoulders slumped and he turned his back on everyone. He blew his nose again.

We were almost there. As I continued chipping around the lower leg, I explained to Bettina," Don't worry. We'll release the whole leg any minute now. The vet will likely be able to save it."

As Al poured more hot water down the channels I'd created, he asked me confidentially, "What do you think are the dog's chances?"

I replied softly so as not to reach Bettina who was within hearing.

"Since the dog had likely been hit by a vehicle, there is no way as yet to know the extent of the dog's problems. There could be breaks and internal injuries."

The trucker turned and started in again, wiping his nose with the back of his hand.

"At least chip faster. You're hardly making a dent in the ice. Time is important. You're too slow to make a difference. Time is what matters ... and getting there fast enough." He stopped and wiped his nose again.

Speed was important but doing it correctly was equally important. Suddenly rage engulfed me. I realized I had let him control my thinking. Instead of arguing, I should have determined if he could help.

I blurted out, "Since you want to be helpful, do you have a blowtorch with you?"

"Yes."

"Well, would you get it?" I was biting my tongue to remain calmer, and letting blood in the process. I took off my L.L. Bean Thinsulate vest, folded it on the ground to kneel on it. My calves and thighs were cramping and burning. Note to self: Add more squats to my exercising and weight workout.

I continuously checked my watch, thinking about my promise to be at the hospital by four o'clock. My sister was scheduled to be induced at four-thirty. As Al shifted his position on the packed snow to gather more in the pan, his prosthesis knocked over the open full canister of fuel that he had beside him. He looked stunned.

"That's okay, Al. Were only a minute or so from finishing. We don't really need more hot water now but let the trucker with the blowtorch heat the last pan of water. The ice has been removed to just above the dog's toes. You've done a wonderful job."

The Keeshond was seemingly going in and out of consciousness. Bettina had stationed herself in the front of the dog, petting its head, speaking quietly to it, continually inspecting the coat to make sure it was tucked around it and not getting wet. I worried about having the hot water too close to the dog's paw for fear of defrosting the flesh too fast and burning it as we completed the job.

I asked Al to fill his camp stove pan one last time. As the trucker returned from his vehicle, he produced a large lighted blowtorch that quickly heated the snow which Al carefully poured it into the hole around the dog's foot.

Because I had already created grooves under the paw, when Al poured the last pan of hot water, I used the screwdriver to push away the softened ice around the paw. I felt the toes loosening.

"Here it comes!" I shouted.

Everyone gathered closely, waiting and watching for the final rescue. Slowly, carefully with my fingers under his toes, I finally pulled the foot out of the hole. Whoops and cheers filled the air. Everyone was patting everyone else on the back, delighted with their accomplishment. Even the trucker quietly joined in the celebration, smiling, again blowing his nose. I carefully picked the ice remnants from between the dog's pads. Taking off my black wool watch cap, I slipped the dog's foot inside it. We had been working on this for less than twenty minutes but it had seemed like hours.

When the joviality ceased, it was obvious that it was time for everyone to leave, to get back on the road to their original destinations. But it was awkward. We all had an investment. We couldn't just leave until we all knew what the plan was, that the dog would be taken care of.

Bettina asked, "Can I rub the dog's paw to warm it?"

I smiled. "Not just yet. It's very kind of you to want to help warm the dog's foot, but the skin and muscles have to warm very slowly. Pressing or disturbing the skin and muscles might harm them." Patting her on the shoulder, I said, "I'm sure your keeping the dog's body warm and talking to it has made all the difference for its recovery." I noticed Miriam glanced longingly at the coat they had just bought.

"Okay, now can anyone direct me to the nearest animal hospital?"

Miriam said, "Yes, I can. Our old gray cat, 'Possum,' used to go there before he died. It's about two miles from here. Straight ahead." She pointed. "There's a large sign. Hadley Animal Clinic will be the brick building on the left."

I thanked her, removed the coat from the dog, and handed it to Bettina.

"Thanks for being so smart for suggesting it. The dog no longer needs it. It will be in my warm car and then go into a warm bed at the animal clinic." She grinned as I continued, "I'll let the dog know of your good deed. You're what's known as a Good Samaritan."

Bettina baby-fat face broke into a brilliant smile, looking very proud of herself for helping. She reminded me of me at that age, but without the baby fat. Maybe she'd become a veterinarian or animal advocate.

Each person seemed to feel obligated to explain why they couldn't further help take the dog to the hospital. As he turned off his blowtorch, the trucker looked sheepish and hemmed and hawed.

"I need to get going. I was just passing through. You know, he'll need long-term care." Then he unnecessarily added, "if he survives."

Ignoring his added comment, I said, "Thanks."

Al smiled. "I'm glad I could help." Then apparently ignoring the cost of his camp stove fuel that he had used and lost, he slipped me $25. "To help defray the hospital costs," he whispered.

I smiled and gave him a hug.

"You worked wonders, Al. Many thanks."

The trucker observing this exchange, furrowed his brow. He walked up to me, reached for his wallet, and dramatically flashed it for everyone to see that he was following suit and more. Slowly he counted four tens into my hand.

"I appreciate your assistance. Your blow torch made a big difference. I'm very sorry about Mooch. I know it's a terribly painful loss." I didn't give him a hug.

That left Miriam. She looked self-conscious. Apologetically, she whispered to me, "I think you'll understand. I'd like help toward the dog's medical bill but right now Bettina and I can't pay anything."

I shook my head and smiled.

"No, no, that's not necessary. You've already done more than enough. Really. Both you and Bettina have been a big help."

Miriam didn't appear assuaged. She obviously wanted to explain and followed Al and me as we lifted the semi-conscious dog over the snow bank into my car where we placed him on the front passenger seat. I covered him with my retrieved vest.

Reticently, she whispered, "My husband had been incapacitated for most of this last year with hypertensive heart disease. After his first stroke, the insurance company where he worked let him go. To give him the twenty-four/seven nursing he needed I had to leave my job as a pathology lab technician at Holyoke Hospital. Then two weeks ago, he died from a stroke. You can guess the rest."

I hugged Miriam. When her back was turned away, I secretly passed the $65 I'd been given to Bettina.

"Surprise your mother with it when you get home. Tell her that I know that when she gets the chance, she'll pay it forward. Okay, you got that?"

She nodded and smiled. I felt warmed by my own altruism ... until I realized I didn't have my wallet with me, not on me or in the car. That meant no credit cards or even a check book. When I had gotten gas earlier, I had paid for it with some cash that I had unconsciously stuffed in my vest pocket along with my license. I couldn't believe what a distracted mess I had become since Mr. Rogers had died. A synaptic flash occurred in my head.

"Oh, no!" I muttered to myself. "What am I going to do at the animal clinic? Dazzle them with my charm and verbal footwork instead of paying for the dog's care? Damn!"

Before Al drove off, he gave the Keeshond a pet on the head and wished him the best.

"Thanks for letting me help. It was so gratifying. I'll never forget it … and you." He started to walk away, paused, and turned back toward me. "I hope if my new dog ever got out and needed help, someone like you would care enough to do whatever was necessary for him."

One by one the other vehicles left making me the last to depart. Before I slipped back onto the road, I put the tools back into the canvas bag. There I stopped, and angrily muttered, "Oh, damn! We didn't have to melt snow. We could have heated the distilled water I already had. I hope my moment of distraction didn't put the dog at greater risk." Shaking my head, I closed the hatch, tucked my vest more tightly around the dog, and closed the passenger door. As I started the car, I whispered to him.

"Hang on, baby. Medical help is on the way."

I took off, driving a little faster than the road conditions indicated. At first the Hadley Clinic looked as Miriam had described, like a tiny brick office building. But then, as I pulled into the small, ploughed, asphalt parking lot, I could see it had been expanded several times toward the rear, giving it greater gravitas and capabilities.

As I presented the dog as an emergency, briefly describing what had happened, the vet techs rapidly carried the barely conscious dog inside. For the first time this afternoon, I tried calling my sister. As expected, there was good service here but the line to her room was busy. I hurriedly followed into the exam room where the tall, athletically-muscular, white-haired, craggy-faced, bespectacled veterinarian was already examining the dog. Trying not to hover, I explained about the ice-stuck leg and mentioned that it was likely that the dog had been hit by a vehicle, probably the night before.

X-rays show fractured ribs and a clean break of the right front leg. Incredibly, there was no sign of internal bleeding.

"This dog's coat and your covering him with a wool coat probably saved it from severe hypothermia though his core temperature a little low, 100 degrees F. He's dehydrated. With poor pulses and a low blood pressure, the dog is in shock. We'll put him on IV fluids. He's malnourished, underweight, and may have internal and external parasites. Once the right rear leg is carefully 'defrosted,' it should be restored to normal function with only minimal therapy needed. Good thing you knew what to do. We'll put a cast on the broken leg."

I was swallowing hard trying to keep my emotions in check. As the pathetic creature lay on the steel exam table, intermittently moaning, I searched for a collar and tags. Of course, as yet unbeknownst to me, since it was a puppy mill dog, no identification existed. I allowed myself to acknowledge that this rescued dog "vaguely" reminded me of a darker version of my life-long companion I had just gut-wrenchingly put to sleep.

It was like a coruscation. I wondered if magic or divine intervention were giving me a new best friend, and a second chance. "Wait, wait," I chastised myself, "maybe there was a microchip." Anxiety tugged at my sleeve until the vet tech could scan to determine that there wasn't one. Enthusiasm and anticipation began to give me goose bumps, making arm hairs erect. I had to temper my excitement because the dog was still in a bad way. I was trying not to cry, happiness competing with my fear.

"Do everything you can to make the dog whole again." He smiled in a grandfatherly way, his blue eyes behind his thick lenses seemingly twinkling, and said he would.

This was promising the moon without a clue about how much this would cost me. I hadn't as yet become the professional I had long planned for myself. While I had been accepted at Cummings School of Veterinary Medicine at Tufts University in North Grafton, becoming a veterinarian became financially out of reach without a series of expensive loans. As a result, I went back to school at Boston University to enter another field, clinical psychology, likewise minoring in animal psychology. Uncle Harvey had promised to help me financially but he had not as yet made out a will stating that prior to his unexpected death.

Currently, I was doing my clinical internship at Beth-Israel Deaconess Medical Center's psychiatric clinic, finishing my dissertation, and working full-time as a counselor at High Point Treatment Center, an alcohol rehab facility. On the side, I was also learning about coaching, which was the up-coming thing. I was a great believer in not being a one-trick pony.

With an invoice and treatment plan in hand, I gave the clinic all the cash I had left, mostly in ones, as a down-payment, and my license number, address, and phone number.

"As soon as this dog," I had already named "Snowpaws," "can be moved, he will go to Dr. Shelby in Southampton." I provided her address and phone number as well. With the paper work done and the pooch being attended to I could leave ... but only for another important task. But before I did, I whispered in Snowpaws' ear what Christopher Robin had said to Pooh.

It again struck me as strange that this big bundle of ebony fluff kept reminding me of Mr. Rogers. They didn't look alike and likely had very different personalities. Still, something stirred. As I started for the clinic door, a backward glance gave me an inkling as to why I had had to stop for the dark shape on the side of the road. It felt like more than simple compassion or a sense of responsibility to help. But I didn't know exactly what it was.

Perhaps theologian and social activist Thomas Merton best encapsulated it, "Love is our destiny. We do not find the meaning of love by ourselves alone—we find it with another. The beginning of love is to let those we love be perfectly themselves and not to twist them to fit our own image." Or the image of a former companion.

Leaving for Holyoke Hospital, I now felt I could finally welcome my sister's first child into the world. I knew that despite my real and devastating loss of Mr. Rogers, I had been wallowing in self-pity, to the exclusion of everything else. Yet, as soon as I did the honors with the Gia, I'd be back at this clinic where I knew I really belonged—where Uncle Harvey and I belonged. Where life was also triumphing over death.

After reading the article about the assault on the puppy mill, which I wished I could have been involved in, I somehow never bothered to report my finding the escaped Keeshond. As they say, "I'd let sleeping dogs lie" ... in this case, happily with me.

5

Even though I didn't become a veterinarian, I continued to spend much of my free time helping animal humane organizations because the trend of homeless animals was increasing. But along with that trend was the increase in animal abuse. Perhaps, as a consequence, this was also the burgeoning era of investigative reporting using secret filming into the horrors of industrial farming as a profitable corporate enterprise as well as federally-funded, torturous animal experiments where companies and individuals were too often cruelly treating and slaughtering animals.

Cats were used in unproductive *what-if* medical research experiments with springs implanted in their eyes in order to collect grant money. Conscious monkeys strapped down wearing metal helmets were struck in the head with a hammer to see what kind of brain damage would be caused. Drooling, dysphagic, crippled Golden Retrievers with muscular dystrophy were being bred for decades to have the disease for experimental research which had, in all that time, produced absolutely no useful treatment or disease prevention methods for humans or dogs.

According to Peter Singer, moral philosopher, "In the real world, 90% of the money spent on medical research is focused on conditions that are responsible for just 10% of the deaths and disability caused by diseases globally."

Wolves in Wyoming were being chased by snowmobiles until they were exhausted, then repeatedly run over by the snowmobilers until they were dead, an activity that was positively sanctioned by the U.S. Fish and Wildlife Service. Exotic animals were fenced into small areas where they couldn't hide or escape so "hunters" could use their "skills" in order decimate them and take grinning selfies with their quarry. The USDA was planting cruel USDA M-44 cyanide bombs on federal lands to kill wolves, coyotes, feral dogs, and foxes, that had managed to also kill all manner of other animals, including family dogs.

The distressingly gruesome list went on and on, with daily e-mail announcements from humane groups requesting help for the latest grotesque incidents. The accumulating reported abuse gnawed at me.

In spite of the efforts of many millions of caring, compassionate people, so many abusers were not caught. Many seemed to be ignored by authorities. Others escaped arrest because they were part of the government, universities, or industries with strong lobbies so their abuse was dismissed as a necessary part of doing business. And those individuals who were arrested, too often were let off with minor sentences, if sentenced at all, because the laws allowed only misdemeanor status for acts of animal abuse, where they should have been felonies with strict, enforced punishment.

Even knowing better, I was still amazed that this cruelty and neglect knew no boundaries. In fact, these abuses were shown to cut across all social and economic strata. Furthermore, they were common in both rural and urban areas. It was depressing that this unacceptable behavior couldn't be isolated to some morally corrupt malignant group.

Feeling down after each new cruelty scenario appeared, I was now sadly seeing societies demonstrating over and over again that as a whole they simply didn't value or care enough about animals' lives and their well-being. That animals didn't have the right to live unfettered existences. In some Western societies this was supported by the Bible-based dictum of "man's dominion over animals."

Too often animals were trivialized and dismissed as useful objects, unworthy of serious concern because they couldn't reason or talk like humans. But worth isn't predicated on the ability to mimic humans. It is based on their ability to experience pleasure, pain, happiness, misery, and suffer. Surprisingly, abuse wasn't particular to any one religion, society, or culture.

About perpetrating this abuse, German philosopher Friedrich Nietzsche warned, "If you gaze into an abyss, the abyss will gaze back into you."

Over time the frequently repeated situation of exposed animal abuse began to poison my soul. I needed to neutralize the toxicity but had no idea how. The answer was just out of reach. It was like having a diaphanous, smoke-wisp-pillow-lace veil over my eyes. The answer was shrouded behind its bobbin-woven threads, tantalizing me. What was required to reveal it was beyond my ken. I only knew I was required to do something more, but the what was seductively teasing me to solve a puzzle that had too many important pieces missing.

The question Peter Singer asked in *Animal Liberation* about humans and animals had been etched into my brain: "If possessing a higher degree of intelligence does not entitle one human to use another for his or her own ends, how can it entitle humans to exploit non-humans?" Where such exploitation occurs, "We have to speak up on behalf of those who cannot speak for themselves." What had become my mantra was applicable to vulnerable people as well as to animals, but especially animals whose rights were all too often sadistically trampled. They depended on our being humane for their welfare and existence, despite our constantly wielding power and control over them.

That anxiety-tinged indecision about what further I could do hung in the back of my mind like a moth-attacked wool jacket. It was riddled with holes but still wearable, if I could ignore its being less than perfect. It goaded me to act irrespective of its incompleteness, but I needed a big shove.

But it wasn't until Snowpaws, who had become my best bud for the last ten years, died of chronic kidney failure that everything surprisingly changed. His death precipitated a new response in me to all this animal cruelty, death, and destruction. Suddenly I was primed to make a sublimely spectacular difference. So, when I chanced to meet animal abuse up close and personal, I discovered I had reached my outrage's final straw.

It happened one afternoon in northeast Rio Rancho. Rio Rancho is the third-largest and one of the fastest expanding cities in New Mexico. Even with its flat dusty topography, grit-cloaked high winds, and arid climate, it's the site of rapid housing development and Intel Corporation, which develops and manufactures their Silicon Photronics, high-speed optical connectivity for data communication, there. Rio Rancho borders sleepy Bernalillo, all four-point-seven square miles of it on the east bank of the Rio Grande, where I lived.

I was approaching the Albertson's supermarket on Route 528 on foot to pick up some Gala apples, fresh kale salad makings, and a few other miscellaneous items. Pausing on the asphalt, a few feet from where I had parked my car, I scanned the messages on my cell phone. What I was waiting for was a call about a prescription refill at my drug plan's designated Walgreen's Pharmacy down on Route 550 in Bernalillo. There was no word yet. I was about to put my phone back in my cross-body, black nylon mini handbag when I saw something that seized my attention. A man who was coming out the store's automatic glass doors suddenly stopped to try to kick a scrawny, gray, bristly-haired puppy that was ambling by. I was shocked and shouted at the top of my lungs.

"Hey, YOU!" He didn't respond.

Quickly, as I jogged toward the front of the store, I began filming the perpetrator, my cell bouncing up and down as I moved. From his demeanor, I knew he wouldn't let his failure to connect go at that. He was deliberately walking after the puppy.

Once more as I approached, I yelled.

"Hey, you! Leave that dog alone!" He still didn't seem to hear or he was ignoring me. I was only twenty feet from him. Getting closer, I was about to charge at him to distract him when I instantly felt afraid. I halted.

What if he were carrying? New Mexico is gun country. You never necessarily knew who was armed, unless they did open-carry, and who might be looking for an excuse to pop someone, especially someone who was trying to interfere with that person's idea of "entertainment."

He was tall, perhaps six feet or more, about one hundred and eighty-five pounds, looked muscular, either from heavy manual labor or weight lifting. I pegged him to be thirty-to-thirty-five years old. He was tanned, either from outdoor work or chronic sun bathing. With little cloud cover in mile-high Rio Rancho, ultraviolet radiation was particularly strong. Beneath his white cowboy hat worn jauntily low on his brow, his sideburns and his hair above his collar appeared to be medium brown, but most of it was obscured by his hat which touted a narrow black braided hat band.

There was no obvious facial hair on his squared jaw. But I couldn't see his full face. He was wearing a tightly-fitted light blue pants of some soft fabric and a fitted light blue shirt of the same fabric with a small collar and black lacing closure. Around his neck was a red scarf tied to the right and a black belt with a silver buckle. There was something familiar about his unusual attire. But what especially caught my eye was the embroidered black leather cowboy boots he was wearing with his pant legs carefully tucked in. The boots had distinctive, metal-covered toes. He could have been dressed to perform in a 1940s-1950s western film being made locally at Lionsgate Studio or at the opening of a local Hummer dealership.

It happened instantaneously. After one long stride to catch up with the jogging puppy, he lifted his leg to do it again. In a fury I impulsively screamed again, "You son of a bitch!" Only this time, just nanoseconds later, he fully connected. It was as if he were kicking a field goal for the Philadelphia Eagles to win the Super Bowl against the Patriots. The puppy flew noiselessly through the air. It smashed with a sickening crunch against the building's beige stucco-ed exterior wall. Then it dropped to the concrete walkway with a soft splat. I thought I caught a slight smile play on the abuser's lips. After glancing at the dog now lying lifeless on the sidewalk, he merely continued sauntering along as if nothing had happened.

"Goddamn dog killer!" I screamed.

He stopped. When he turned around, my heart dropped to me knees. My phone slipped out of my sweaty palm to the ground. He looked straight at me and gave me a one-sided smile. Then he drew his thumb across his throat. In five steps he could have assaulted me too. Instead, he turned and calmly resumed his departure.

Totally stunned, I couldn't move. My heart was galloping. Seconds went by before I realized that while I had caught his action before I dropped my cell phone, I had only managed to capture the side of his face. Fear and anger struggled within me.

My first impulse was to run after him. And do what? I asked myself. Tackle all six feet of him with my one hundred and thirty-five-pound, 5'11" body? Give him a hard, upward karate palm strike to the nose? Disable him with a Vulcan nerve pinch? And then what? Apply plastic cuffs, which I didn't happen to have. This was not some macho police show; this was real life. And after

I'd done all that? Manage not be personally charged with assault?

Stop it! I rebuked myself almost aloud and switched gears. He wasn't the priority. The puppy was.

I instantly ran to the sprawled puppy that bystanders, who had realized what had happened, were gathering around. Kneeling, I checked that it was breathing, but barely. Blood was seeping from one of its floppy ears and slack mouth. And one eye was protruding slightly from its socket. Painstakingly, I scooped up the limp body. Trotting to my ten-year-old Civic, I placed him on the front passenger seat on an unfolded newspaper. Serendipitously, the nearest animal clinic, Coronado Pet Hospital, was less than a mile to the north just short of the intersection of Routes 528 and 550.

As I drove, I talked to the unconscious dog with encouragement.

"Hang on, sweetie. You'll have help in just a few minutes." Snowpaws' first trip to the vet came to mind. The lump in my throat made my words squeaky and intermittent. "You know," I started to cry, "you look like a 'Teddy.' How about I call you that? Is that okay?" He didn't respond.

Because of the walrus moustache-like hair that was beginning to cover his upper lip, he vaguely reminded me of Rough Rider Teddy Roosevelt.

"Teddy? Come on, baby, stay with me."

I was full out bawling now as I incautiously cut across three lanes of traffic to get into the right lane and roar into the animal medical facility's parking lot.

"We're almost there. I promise I'll make things better for you. You have my word so don't you dare leave me."

Once inside the hospital, bearing the puppy in my outstretched arms, I could barely speak. The receptionist immediately called out their ER veterinarian, Dr. Smith, who appeared and took Teddy in.

"Follow me," she said as I stumbled after her, hardly able to see through my tears.

All I could whisper in response was, "He was kicked against a wall."

Scrupulously examining him, the thirty-ish, blonde veterinarian, who had been Snowpaws' primary vet for the last four years, quickly assessed the extent of Teddy's condition.

"He appears to have internal bleeding. That needs to be addressed immediately. The same with bleeding from his right ear." She did x-rays. "The radiographs showed he has a skull fracture. His ribs and pelvis appear to be broken. Front and back legs on right side are broken as well. And his right eye needs to be removed."

I stared at him, disbelieving, on the one hand glad he was alive and on the other heartbroken that he was so badly injured. Would he die anyway ... after all I had promised him? I thought if only Dr. Smith could also have been trained at the Hogwarts School of Witchcraft and Wizardry. Then maybe she could have waved Harry Potter's holly-wand-with-phoenix-feather-core and incanted a healing spell to create a puppy miracle, to mend this baby immediately. Make him happy, healthy, and whole again. *Brackium Emendo*. That could take care of his ribs, pelvis, skull, and legs. As for his spleen, eye, and bleeding from his ear, I didn't know if *Reparo* would work but it was worth a try.

Part of me felt it was my fault Teddy was hanging on by a thread. I should have done something more than repeatedly yelling before the man caught up with the puppy. I assumed he was going to try to kick Teddy again and should have acted accordingly. I should have physically stopped him ... somehow. But I didn't. Fearing the consequences of my actions, I didn't interfere with his. That meant I was complicit in Teddy's demise. My tears were drying but I was getting a headache as the muscles in my shoulders and neck tightened into spasms.

When Dr. Smith looked at me and then back at Teddy. I noticed Teddy's tummy was enlarging. That was likely the accumulating blood.

"His chances are probably good, depending, of course, upon if we find anything else. We need to do surgery immediately."

I bit my lip, then slowly nodded. My face was saturating with blood once more. Dr. Smith left the exam room to talk with Dr. Mitchell, one of the hospital's surgeons, to fill him in on Teddy's problems as the vet techs prepared for Teddy's surgery.

For only a split second, I saw Teddy's good left eye's eyelid flicker. He opened it and seemed to focus his cinnamon-tinted iris on me. I had been stroking him, whispering to him that I'd make it all okay. In that millionth of a second we connected. I knew without question that he knew I was there to help him. I could feel his trust, his puppy gratitude, despite his devastated body wracked with indescribable pain. Then, just as quickly, his gaze faltered and the linkage disappeared. The vet tech, Sarah, returned.

I squeezed my face together and whispered in Teddy's ear again.

"Just relax, sweetheart. Everything will be better. Good news. We're not sending you over the Rainbow Bridge." To myself, I murmured, "I hope."

I began to cry angry tears. Instead of letting Sarah scoop him up, I bent over his crumpled body on the exam table. Even though time was of the essence, I wanted to cradle him against me, but didn't. Blood from his mouth, ear, and rectum were dripping. Instead, I picked him up in my arms and carried him flat into the surgical suite. My tears bathed his rough coat. His bladder let loose on me. Placing him on the flat, hydraulic-base, stainless steel operating table, I left to use the rest room.

This senseless destruction of the puppy exploded in a sweeping fury. I raged at the universe.

"We're supposed to protect the vulnerable! How can there be so much unspeakable cruelty that's never avenged?"

I used the toilet and scrutinized myself in the mirror above the sink. Deep within the convolutions of my brain I knew there was no such thing as "fairness" in this world, as much as I truly wanted such an attitude to exist because it "should" exist. Sadly, it was wishful thinking. In a daze, I washed my hands but nothing else.

I re-entered the surgical suite on its periphery. As Dr. Mitchell prepared Teddy for his abdominal surgery, Sarah put her arm around my shoulders and led me to the waiting room. Dr. Smith was nearby talking to another client who was holding a cat with an abscess on its paw. When she finished, she walked to me, looking downcast, and whispered.

"What was done to that puppy is so criminal. It's disheartening too. I see way too much of this."

Sarah who was still standing with me.

"I shouldn't say this but I can understand how people could feel justified in killing someone who'd do that to such a defenseless creature."

Then as Dr. Smith left the packed waiting room and Josie, another vet tech, escorted the client with her cat into one of the "cat" rooms where Dr. Smith would examine the feline, Sarah took a moment to continue. Coming closer to whisper in my ear, she began as words flew from her. Trying to keep her composure, she shared that she had experienced this abuse too.

"Someone stole 'Delilah,' my beloved Yorkipoo, from my fenced yard." Her face reddening and voice cracking, she explained, "She was the sweetest, most cuddly dog. She loved everybody but they beat her and then left her battered body inside my fence. The emergency specialty hospital in Albuquerque did everything they could but she was so injured. From head injuries, she was left blind in both eyes and had trouble walking. For months I provided her therapy, hoping for a miracle. She gets around with a little difficulty and pain meds but she seems content most of the time, especially when she's snuggled in my lap. But she's getting old and arthritis is settling into her previously damaged joints."

I hugged her. "What happened was awful but I'm glad she's back with you."

Echoing Dr. Smith, she said, "We see so many more abused animals. It makes it hard to have to deal with them and makes me, sometimes, question my profession. No one was ever charged with Delilah's theft and abuse even though my landlord had outdoor surveillance cameras."

Then she paused. "Dr. Mitchell will do his very best to save Teddy. In fact, he just did abdominal surgery on Dr. Smith's Irish Setter, 'Maiti,' who had an intestinal blockage. Maiti had been a naughty girl. She got hold of three banana skins and ate them. In the scheme of things that was somewhat better than her trying to eat a lizard, which I understand she has also tried to do. In the meantime, if there's anything else we can do to help, please let us know."

I clasped her hand. "I'm so sorry about your Delilah. Give her a pet for me."

As her nose reddened, she lowered her head and nodded, then left me sitting in the reception area. I was still stunned, picturing Teddy, lying lifeless on the examination room table. I didn't want to leave the puppy, but surgery would be lengthy. The barbarity exercised upon Teddy brought home everything I had ever seen, read, and heard about animal abuse. It was like the culmination of all the indescribable past, present, and future cruelties against animals on the planet.

Wet eyeliner and flaking mascara had run down my red cheeks in rivulets, some settling into dark circles under each eye like soot. I looked like a raccoon wannabee for Hallowe'en. My blouse was wet and stippled with waxy black detritus like gun powder residue. Teddy's blood and urine had pooled on me, making me look like the victim of an accident, but I ignored it all. Making sure I looked presentable in public at this particular moment seemed inconsequential.

Before I put a down payment on Teddy's bill, I asked Sarah to have Dr. Smith write up Teddy's medical evaluation for me. She said, with a slight smile, "I was already going to do it. But I'll wait until Dr. Mitchell determines whatever else may be going on so we can have a full and accurate medical status and a prognosis."

My goal was to take the video and Teddy's medical assessment to the authorities ... Suddenly, I realized, I didn't know to whom I should take them. Was it to the police or Animal Control? The police seemed like the logical place to make a report but regulations for that sort of thing could vary from state to state and community to community. I didn't know what it was here in the county of Sandoval or within the boundaries of Rio Rancho.

I was too antsy to sit and wait so I began pacing. Annette, the pregnant receptionist who was overwhelming her teal scrubs, waved at me subtly, trying repeatedly to get my attention. My constant movement was disturbing other clients and their animals. When I finally saw her, I apologized to everyone present, and took my pacing outdoors. Before I left, however, I got the police business and Animal Control numbers from her. I'd phone from the parking lot.

When I made my first call to the police, the line was busy. After fifteen minutes of sitting in my car and not getting through, I tried Animal Control's number. What I needed to ask was a straightforward, simple question, or so I thought. I reached whoever answered the phone and tried to explain that the abuse had already happened, the animal was in surgery and hanging on to life, and I wanted to know to whom to report it.

"You recorded what? Christ, that's sick! Why in hell are you calling me? What do you expect me to do about it? Go clean up the blood? Shit, lady. You've got some damn nerve! Fuck off, dumb ass."

What the ...? Had some smart-alecky kid who was delivering lunch to them answered the phone in the supervisor's absence? Had someone been snorting a line or two at lunch time? Or taking more than a nip? I had heard that Animal Control was very responsible. But there had been no sign of it on the phone. It seemed to me that what I said was being received that I was either making videos for "crush" films or making a prank call.

Before I could make a valiant attempt at clarification, the person on the other end of the call had hung up. I sat staring at my cell phone. Had I really reached Animal Control? The call left me with the anxious feeling that Animal Control was going to locate me through my caller ID and send someone banging on my front door with a warrant to search my premises for abused animals and/or abuse-related DVD-making equipment.

I tried the police again with no success then returned to the waiting room to ask Annette what I should do. She reminded me that Drs. Smith and Mitchell would do the report as soon as he finished with the puppy's surgery but it would still be a while.

"Regarding whom to call, Dr. Smith says you should start with Animal Control. If the case needs to go to the police, it would eventually filter down to them. But I wouldn't hold out much hope for anyone finding the perpetrator even with your video."

As much as I wanted to go report this, I couldn't leave. It was two hours later that Dr. Mitchell came to the waiting room, which now had only a few scattered clients, and took me into an empty examination room.

"Teddy did have internal bleeding because his spleen had ruptured, probably from the kick itself, so I removed it. Then I repaired the right eardrum laceration which caused bleeding from his ear. Those both have a good prognosis. I also removed Teddy's detached eye. That isn't a problem. His other eye looks undamaged."

Hoping he was finished, I let out a sigh of relief I'd been holding on to tightly since Teddy entered the operating room. But then he continued.

"His right front and rear tibias—lower leg bone—which both had complete transverse fractures—clean breaks—were stabilized in fiberglass casts. He's fortunate the breaks weren't of his femurs—upper leg bone—because they would have had to be pinned. And doing casts on them is trickier. Healing time for puppies for these current breaks is about four weeks. He had both a fractured pelvis and broken ribs which will probably heal with cage rest."

"What about his head? His head struck both the wall and sidewalk?"

"Luckily, his skull fracture was only hairline. If it had been otherwise, there likely would have been trauma to the brain which would have required heroics and had a poor prognosis."

I couldn't believe what I was hearing. When I had rushed him to the hospital, I didn't think he had a prayer. It was "Adios, Teddy." But, that little body of bristly hair was going to survive his injuries. I wanted to cry all over again but this time from happiness.

"He's on anti-inflammatory, antibiotic, and pain medications. So, while he's currently in serious condition, he has a good likelihood of full recovery. We'll see from day to day. He's going to have to stay here a while so we can monitor him for any complications. But given how he looks right now I don't expect any."

After Dr. Mitchell finished explaining Teddy's prognosis, Sarah gave me Teddy's report with a quick grief-stricken hug.

"Thanks for recuing him. He's such a little sweetheart. He has a long haul ahead ... but now he has a future ... thanks to you. I wish someone like you could have been there to rescue Delilah in time to prevent her from being hurt and so damaged."

Feeling torn about leaving, I checked the hospital's phone book again. I re-checked the Animal Control number. I had copied it incorrectly. So maybe I wouldn't be visited by a SWAT team after all. With directions I drove there immediately, muttering angrily that I should have gotten even better pictures of the abuser. Of course, it wouldn't have hurt if I hadn't been trying to film while hurrying closer, and more importantly, if I hadn't dropped my phone when he turned to stare threateningly at me.

The Rio Rancho Animal Control was a large, two-story, brick and pink stucco building, off Northern Boulevard, set on the edge of an arroyo, surrounded by shade-providing Siberian elms and Russian olives, with chain link-fenced kennels and dog runs out back. As I entered, my blood-stained blouse, urine-soaked slacks, and runny eye make-up caused others to look askance at me. If I'd also have had gray, peeling skin, I could have auditioned for yet-again another remake of *Night of the Living Dead.*

I found a heavy-set officer at the front desk who seemed to be the one with whom to speak. He was about 5'8", weighing close to three hundred pounds, and looked as if he had never met a pizza, honey-drizzled fried bread, or creamy dessert he didn't like. Scattered wisps of dull, dun-colored hair from a lower fringe were combed over his spacious balding pate. He had dark bushy eyebrows, like clinging hairy caterpillars, which partially obscured his eyes, and the lax jowls of a Bloodhound. His physique surprised me since I expected Animal Control and police officers to be required to be in reasonable shape. He must have been desk-bound because I could not imagine him "running" after an escaping dog or perp, risking a stroke or heart attack.

His name tag said "Hardess." I explained what had happened. He raised his untamed eye brows and the corners of his lips curved up. At first, I thought he was going to laugh. But then as he more carefully studied my body-fluids-soaked attire, he frowned. Suspicion replaced his questionable initial joviality. I didn't understand his reactions.

As I described what had happened, his eye brows lifted again. He pursed his lips in incredulity. Even after I played the video for him and showed him the medical report, he seemed to find it all a bit dubious.

Now glowering at me, he dramatically shook his head.

"You're saying you actually just stood there and filmed this person abusing the dog and you did nothing about it?" He raised his voice, "What the hell is the matter with you?"

Others turned and stared. I was stunned. My brain had disconnected with my tongue. Finally, I squeaked.

"Officer Hardess, I yelled at him three times as I ran toward him, filming just in case my shouting didn't stop him."

Hardess looked me up and down and shook his head as if sickened by my "lack of acceptable actions."

I gathered my courage together.

"Okay, so, just what would you have expected me to do ... on the off-chance he *might* try again to kick the dog? Charge into him and get myself arrested for assault when he hadn't actually done anything ... yet?"

He ignored my questions and took another tack.

"It strikes me as strange that you filmed him just as he abused the dog. That doesn't sound reasonable to me. It sounds as though you *knew* he was going to do it and were there to film it. Maybe for Facebook or YouTube?"

My blood pressure was climbing, I thought about my knee connecting with Jim and the Twins, if it could find them under all that pendulous fat.

"Look, I'm a clinical psychologist. I know about the psychology of abusers and have seen animal abusers before. He tried once, missed, and looked *very likely* to try again. But I'm not psychic. I hoped my yelling and filming would dissuade him. His trying again was only a possibility, not a fact."

"Yeah, but if you had done something more than 'filming,' you might have prevented the dog being severely injured in the first place."

I wanted to scream, "You son of a bitch!" That was a low blow and totally unnecessary. His job was to take the report, not pass judgment on my reactions to what I'd witnessed. I pictured my fist snuggly ensconced in his puckering pig-butt-shaped mouth.

"Yeah, sure," I mimicked his tone, "I should have attacked him on the chance he'd kick the dog and been arrested for assault and battery." My brain was swimming in black anger. Why did I have to deal with this antagonistic jerk!

He looked at me with indignation building. I suspected he was tired of me and my story but, mostly, of my not genuflecting to his authority. I didn't care. He was choosing not to believe any of what I'd said. I imagined him thinking that using a rubber hose on the soles of my bare feet might make me shape up. And, perhaps, confess that I was the real co-perpetrator of a crime and not a witness to the abuse.

At this point with a deep sigh he finally got down to business. "You are required to file a short, concise, factual report specifying what you observed. That includes the date, location, and approximate time. So where are your witness statements?"

"Witness statements?" I asked, my voice rising, hinting at my doubting his sanity.

"Yes," he asserted patronizingly, "you need witness statements to support your report."

"Are you serious?" I blurted out.

His eyes reduced to slits. Catching myself, I tried to calmly point out.

"There was a broken, bleeding, barely breathing puppy in overwhelming pain. I wasn't going to stand around and collect recollections like a journalist for a story when Teddy's life hung in the balance." My exasperated response dripped with sarcasm. "It's not as though I witnessed a nice, clean-cut, no-injury robbery."

His barely-submerged spleen concentrated his stare at me, as engorged capillaries rose closer to the surface of his skin, producing a magenta which climbed from his neck, under his dewlap, to his hairline. He clenched his fist and shouted at me.

"Watch your mouth, little lady! Don't you dare smart-ass me!"

My face reddened as my blood pressure rose too.

As others in the Animal Control facility again turned to see what was happening, he took a breath and resumed his lecture on witness statements.

"Witness statements are essential to your report so we know details of what happened. For example, maybe someone there knew him." Then something interrupted his thought. "Wait a second. You just called the dog 'Teddy.' Was he your dog? If not, how did you know his name?"

"Kee-rist!" I almost exclaimed as I too made a fist I wanted to slam on his desk. I was letting him push all my buttons. "No," I seethed, "he wasn't my dog. I didn't know him before the incident. He was just a stray that chanced to trot by."

"Oh, yeah. But you knew his name."

"No," I took a deep breath, counting to ten. "I didn't *know* his name. I *named* him on the way to the animal hospital because I didn't want him to die without a name."

He mattered whether or not he had an 'owner.' I was on the verge of crying again but I held it at bay. No way. Not in front of this bozo.

"And, yes, I do understand about the importance of witness statements," I sighed, thinking I'd watched *Law and Order* more than enough times to know. "But ... that's why I'm giving you a video which describes precisely what happened. It doesn't include other people's observations and knowledge but it should certainly speak for itself."

Hardess didn't look convinced but made a copy of my video and the puppy's medical evaluation. I wondered from his demeanor if he himself gave a damn about animals, really saw this incident as a crime. Maybe he was one of those sub-humans who beat their dog or essentially abandoned it, chained outside, starving, alone, and neglected all year long, irrespective of weather.

As much as I already knew the answer, I asked anyway, "How likely is it you will find this animal abuser?"

He smiled.

"Unless we get a solid tip or can catch the guy in the act, it's unlikely we'll find him. But, as I indicated, *if* you locate the other witnesses and take down their signed statements, it could possibly help. You won't know until you actually try."

Imagining him waving his sausage-like index finger in my face, I attempted not to roll my eyes at what he was saying. Find the other witnesses? You mean, strangers going into and coming out of Albertson's? And even if I could secure witness statements, would this officious dolt give a goddamn and *really* do anything about them?

6

Once I was home in my twelve-hundred square-foot, beige, pueblo-style rental house on Camino Vista Rio off Sheriff Posse Road and near the Rio Grande, I debated what to do next. First, I decided to post the video containing his facial profile on Facebook and other social media sites. As I turned on my desktop computer in my office, the ten-by-twelve square-foot second bedroom which was equidistant from the living room, kitchen, and dining room, I suddenly stopped. Was it really a good idea to draw attention to myself by providing it in a post with my identity attached? The potential negative consequences swirled around me. The abuser could see it, recognize me, become angry, even vengeful, and try to track me down. I needed a better way of getting the word out and the sooner the better. It was clearly up to me to do something.

In lieu of any better plan, I started making up color fliers with the abuser's facial and physical profile, his western-style dress, a screen shot of the broken, bleeding puppy on ground with a detailed description of the abuse event and an urgent request for witnesses to call the Animal Abuse Hotline with tips. Someone was sure to recognize him by his face or his unusual attire and could report him, at least to the hotline. Contacting all the animal rescue groups and rescue shelters in the area by e-mail, I asked for their assistance in distributing the attached flyer throughout the surrounding towns. It was a very close, active network of vigilant animal activists with whom I had worked for several years.

I didn't tell them I was the one who filmed the event from which the stills were derived and, furthermore, asked that my name not be associated with it in any way. Moreover, if they had Facebook, Twitter, Instagram, and website accounts, I asked if they could post the anonymously-produced video? While everyone I contacted promised to help with the posters, they added that putting the video on their sites needed an okay from a higher up. The consensus was not to count on it. I figured that was a legal liability issue.

Two days later when I drove through Albuquerque to go to the University of New Mexico where I taught psychology, I saw the posters. Over a short period of time they would become faded from the ultraviolet radiation or wind-torn from our frequent high winds. But in the interim, they were useful. If necessary, new copies could replace the old. Some of the organizations had encased the flyers in clear plastic envelopes to increase their longevity. After several days when I called the Animal Abuse Hotline, I discovered there had been no tips yet.

But what about Animal Control? Hardess's dismissiveness and pessimism made me feel even more frustrated yet I had to check to see if they had learned anything. When I inquired, unfortunately I got Hardess. He didn't sound thrilled to hear from me.

"Where are those witness statements?" he challenged me. "Without them we have very little to go on."

Likewise, he reported no progress. The perpetrator had not as yet been identified much less caught. Even with that unusual get-up he was wearing? It had been a week since the incident and nothing had come to light as a result of all these efforts.

Teddy was still in intensive care, hanging on somehow. I visited him every day and wanted to cry all over again. Thinking about having helped save Snowpaws a decade ago, I tried to convince myself that it wasn't beyond the realm of possibility this could work out too. Despite what Drs. Mitchell and Smith had optimistically said, I wasn't as yet convinced of it.

And, as the second week ended, things had not changed information-wise. Still no tip calls meant that the abuser was free to continue to abuse animals, publicly and privately. I also sent reminders with his profile photo and description to all animal shelters and rescue organizations to be on alert for him so they would be sure not to adopt any animals to him. If only I could have filmed his full face, even a three-quarter view. I mentally punished myself again for dropping my cell.

From my volunteer work with homeless animal rescue and psychological research on animal cruelty, I knew the sad statistics about animal abusers. It was a frightening fact that they frequently were ticking bombs. While they may have been expressing their anger, violent tendencies, and maybe their psychopathic personalities against animals initially, they tended to progress to expressing their anger and violent tendencies against humans as well, especially toward the more vulnerable, women and children.

Researchers had found that in seventy-one-to-eighty percent of domestic abuse cases family pets were targeted as well and killed. Likewise, pet abuse had been found to occur in eighty-eight percent of families under supervision for physical abuse of their children. There was a strong correlation between intentional cruelty to animals and amplified violence toward vulnerable people.

Seated at my desk as I thought back to Teddy's attacker, he didn't seem outwardly angry. He wasn't ranting, raving, or gesticulating wildly. In fact, he seemed cool, controlled, and calculating when he had to speed up his pace to position himself correctly to try to kick the puppy again.

In a dark phantasm world of my primitive reptilian brain's creating, I wanted to confront this abuser, pull out an AK-47, a gas-operated 7.62x39 mm. assault rifle developed in the Soviet Union by Mikhail Kalashnikov, and shoot him in the bah-doo-bees. Or, perhaps, better, since I wasn't fond of guns, I could string him up by ankles in the town square slathered in peanut butter for the dogs to nibble on and everyone to scorn. But, perhaps, fortunately, this parallel universe wasn't reality. Zapping him or letting him swing publicly in the breeze wasn't going to happen. But, by God, something had to be done to avenge Teddy and all the animals who had suffered at the hands of such monsters!

That so many abusers were essentially being given carte blanche by society's apathy or justice's inadequacy to hurt, torture, and destroy more and more animals drove me crazy. I was sick and tired of the brutality surrounding the existence and survival of the voiceless non-humans. If only the prohibition against cruelty to animals were a commonly accepted value and attitude. However, it was only in a benign dictatorship that kindness, care, and compassion for animals could be required to be taught, controlled, and its transgressions punished. But as much as I wanted kindness to prevail, I didn't really want an authoritarian government, benign or otherwise, to effect it.

What I wanted was someone to stand up, like a Superhero or Caped Crusader, for the animals. I wanted something done that was more than what animal humane and animal rescue organizations—and even Animal Control and the police, when, unlike Hardess, they truly cared and acted—could do.

What humane organizations did was great, as far as they could go. They rescued all kinds of animals, like neglected dogs that were tethered and left to fend for themselves outside. They rescued the homeless and saved the abused, worn-out, and sick from puppy mills, farms, and dog fighting rings and provided them with medical care and sanctuary. They worked hard to legislate, to change the laws regarding cruelty to animals. From what I had read, a majority of anti-cruelty laws were limited to misdemeanors and varied with respect to definitions of aggravated cruelty, torture, or cruelty to companion animals. Moreover, they varied from state to state, wherein enforcement could likewise vary from community to community. It wasn't acceptable!

What I wanted deep in my heart was in-your-face revenge! YES! Maybe that was "vigilante-ism" ... but maybe this situation demanded being some sort of a vigilante to make a real, immediate, positive difference, acting against all the existing probabilities. Whatever it took—well, not really breaking the law ... too much—these animals deserved it.

It was clear to me that *I* needed to so something more. But what could I, a single individual, do that millions of others hadn't already done? While I knew I couldn't save each and every abused animal—and I certainly couldn't prevent all the despicable acts of every kind of abuse—maybe, I could develop and initiate a campaign which provided some form of pay back to the abusers.

A malicious grin slowly creased my cheeks as evil fantasies exploded in a breathtaking display before my eyes. Yes, maybe I could help bring public, social, psychological, financial, and, perhaps, even physical pressure to bear and make these bloodthirsty creatures from Hell examples of what could happen to animal abusers. Maybe then a positive societal attitude change regarding compassion toward animals could occur, controlled by peer pressure, along with encompassing legislation and enforcement of stringent anti-cruelty laws.

After Teddy's attack, I had discovered that I couldn't merely continue to angrily agonize over the daily reports of only an infinitesimal percentage of world-wide animal abuse. No one individual had taken the lead to come forward in all these decades of abuse to do something amazingly righteous to change things. As my momentum increased, I realized a great graphic-novel avenger with girded loins, six-pack abs, and great pecs—someone like Ricardo Montalban as *Star Trek*'s "Khan (Noonien Singh)," the genetically-enhanced superhuman who, with strength and superior intellect, ruled Earth—had to come forward ... soon ... to make that difference! But, unlike "Khan," this avenger would make an overwhelming *positive* difference.

"No!" I stood up and shook my fist at the heavens, proclaiming, "We can't wait any longer." Nearly shouting now, I declared, "That someone has to be *me*!" Taken aback, I shook my head in surprise at my own outburst. "Yes," I stammered, "*I* alone have to be the one to start the ball rolling, to take revenge on these abusers." This was a whole new side of me coming out. From being a non-assertive youngster to a full-throated avenger was an incredible and totally unexpected transformation.

Seated again, I still couldn't quite believe what *I* had vowed to achieve. I wasn't a promulgator of hate and violence. As my adrenaline slowed its circulating, reality tapped me on the shoulder. This needed a plan. Not just any plan, but a complex, intricately developed, full-blown plan to even the score a little. Crazy ideas swirled around me, some more vindictive than I would have imagined.

But before I got too far, my rational side irritatingly intruded. It reminded me that I had to determine what "revenge" for animal abuse really meant to me and precisely what it would and would not entail. That definitely took some of the bloom off my impassioned rose of retribution.

Oddly, in retrospect, I recognized that I had never, as far as I could recall, ever participated in revenge. Even as a shunned tall child, I tried, often unsuccessfully, to ignore the bullies and derogators. One might say I had a wishbone where my backbone should have been. Too often I let them see my hurt and confusion which was, no doubt, what they wanted and acted to promote.

As I grew older, I learned that how I chose to respond depended on the situation. I might walk away when I could. I might ignore them by pretending I didn't hear, distracting myself, or concentrating on what I was doing. Or I might calmly address the bullying directly. The latter approach seemed the most positive whenever possible, showing that I could stand up for myself. That, however, did not come easily. Irrespective of what I did, I was determined I wasn't going to let them play with my head. By not reacting emotionally, I kept them from receiving the full satisfaction they desired. That made me one-up.

But this wasn't about me and how I responded to personal attacks. This was about the abuser. It was also about the many millions of people who felt powerless to prevent animals from being abused and who, like me, daydreamed about paying back those who so cavalierly tortured and lustily dispatched them. Those who loved and respected animals who wanted them to be able to live unharmed and be appreciated for being a part of Nature and their own lives.

My mind was radiating like a chunk of plutonium-239, sending out alpha scintillations in all directions. I was energized. My body felt lighter. I suddenly felt emboldened and empowered. I—yes, I—was the one who would embark on this sanctified mission. In my mind I pictured myself standing atop a tall building, sheathed in a clingy white bodysuit—all 5'11" of me—with a golden AAA for "Animal Abuse Avenger" (not "American Automobile Association") emblazoned across my breast, legs apart, fists on hips, head up, a red cape unfurling behind me in the wind. I was a Superhero right out of Marvel Comics. I might not have the full range of super powers Marvel heroes had but I was *going* to do this ... and I couldn't ... no, wouldn't ... fail. I straightened my back as my face lifted in an omnipotent smile.

As I considered the concept of revenge, it was plain that analytically it meant to me imposing costs to the abuser as a type of deterrence so he (and others) would feel less incentivized to continue practicing his harm. Emotionally, however, it was a profound moral desire inflaming my heart, soul, and gut for me to keep faith with the abused animals, to honor their lives and memories, and ... somehow "even the score," to set the world right. I couldn't go back and fix what had happened to Teddy. I couldn't erase it either, but ...

The more I thought about it, the more I knew I wanted to make those cruel sons of bitches truly suffer for making animals suffer. Basking in the glow of sanctimony and self-righteousness, I realized, with dismay, I had no idea how I was going to strategize this battle.

Its enormity was becoming clear. It wasn't going to be as simple or straightforward as I imagined when seeing myself in my nifty red cape. Killing these people was clearly out of the question. It wasn't just that it was unethical, illegal, and against my strongly-held principles. Violence as a way to achieve justice was clearly impractical. Besides, killing them was just too quick and merciful. That also went for physical harm. I wanted them to linger in their psychological pain, wherever it was that would hurt them the most and dissuade them from violent repetition. Their suffering had to become a strong symbol of what *not* to do.

As a clinical psychologist, I knew that attacking them publicly, socially, psychologically, and financially would likely hurt them worse than any physical pain I could possibly inflict. It would undermine their self-esteem and sense of security and make them feel anxious and fearful. Maybe their friends and family would turn away from them as well, not wanting to be associated with the abuser's public excommunication from society for having been labeled as a "brute" and "pariah."

But that meant I had to be very careful, if not practically clairvoyant. I didn't want to do anything to make these abusers feel I was attacking them personally, instead of their behavior, at least initially. So as not to allow their boldness, disinhibition, and egotism to be further inflamed and directed at animals. In reality, their chosen response to whatever I did, however, was going to be unpredictable. Specifically, no matter how much personal data I collected on them, there was no way to be sure what my strategies and tactics would precipitate. Positive results would require a *lot* of luck. As I considered the possible ramifications of my actions, I suspected I might be expecting way too much.

Whatever I planned, the tactics had to be unexpected, seemingly random at first, and anonymous. Like a series of Blitzkrieg attacks. As I ruminated upon it, I smiled as I considered that—gee, whiz—if I *just* happened to somehow "accidentally" inflict a little physical discomfort in the process—like Tasering them unconscious, flopping around, convulsing, pissing all over themselves—well, that couldn't be helped and wouldn't deter my other efforts.

No. No. No! I quickly scolded myself. I didn't have a Taser or other electroshock device. Physical abuse was out, which in my darker moments felt like a bad deal. However, my slipping into such sadistic thoughts could not and would not be allowed. As Nietzsche also said, "Whoever fights monsters should see to it that in the process he does not become a monster." Those thoughts would defeat my whole purpose.

For my overarching campaign, initially I considered choosing either personally-observed abuse or abuse found in social media or newspapers. It had to have occurred near my location for me to work on it. Later on, ideally, as I expanded my far-reaching Caped Crusader efforts, I might also be able to address animals abused in every situation, including factory farming, medical and pharmaceutical research, entertainment, etc. Grandiosity was nudging me in the ribs as I contemplated my avenging future. However, as the magnitude of what such an effort would entail slowly dawned on me, I knew that much of that was merely an ambitious fantasy.

I was, after all, only a minor Marvel hero. I couldn't swoop in like Superman and create supernatural phenomena. However, when I thought of Snowpaws, what I really wanted to do was travel around the country lawlessly destroying puppy mills. Rescuing the animals, providing them with medical care, getting them adopted into loving homes, and blowing these "manufacturing facilities" and their owners to kingdom come. "Domestic terrorism"? Well, yeah … maybe … a little around the edges.

My brain was again exploding with ideas. Brainstorming, I started making lists of possibilities, no matter how outsized, silly, or grotesque. I'd evaluate each of them later when I was done:

1. My initial outing would be for Teddy's abuser.

2. Next, maybe I could make my services known to animal lovers through an obvious pattern of abusers getting their comeuppance. This, of course, would have nothing to do with Animal Control or the police. My work would touch the nerve of all animal lovers who would revel in my activities, doing what they so passionately desired to do themselves.

3. I'd have to keep police in the dark about my actions.

4. As more and more people wanted to contract my services to avenge their or others' pets' abuse, I probably couldn't continue on my own.

5. If I wanted to counter the unconcern of the legal system in dealing with animal abusers, I probably couldn't continue on my own.

6. Eventually, I'd need to create an organization of like-minded people.

I was pleased with what appeared on the paper. Items numbered four through six particularly sounded good to me. Nodding with enthusiasm, I knew I couldn't do everything on my own.

Whoa! Wait a minute! There was a glaring problem that I couldn't wait to finish the list to address. Being publicly recognized? Inviting others to join me? My going public would pose some real potential problems. Having many others involved would put me at considerable risk. As I wrote down the possible initial problems, more came to mind:

1. One obvious problem with people wanting to join me would be that if I refused to let them in, for whatever reason, they might become miffed for being rejected and report me.

2. If they wanted to do something I thought was out of bounds, they might become miffed for being rejected and report me.

3. If someone were unhappy with me for *any* reason, they could retaliate by working with the police to set a trap to ensnare me for my skirting the law.

4. Sadists and others with Anti-Social Personality Disorder who were looking for an acceptable way to hurt others might want to join.

5. I couldn't trust others to be silently involved with me in such a questionable, nefarious endeavor. There was nothing to prevent them from sharing what they were doing with anyone, potentially making it public.

6. Was there *any* way I could have others join me so we could accomplish so much more, quickly, without putting me at risk?

In reality, having others join me negated my control over any of it. There were too many formidable problems with involving others. That meant, at least for the moment, whatever I did, I'd have to do it on my own. That would slow me down, but not stop me. But then again, what if I hired people who couldn't afford to rat me out, like contract killers? I would still want to do it secretly so I couldn't be tied to them. Being discovered in a conspiracy with or as an accomplice of criminals, especially murderers, was too risky and not great PR. Besides, they'd probably charge too much.

Suddenly I realized I was skirting the boundaries of the *Outer Limits* with my extreme ideas. I needed a break. A hot cup of Celestial Season's "Red Zinger" tea and fifteen minutes of meditation helped. After my break, my brain's seizure of the creative outlandishness had resolved itself.

7. Although, maybe, in the future, while I would still work alone finding and targeting abusers, I could create an Animal Abuse Registry. It would list and describe in detail, with photos, all known animal abusers in an area, state, or nationally, like a Sexual Abuse Registry, and make it available to everyone. I might be able to get animal humane organizations to set it up, keep it up to date, and monitor it.

Oh, crap! It occurred to me that even that could be problematic. There would have to be people responsible for making sure the information was totally accurate. It wouldn't be practical or helpful if innocent people mistakenly were included, making the animal humane organizations liable for defamation civil suits. Still, that did have some potentiality for being the basis of a worthwhile project much later on.

I went back to my original list of possible things the "Animal Abuse Avenger" could do:

7. What about my filming revenge and posting it on social media to humiliate the abuser and warn other abusers? I remembered that a man had posted a video of himself whirling a leashed puppy in the air then slamming it into sidewalk, breaking its legs, and undoubtedly causing internal injuries. The man struck a macho pose and had a supercilious smile spread across his face for a friend who was filming him. What

if I could then demonstrate how I rescued the puppy and made life ever-so-difficult for the abuser?

Doing that, however, could be particularly risky for me as an avenger unless I were in disguise. Yes! No! I couldn't put out a video of myself stalking him, "rescuing" (aka, stealing) his dog, and harassing him, even for a good cause, without ending up in the slammer. This was absurd and had to be rejected out of hand.

Something else was also slowly dawning on me.

8. I had to be careful of my filmed actions, if any. I couldn't do anything that might encourage "non-Superheroes" to do something on their own which could cause them and me legal repercussions. That meant that if I shared anything with others, it would have to be only my talking about bringing animal abusers to justice. It couldn't be anything that would make me responsible for how others acted on my words or actions. Specifically, I couldn't be seen as instructing them, encouraging them, or suggesting they take the law into their own hands.

"Real" Superheroes weren't constrained by all these legal and ethical problems.

9. My overall goal was to reduce the number of animal abusers by peer pressure and motivate legislators to make animal abuse a clearly-spelled out felony with significant penalties for it—a law that would be strictly enforced by the police. This was an outrageous challenge, but a sublime goal.

"Whoa! Good grief!" I exclaimed, shaking my head in amazement. "I'm getting way ahead of myself." This was supposed to be about my Caped Crusader's first and most important endeavor: Finding and dealing with

Teddy's abuser. "What I need to be doing is constructing a real, executable plan for this and only this. Only once this deed is accomplished can other things be considered." Now the *real* work would begin but I hadn't a clue what that was likely to mean.

7

First of all, I had to figure out who Teddy's abuser was. I knew that some animal abusers took immense egotistical pleasure in sharing with the public their so-called "creative fun." They demonstrated how unafraid, strong, and clever they were in inflicting harm, like a smiling young Brit who filmed himself repeatedly throwing his bulldog puppy down a flight of stairs and then slamming it into walls. Teddy's abuser might be one who was so inclined as well. That meant researching social media sites and YouTube.

I tossed together my dinner, a veggie burger and a salad with all the vegetables I had creeping toward their demise in the refrigerator, and bolted it down without even tasting it as I stood at the kitchen counter. I was incredibly motivated. Examining social media seemed like a brilliant way to begin. I knew I'd find him.

But after hours of searching, I found to my extreme displeasure the Internet was rife with proud videos, photos, and proclamations of a super-abundance of animal abusers' past "accomplishments." People appeared to be trying to outdo one another in how extreme or outrageous their cruelty could be. There was so much blood, gore, and mayhem displayed with so many delighted faces that I gave up, with a headache and a sour stomach. It was like touring an abattoir.

It reminded me of the 1962 documentary *Mondo Cane*, which detailed some of the bizarre and horrific rituals and practices from around the world at that time. By today's crystal-meth social media standards this film was now nearly G-Rated. At the time the film title was loosely translated, "a world gone to the dogs." Today social media abuse posts had out-paced the film by hundreds of miles. The display of violence and blood lust was a "world gone to the depraved." It was obvious that while the technology had its good applications, this definitely wasn't one of them. Application of the First Amendment here was likewise questionable.

Yet, as I tried to keep my gag reflex from spilling my stomach contents onto my keyboard, I was surprised by how much personal information could be gleaned from the abuse posts. Maybe getting personal info about the puppy kicker might be found there after all. If only I could find it right away. Looking much further was quickly becoming an emotional and physiological non-option.

Since I had personally witnessed the incident, I was already ahead of the game because it happened near where I currently lived. That suggested that, perhaps, the abuser lived near Albertson's as well. With that in mind, "all" I had to do was identify the abuser, locate him, stalk him to learn about his personal and public life and schedule, and make a specific, personalized plan to psychologically "crucify" him for his deeds. A piece of cake.

It occurred to me that using the media would help. However, without any thought, I rejected it out of hand. The idea of newspaper articles, TV coverage, and radio announcements superseding my "personal" efforts—it was *my* project after all—seemed to take me out of my revenge picture. Slapping myself, I exclaimed, "Dummy! They would be doing the hard work that you can't do, spreading widely the word of the abuser and his crime."

Unenthusiastically, I acknowledged that I was allowing my ego to get in the way. That was bad. What did I care how I found out who he was? Identification wasn't the end-all and be-all of my work. My mission was to make the identified animal attacker feel like an outcast in public, be legally punished, and exceedingly sorry for his actions. Well, his being sorry for his actions was likely another example of wishful thinking.

Employing a pad of news print I used when teaching seminars off-campus, I began to outline a plan as a flow chart. With my mood now more subdued, I took time to consider the different phases of my project. Once I found him, it would have to involve a series of relevant, well-organized, public and private attacks. In combination they would have to have a lasting impact on him: Feeling public shame at work and in his community.

That was what I craved. Psychological methods that would make this person look "bloodthirsty," "barbarous," and "cowardly." Well-placed photos, flyers, abuse videos, and newspaper articles could impact the abuser's reputation negatively. There were so many possibilities that it made me smile.

As I warmed to my subject, I suddenly realized that I likewise had to plan how I was going to go about doing all this while not being detected by the abuser or Animal Control. I couldn't allow myself to get caught. A moment of doubt settled its fingers around my throat. In all seriousness, how did *I*, of all people, think I could do it and get away with it?

My immediate goal was a satisfying revenge for Teddy, while not being beaten to a pulp by the abuser, or spending years behind bars fending off unwanted sexual advances by guards, physical conflicts with female gang members, or haranguing attacks by those royally pissed off by their experiences with half-baked behavioral scientists. I had to consider every potential situation in detail and have as many fallback positions for as many unintended consequences as I could imagine. But not everything that could possibly happen could be planned for. That gave me a moment's pause. Reality was creeping in again. This wasn't going to be as much fun as I had hoped. In fact, it was going to be hard, grinding work. The presumed "glamour" of being a minor superhero was rapidly losing its cachet.

As my mind circled around the plan, I knew it likely would take weeks, maybe more, to painstakingly work it all out in order to successfully make my first "hit." And then, if I were lucky, the results would be what I so dearly wanted.

However, in the meantime, I daydreamed that maybe karma would make Teddy's abuser take an NFL kick at another dog, miss, slip on a pebble, crash-land on it on his coccyx bone, and wind up in a wheelchair in un-relievable chronic pain, that couldn't even be addressed by a spinal cord stimulator, and furious with his life. Or maybe he'd own a .44 Magnum to slaughter anything that came into his yard and manage to shoot off his metal-toed boot and foot as he tried to follow the zig-zag scampering of a squirrel. Or maybe he'd be hunting, stalking a bear cub, so intent on killing he was not looking where he was going, fall off a cliff, be knocked unconscious, and then eaten slowly, relishing each tasty morsel, by the mama bear. That could make him a Darwin Award contender. Smiling, I shook my head and chuckled, "Ah, if only."

While I may have wanted karma to intrude, I didn't really think it would step in to demonstrate that what goes around comes around. As far as I could tell, it hadn't happened yet, at least not with any consistency or frequency. "So," I sighed, "I guess I had better just keep on developing my plan."

However, as I worked on its evolving structure, emotion and my personal connection to Teddy kept wading into the fray. That was dangerous. It was too easy to slip back into that tearful, uncontrolled anger, and its associated impulsivity. For everything to work, I would have to remain rational and objective. My plan would have to be executed as an intellectual exercise with me remaining detached. Maybe that was the meaning of the popular expression, "Revenge is best served cold."

Furthermore, if I managed to remain as detached as humanly possible, when I achieved my goal, I would more likely enjoy my sense of success. It was simply the accomplishment of a project. Feeling "successful" was less likely if I let my emotions rule as my focus and prime motivation. I would *never* "feel" the abuser's pain was enough to compensate for Teddy's trauma and suffering.

I spent the rest of the day working on a press release to submit to the *Albuquerque Journal,* public service announcements for radio stations, and making copies of the cell phone video for the TV affiliates. With permission, I used a local animal humane organization as the distributor. Calling all those media organizations the next day, I made sure they had received the information and inquired if they needed anything else. Around seven-thirty that evening, Judy at the Animal Abuse Hotline called.

"Someone—didn't leave their name—left a tip that your abuser might be named 'Marr.' You want to check it out before I call Animal Control?"

"Yes, that's a good idea. I'll check it out starting tomorrow and let you know. Thanks."

I scanned the phone book for the name. There was one person listed under that name who was living on Albuelitas. I'd drive over around 5:30 P.M. in case he worked regular hours. At 5:45 P.M. with my Civic parked across the street from his house, I was all set up for surveillance. With me was a thermos of coffee, a granola bar, a city map and phone book, a camera with a zoom lens, my cell phone, notebook and pen, and a bulky Depends diaper I had purchased at Walgreen's just in case I was stuck there for a while.

When a man drove his gun-metallic Nissan Altima into the driveway of the house, I readied my camera. Hunkered down on the driver's side, I began snapping pictures. This man was wearing a dark blue sports jacket with gold buttons, light blue shirt with maroon tie, tan chinos, and cordovan loafers with navy socks. Without his cowboy hat it was easier to see him. But he didn't remind me of Teddy's abuser. Maybe he was just visiting or lived with the abuser. Confusion overwhelmed me about what to do next.

As I snapped photos, he opened the door with a key and was greeted by a big black dog with rust markings and rust paws, possibly a Rottweiler. The dog looked healthy and without injury. I was astonished when he responded lovingly to the dog, petting it, playing with the rope toy it had brought to him.

"What is going on?" I questioned myself. "This can't be the same person, can it? If the dog had been abused, it would have been cowering and submissive, instead of leaping with joy at his presence. I need a closer look." Maybe he was just visiting or lived with the abuser. Confusion overwhelmed me about what to do next. I had to see him up close.

But, surely, if he were the abuser, despite his attire and the dog's behavior suggesting otherwise, he would recognize me from Albertson's. It would be risky to approach him to get a better look. Yet, ...

After pondering a believable excuse for about five minutes, I walked to his door, rang the bell, and waited. The dog began barking wildly and jumping against the door with its nails undoubtedly engraving tiny worm holes in the wood. I swallowed hard as he opened the door.

"Yes? Roddy," he commanded the exuberant dog, "Just relax." The dog lay down at his feet, still displaying his doggy expectation.

"I'm sorry to bother you." I smiled. "I'm new to the area and am looking for Noreste Drive. I seem to have made a wrong turn somewhere."

I looked at him pleasantly as I examined his face. Suddenly I was aware this person was not only shorter, less muscled, and had lighter hair than the abuser but also was less tanned than the face I had recorded. Up close there was really no resemblance.

"What you need to do," he responded, stepping onto his small front stoop, "is go back two blocks, look for Sabroso NW on your right, turn there, and that will take you where you want to go."

"Thanks for the help. You have a beautiful dog. He looks friendly. Would he mind if I petted him?" I was vamping, trying to figure out how to discover if the abuser might live there as well.

"Sure. Roddy, Up."

Roddy jumped up. I extended my hand to him which he licked jubilantly, ready to place his front paws on my shoulders to give my face a slurpy bath if given half a chance. Nothing else came to mind to ask. Now I felt awkward. After petting Roddy's large head, I thanked the man again and returned to my car. I gave a quick wave as I turned the car around and left but he had already closed his front door.

Considering this situation, I wondered what had the tip been about. Was it an honest mistake? Was someone playing a joke? Was there an error in the name? There had been only one "Marr" in the phone book. Was this really that man's house? Did he have a roommate? Was this man visiting? Had the house been sold and this was the new resident? I was back at square one again. Maybe I should listen to the hotline message myself. Tomorrow would be a good day to do it. Since I was an associate professor in the psychology department at the University of New Mexico, I couldn't just hang around, contemplating. I had students' papers to correct. These were on what the humanistic psychologists had contributed to the field. I returned to Bernalillo, feeling confused.

Back home my initial chore was to put cat chow and fresh water dishes out front for neighborhood cats. With so many people allowing their cats to run it was difficult to know which cats had been abandoned, neglected, were feral, or were just roving their home territory. Hopefully, wandering raccoons wouldn't get to the crunchies first. It took an hour to correct most of the papers, delaying dinner. Then after eating a microwaved Amy's frozen vegetarian, pseudo-Mexican enchilada dinner and watching the evening news, I migrated back to my office. It occurred to me it would be useful to further survey the name as well as the address online.

To my surprise what I discovered was that the name on the hotline tip could be spelled numbers of different ways. It sounded like "Marr" but could also be spelled "Mahr," "Mahar," "Maher," "Magher," or "Meagher." If I had been an Irish genealogy buff, I might have toppled to that sooner.

Under each spelling I checked the phone book, Googled the name, and researched Facebook, Instagram, LinkedIn, and Twitter. My search came up with six possibilities located in Rio Rancho, Albuquerque, and nearby Algodones. After correcting the remaining twenty percent of my students' research papers, I went to bed, vowing to explore these possibilities after classes tomorrow.

During my last class of the day in abnormal psychology, I asked my students, "How would you handle the following scenario? This is something that you've probably already read about in the newspaper or heard about on television or radio." I described what had happened at Albertson's. Going around the room, I asked each psychology major, "What would you do if you had witnessed the incident?"

Some said, "I'd shout at the abuser."

Some males said, "I'd chase him."

Whereas some females zeroed in on the injured puppy, "I'd check to see if I could help him."

Then I asked, "How would you psychologically characterize the abuser?"

Most said, "He's a psychopath."

A few offered, "He has Anti-Social Personality Disorder."

One suggested, "He has serious anger problems."

Then I asked what I really wanted to know, "Do any of you know of anyone who abuses or has abused animals? If so, would you please describe the person physically and emotionally to me. Also, what would *you* do, if anything, about these individuals harming animals?"

They looked furtively at one another as a heavy silence became a pall. Time dragged on until one male uttered, "Yeah, but telling on someone you know would be like squealing on them even if you think they're wrong."

A couple added, "I'm not sure, but I think so."

While a few said, "No, but I'd be afraid to say anything for fear of retaliation if I did."

"Okay," I continued, "those of you who know someone, please give me a description of the person. I'm not asking for a name or where this person lives, just a physical description."

No one raised a hand. Although, one graduate student, Carrie, jerked her head toward the classroom door as if she wanted to talk to me privately.

"One more thing. I've been doing research on animal abusers, which includes all aspects of their lives and occupations. I'd like you to consider sharing with me more about the animal abusers you know, *without* identifying them, including how they dress, act, anything unusual about them, and what kind of work they do." This was very probably a non-starter.

After class, Carrie followed me to my office. As soon as the door closed, she began.

"A guy I used to live with off-and-on was always taking out his frustrations on his dog." Words rushed from her as if she'd been hoping for the opportunity to share this with someone who'd understand.

"I once saw him slam his cowering dog across the side of its head with a large, heavy metal flashlight. It made a huge dent in the dog's skull. Some of its teeth popped out of its mouth with lots of blood. The dog collapsed on the floor. I wanted to take the poor animal to the emergency veterinary hospital on Montgomery but he wouldn't let me. When I insisted, he flew into a rage and flung me across the kitchen into the stove. I thought he'd punch me out as well, but he didn't. Instead, he commanded me to quickly clean the blood from the floor before it dried. He was a nut about cleanliness. The next day the dog was gone. I wasn't sure what that meant. I've been growing more afraid of him. Afraid to stay and afraid to leave. After this, I desperately wanted out."

"What did you do?"

"I took a big risk because I never knew what would set him off. I told him I was pregnant by my ex-boyfriend and that my parents wanted me to visit my uncle and aunt in San Ysidro until I had the baby. I thought he might kill me but hoped he might only think of me as 'tainted goods.' Lucky for me that news seemed to make me a problem he didn't want so he let me go. Good riddance to bad rubbish."

"Carrie, that's very frightening. I'm glad your plan worked for you. You were fortunate he responded as he did. People who hurt animals often begin to hurt people, especially women and children."

"I have a friend whose husband beats her and when she tried to leave him, he mutilated and killed her beloved cat."

"How would you describe your former-boyfriend for me physically?"

"Why do you want to know?"

"I was wondering if he might be the one who attacked the puppy at Albertson's."

"He's big, over six feet. Muscled because he works out. He's very proud of what his muscles can do. He likes to dress like a cowboy, you know, with the boots and hat, but with a very specific look. That's when he's not at work. No Levi's. He has multiple outfits all the same which he changes every day so he's always in a clean one. His boots are very distinctive in that they have metal-covered toes. He loves those boots and cleans and polishes them all the time."

"How would you describe him emotionally?"

"Besides being violent, he's a control-freak. Everything has to be just so. He was always criticizing me for not putting things back exactly where they had been, even his gun magazines on his coffee table. According to him, I never did anything right. I never made things clean enough for him. I had to change the bed every day. Living with him was like being a prisoner and a slave. While he never actually beat me, he did use force, especially when he wanted what he wanted, if you know what I mean, and when he was angry."

"What kind of work does he do?"

"He used to work at a Walmart warehouse but that was several years ago. I don't know if he still does. He hated all the dirt and took to wearing latex gloves. I know he wanted a more prestigious occupation, something associated with the professions."

"Thanks, Carrie, for sharing with me. If you have anything further to add on the topic, please drop me an e-mail or catch me after class."

She looked a little brighter and less burdened when she left. I suspected she didn't know how truly lucky she was to have gotten out of that situation alive.

At home I searched online to see if Walmart had separate warehouses from their stores, if their shipping center were considered a warehouse, and the locations of their respective facilities. The idea of wandering around the stores, warehouses, and shipping facilities to look for him was not only unappealing but also awkward and risky.

8

Searching the six possible names on Google for their addresses then on YouTube for related animal abuse videos took hours but revealed nothing. If he were on either or both, I probably had missed him. After the first few videos, I began to race through them, feeling nausea and pre-vomit saliva collect in my mouth. That meant having to continue to look for him by surveilling the located addresses.

On my local map I marked the locations of the six. While I was glad Carrie had finally parted company with "my" cowboy, I wished she had given me more information about him. It was going to be a long couple of days as I staked out the addresses, unless I was super-lucky to find him the first day.

At 5:30 P.M. I was back in my Civic with thermos, an apple, map, phone book, camera, cell phone, notebook, and Depends, easing up to the first address. Since this house number, which was painted on the curbing, for "Mahr" was a vacant lot, I went to the next one on the list. This one's name was "Mahar." As I arrived, a copper-colored Chevy Camaro was pulling into the drive of the small stucco, pueblo-style house which was landscaped with grit and desiccated brown grass stalks, surrounded by a five-foot chain-link fence. When the driver shut off the engine, which continued to tick, and rolled out of the car, he was in his fifties, heavy-set, red faced, balding, and wearing denim work clothes.

He certainly wasn't the abuser I sought but perhaps he might be the abuser's father. There was no sign of animals present. Of course, the animals could already have been hastened to their graves. I took a couple of shots of him anyway. As he approached the front door, an older woman opened it. Could this have been "Mom"? While there was no sign of a thirty-year-old on the premises, this still could be valid. It was time to move on to investigate the next address.

This one was "Maher" but the phone book didn't indicate if it were a male or female. Since the listing used an initial instead of a first name, it might well be a woman trying to protect herself from obscene phone calls. As I began chomping on my apple, a woman arrived. With long light brown hair parted in the middle, white t-shirt, stone-washed jeans with pre-ripped designer holes, and baby-blue Sketchers, she appeared to be in the right age range for the abuser's friend. There was no one with her and no one came to the front door as she inserted her key.

I finished my apple and decided to wait a little longer. Fifteen minutes later a meadow-green metallic Chevrolet Silverado 1500 truck pulled into the driveway, remotely opened the garage door, drove in, and automatically closed the door before I could even get a glimpse of the driver. As the person pulled up, it was more likely male than female but I couldn't be sure.

That was another one that couldn't be crossed off my list. I took one photo of the house.

Frustration was dampening my mood. On my way home I'd try one more address. This was the first "Meagher." By the time I arrived, apparently whoever was going to arrive after work had already arrived or worked another shift. The lights were on but the curtains were drawn. Still, the curtains allowed detection of some movement via shifting shadows on their insubstantial fabric.

That was enough for the day. It was time to head home. But on the way, I stopped at the animal hospital. Teddy's condition had been upgraded to "serious." I viewed him in his cage, curled up on a thick towel with an IV in his left foreleg, sutures in his abdomen, bandages, and two wrapped right legs. He opened his remaining eye to glance at me then dropped off again. I almost started to cry. Just maybe this tough little puppy could make it after all.

After skipping karate and weight lifting at the gym, I changed into my sweats to have a quick six-mile run. As I tried to get my second wind, I thought that after a shower, a glass of some cool white wine would smooth out the day's wrinkles. Following that I would have another quick and simple dinner and either watch a DVD or read a couple of chapters of a new David Baldacci novel. I needed something, anything, diverting. My mind and heart were still with Teddy and his slow but hopeful progress.

After being well-scrubbed and refreshed, with some chardonnay and a smoked salmon salad soothing my hunger pangs, I chose the DVD of National Lampoon's 1983 *Vacation* and settled in to permit myself to relax and laugh a little at the expected Chevy Chase slapstick insanity.

My currently disappointing search activities made me wonder what a private investigator would do. Would she or he have access to databases that were not available to me? That was a possibility. In that case, what was there on the Internet that would be available to me that could duplicate, at least in part, a P.I.'s data access? "People search services" came to mind.

The first people-search service I checked was one I stumbled across in an ad before I actually Googled them. It was ExclusiveIntelligence at $9.95 per person per basic search, providing address and social network. But if I wanted to find out the nitty gritty about a single person, including employment, criminal interaction with the law, liens, bankruptcies, judgments, lawsuits, marriage, divorce, etc., it was $49.95. It appeared that was for each individual search. If so, with five people to examine that wasn't going to be an economical choice.

However, when I Googled "people search engines," I found a list of ten possibilities. Of them InstantVerification was the most positively reviewed. It offered one month of unlimited reports for $22.86 per month. "That could work," I said to myself. It hadn't occurred to me before how expensive this "avenging business" could be. It wasn't just gasoline and shoe leather. Naïvely, I had thought it could be done quickly and for free. Discovering otherwise was an unpleasant surprise for this Superhero. Given that, it might not be a bad idea to keep track of my abuse campaign expenses, especially since this was not a project for which I was being paid.

With only one class the next morning, I planned to nail down the abuser through InstantVerification that afternoon. Of course, it was still essential that I see him in the flesh. I needed a full-face photograph. By the time I had returned home for lunch, there was a message on my answering machine. It was Judy at the Animal Abuse Hotline.

"We've had another tip. The person who wouldn't leave her name said she had seen the man kick the dog at Albertson's and thought she recognized him as someone who might work as an orderly at the university hospital."

I exclaimed, "The hospital? Oh, no! And I thought his possibly working at a Walmart in some capacity was bad enough." She laughed as if unsure what I was talking about.

Maybe when I searched InstantVerification, there might be "Marr" name-sounding people who worked in medicine. But when, I wondered, was this ever going to start to become a little easier and more straightforward.

Having signed up for a month with InstantVerification, I researched "Marr." In fifteen minutes, I had his life in distilled format. He with the Nissan Altima and Rottweiler was a hedge-fund manager working in real estate, not married, had had an appendectomy, no criminal record, was active on LinkedIn, and was a season ticket holder to Popejoy Presents, the University of New Mexico's performing-arts theater which hosted national acts, Broadway shows, and dance companies. That was more than was necessary to know about this stranger's private life.

At some point before my subscription ran out, I thought I might search for my own information. At the same time, I wasn't so sure I wanted to know what I'd find. It was shocking how everyone's life was an open book, available to anyone with *any* kind of intention. I wondered what women who are running from domestic violence do about that. It was clear this convenient search engine could put a lot of private people in public jeopardy. Suddenly, I felt guilty I was financially supporting this unconsented invasion of privacy, even if it were merely an aggregate of everything already available online about particular individuals. That was something to always remember when saying anything at all online: *The Internet never forgets. And someone can always find it.*

The next was a "Mahar." While the fifties-looking man in overalls with the copper-colored Camry obviously wasn't the abuser but might have a son who was. Not so. It turned out his only child was a female who lived in Utah. "Maher" was indeed the female with long hair I saw but the report didn't say anything about the owner of the Chevy truck. Maybe it was a brother who wasn't listed in her relatives, someone visiting with her, or a live-in companion. That one required a re-check.

"Meagher" was the house with lights on but no cars arriving. This was an elderly couple with no children and who were no longer working. The second "Meagher" and the last name on my list was the one I hadn't as yet surveilled. This was a divorced orthopedic surgeon who worked at the University of New Mexico Hospital and lived in Sandia Heights. That was unlikely but should be explored anyway.

First thing Saturday morning, after lifting weights and doing my run—I had decided to have my karate practice later—I packed my car with surveillance essentials and headed out to check on the "Maher" with Chevy truck. Parked on the driveway was the green pickup which was being washed. The one handling the hose and sponge was male but he had black hair, tied at the back of his neck. As he sprayed the soap suds off the hood, he glanced over at me, parked across the street, one property back. I hadn't as yet had the chance to take any photos.

His hair looked wrong but his face bore a resemblance to the profile I'd taken. However, as he moved around, he looked more tanned and Native American. I didn't want to come back again unless absolutely necessary. As he went back to rinsing the truck, I whipped out my camera a took a couple of less than perfect shots. With that, I casually pulled away from the curb to examine the last one, the previously missed "Meagher," in Sandia Heights.

Sandia Heights was a modern suburban development east of Albuquerque at the base of the Sandia Mountains where the current median home value was $438,000, as compared with the national median value of $184,700. The houses were mostly one-story pueblo-style, with at least three bedrooms and two baths. My trip there reminded me that when I first moved to New Mexico four years ago, I had checked out that area. However, the rentals were starting around $1,200 per month. A bit too pricey for me.

At the expensive-looking Sandia Heights address there was a youngster who vaguely resembled the abuser playing roughly on the grass with what looked like an Australian Cattle puppy in the front yard. The boy seemed annoyed the dog wasn't doing precisely what he wanted. Instead, it was jumping around excitedly, being a puppy. The next thing I knew the kid tried to kick the dog. He missed its head by only a fraction of an inch and slipped on the trimmed buffalo grass, landing on his bottom which made him even angrier. Immediately, I jumped out of the car and strode across the street, not sure what to do, but knowing I had to do something.

"Did you know that as a young kid you were just like that puppy. You were so excited about everything. You jumped around a lot. You always wanted to play. You didn't yet know what adults wanted you to do so you didn't do it. Hopefully your parents didn't kick you because you were just a child and not able to understand."

"Stuff it, bitch! He's my dog and I can do what I want with him and you can't say different."

"Does your dad feel that way about him too?"

"I don't have no dad."

"Was your dad a doctor working at the hospital?"

"Are you shittin' me?"

"Does your mom have a friend who dresses like a cowboy, with boots that have metal toes?"

"That's none of your business."

"Is your last name Meagher?"

After giving me the finger, he roughly grabbed the puppy that was pulling on his pant leg with its teeth to get him to play, and went inside. Good luck, puppy.

Now I was really confused. Had I copied the address incorrectly? Had InstantVerification gotten it wrong? Did the cowboy really live or visit here?

I still hadn't listened to the first hotline report about "Marr." Listening to both tips that were received would be smart to see if the voices were recognizable or if there were any other information that was detectable in the background. With no other pending obligations, I drove to the humane organization office that had the hotline.

Judy was staffing the office when I arrived.

"We've had several tips since I talked with you yesterday. You'll want to listen to them."

"Absolutely. And then I want to listen to the first two."

Number three said, "I think he lives in Rio Rancho and has a criminal record."

Number four said, "If it's who I think it is, he has a terrible temper and you need to be careful looking for him."

Number five said, "I think he breeds Chihuahuas but I don't know his name."

And number six said, "I'm sure he steals pets as bait dogs for dog-fighting. I hear horrible sounds coming out of his house, like something being tortured. I've reported him so many times but Animal Control hasn't done anything."

"And no one left their name, the assumed assailant's name or address, or how to get in touch with them to follow up on. This is getting more frustrating by the day. Let me listen to the first two first."

The first one was hard to understand because the female's voice appeared to have a heavy accent and she spoke softly. What sort of sounded like "Marr," also could have been "Marn" or "Marne." Or maybe it was something else entirely. I mumbled some choice expletives to myself.

"Hand me the phone book, would you." Quickly scanning each variation, I found two possibilities: "Marn" and "Marne." "Okay, how about the second tip?"

This was the one by a female who said she had witnessed the abuse and thought she had seen the abuser acting as an orderly at the university hospital. There was nothing else useful on the call. She sounded middle-aged and could well have been one of the people outside Albertson's at the time. It was a shame that the callers hadn't been more detailed, more informative. Maybe they felt they had to do something but not enough to get themselves involved.

Disappointed, I trudged home again, planning on once more running names through InstantVerification. All the outrage I had experienced watching the incident then all the enthusiasm of making the momentous decision about how I alone would address it were both waning. In a way not running on emotional fuel was good, particularly since how I'd reach my revenge goal was still too nebulous. If only the work weren't so slow, tedious, and unsatisfying. I knew that Dr. Martin Luther King, Jr., had said, "Every step toward the goal of justice requires sacrifice, suffering, and struggle; the tireless exertions and passionate concern of dedicated individuals," but at moments like this, this quest felt almost ridiculous. Still, I knew I couldn't stop ... it was too important. Something positive *had* to happen ... soon ... to help keep me going.

My time on InstantVerification turned out to be for naught, a total waste. This was beginning to feel like the off-kilter adventures of *Ace Ventura, Pet Detective* but with less success. It left me with a headache. Scouring the bathroom for something analgesic which I didn't use often, I discovered both the small bottles of acetaminophen and aspirin were empty. Pocketing my car keys, phone, and slipping on my cross-body mini handbag, I took the mile trip to Pharmacy-Plus on Rt. 550 just before the intersection at Camino Don Tomas.

When I located the analgesics aisle, I squatted to look on the bottom white metal shelf for generics of what I wanted. I wasn't interested in paying for Bayer or Tylenol's advertising. As someone walked behind me, the sound of heavy heeled boots riveted my attention. Curious, I carefully looked down to my left side, trying not to be too obvious. I couldn't believe what was there. Metal-toed, embroidered black cowboy boots! As he passed, I looked up. There before me was the fitted light blue pants, fitted Western-style light blue shirt with black lacing, a red bandana, and a white cowboy hat covering medium brown hair.

A cheer nearly escaped my lips but there could be nothing to draw attention to myself. Head down, I collected small-size bottles of pharmacy-branded aspirin and acetaminophen. Then I debated about retracing my steps to the next aisle in case he was browsing. However, seeing his face without revealing mine would be tricky. I had to see him but how? Unfortunately, he had gone straight to the rear prescription desk so his back was to me. There was no way to know how long he would be there. He might be dropping off a prescription or picking one up. I couldn't stay squatting out of his line of sight. And I couldn't just hang around the store without being suspiciously observed.

At the front register I lingered by the large candy selection with my head down, as if mulling over what I wanted to buy. He was still talking to the pharmacist. As time dawdled, the cashier seemed to scrutinize me as a potential thief. Keeping my face obscured, I finally chose a small *PayDay* bar, paid for my purchases, and exited through the glass front doors.

By chance, my car was parked two slots over to the left of the door. Hopefully that would allow me a good shot of him as he left. Standing on the other side of my car, I had my cell phone poised to take a shot. Ten minutes later when he opened the door, he immediately turned right with his head down. His face was still obscured. There was no way I could clearly photograph it before he climbed into a vehicle, a silver-colored Dodge Ram 1500 SLT Laramie Extended cab pickup truck which was five vehicles away. However, as he pulled out, I did manage to capture the first three letters and first number of his New Mexico license plate.

While he slipped easily into an open spot in traffic on Rt. 550 before the light turned green on Camino Don Tomas, the cross street, I wasn't so lucky. Heavy traffic left me stuck as car after car passed. He was still visible ten cars ahead. But as I approached Camino del Pueblo, the next intersection, the light had turned red and he had disappeared.

It was clear that his truck hadn't gone straight up the incline toward the exit to Interstate 25 North toward Santa Fe or South to Albuquerque or continued on to Placitas. He had to have turned left toward the Bernalillo High School or right toward Bernalillo's main street restaurants and shopping area. But it was a coin flip which. So close and yet so far, I slammed my fist on the steering wheel.

When the light turned green, I turned left. I'd scope out the road for a mile or two. Then, if I had no success, I'd drive into Bernalillo for a mile or two. With no cars behind me, just cruising along and taking my time, searching was easy. It was two miles of widely-spaced, unadorned, dusty yards pinned in place by indistinguishable stick-built or cinderblock houses. Some were covered with stucco, nearly all with pitched roofs, and most with metal sheeting instead of shingles. Aside from that, nothing remotely useful had appeared. I felt bereft, almost sorry I had started this crusade, and turned around.

Almost back to the intersection, I suddenly thought I had spotted something up ahead on the right. It wasn't directly on the road or even close to it. Pulled into a yard, it was the silver Dodge Ram. It was parked along the side of a small stucco house surrounded by the dark green, highly-invasive sumac trees with their long bi-pinnate leaves dipping low over the house. Sumac grew everywhere. This time the silver Dodge's whole license plate was visible. I scanned the front of the house for its street number. Nothing. But as I was about to drive away, I glanced at the arbor support at the beginning of the gravel front walk. There it was!

Surprise and delight engulfed me. A tear threatened to overflow my lower lashes. Unconsciously doing a wave, my hand hit the car horn. People in their yards and walking along the road stared at me. Quickly, I hunkered down and slowly pulled on.

My brain cells were bursting. I couldn't believe it. I was actually making some progress! I was beside myself with expectation. My only thought at that moment was to do an immediate reverse address look-up. This couldn't wait.

Before I knew it, my Civic was heading north on Rt. 550, turning left onto Rt. 528, and automatically driving south to the Rio Rancho Public Library on Pine Street. In a fugue state, I arrived at the library which had already closed. My brain was still dog-paddling in emotion. I was getting close finally. He was within my reach. Visions of this arrogant cowboy having his narcissistic hide nailed to a fence post was all too sweet as it danced before my eyes.

It was only on my way home that reality struck hard. I berated myself.

"Oh my god! What's the matter with me? Where was my brain? Why did I go to the library? I didn't need to do that. Duh! All I had to do was locate the White Pages reverse phone/address look-up *online*." I suddenly felt very stupid.

I hated when I did something so incredibly thoughtless. My synapses weren't snapping. The lame excuse I scrounged up for my dissociative state was that I had been re-reading Sue Grafton's Kinsey Millhone alphabet novels where the 1980s investigator Millhone frequently has to use the library's crisscross directory for a name.

Once home I followed up on the address look-up. The home belonged to a Clayton Moore. "Moore?" Was *that* what the woman with the accent was really saying? That would never have occurred to me. The wild goose chase for 'Marr' had wasted a lot of time and effort. It was only now that the actual work would begin to exact my revenge. I sighed and briefly smiled but without much mirth behind it. At least I'd moved one square ahead on the game board.

Then it hit me. "Clayton Moore"? That was the name of the good-looking, trim 1940's actor with the mellifluous voice who played the Lone Ranger on television." Except for a three-year interval during a contract dispute, Moore occupied that role in the TV series 1949-1951 and 1954-1957. If truth be told, I watched his show re-runs religiously. Even as a youngster, I was mesmerized by his slightly breathy voice, which as an adult I would now call "sexy." The abuser's mother must have been a big Clayton Moore fan too.

It suddenly occurred to me the Lone Ranger stood for "truth, justice, and the American way," just like Superman, only on his horse and wearing a mask. He was the antithesis of the abuser. Their sharing this name was so disagreeable. Was that why he dressed as he did? He was mimicking the real Clayton Moore in the character of the Lone Ranger? Ewww!

I still wanted to double-check for his photo online, not only so I could see it but also so I could pass it along to the animal humane organizations and rescue shelters so they wouldn't adopt to him. Since there was no photo as part of the InstantVerification report, I scoured all the popular social media sites in case he might have joined recently or recently added a photo. There was nothing to be found.

As much as I knew this Clayton Moore was incontrovertibly Teddy's abuser, I had to ask myself if there could conceivably be *two* men in this area who dressed like Lone Ranger in *public*? No way!

9

As torrents of possibilities about what to do flooded my mind, I wondered about sending a restricted certified mail to Clayton Moore. Perhaps it would be possible to determine when the postal carrier would deliver it to the address I had. That would have permitted me to wait in hiding to see who would sign for it. With "restricted" certified only the addressee could sign. Inside the envelope it would have to be something that was non-personal but important-sounding, like a legal notice, in case he wasn't the abuser. If he were the abuser, it also could be nothing to tip him off that he was being targeted. But so far there was no way to know when Moore would be home to sign for the letter since his place of work and schedule were still a mystery.

But that wouldn't work. If he weren't home to sign for the restricted certified letter, the mail carrier would leave a slip in his mail box indicating he had something to sign for and pick up *at the post office*. Okay, so much for that trick.

However, if the caller to the hotline had been correct about his working at UNM hospital, his schedule might be available. It would mean calling the hospital's human resources department which was most unlikely to give out employee information. Was there some kind of excuse that had a greater likelihood of working? Perhaps my claiming to be a human resources person from another medical facility who was probing his employment record "because he was seeking new employment" could work.

But, then again, if that person weren't the real abuser, that could create a problem. It didn't take much to imagine an innocent person being asked about my call by his employer to which he would say, "I'm not looking for another job. Why do you ask?" and being tagged a liar. That might be okay if he were the abuser. Except, of course, that would make him angry and who knew where he would take out his anger. There was no question that even getting started on my revenge plan was ethically becoming ticklish and tortuous.

Being a Marvel Superhero in real life wasn't as slam-bang productive as I'd thought it would be. If he hadn't seen me at the scene of his crime, I could knock on his door in early evening when he'd likely be home, present myself as doing a survey in his neighborhood on some community issue. But since he had seen me, I could employ someone else to do the survey while I hid and watched. However, I didn't want anyone else involved who could lead to me. Moreover, if another male, or female, answered the door, what would that mean?

My mind was in a constant whirl. It occurred to me I might be overthinking this situation, although it didn't seem I had a choice given the complexity of it. One obvious and simple solution was to do a stake-out at Clayton Moore's address on a weekday morning then follow him when he left. It could be worth setting my alarm clock for five o'clock in case he left early. I decided to do it on the following Monday morning. However, sleep that Sunday evening was nearly impossible. All night long I ruminated about the whole situation, twisting in my sheets, punching my pillow which wasn't comfortable enough no matter what I did to it.

When the alarm buzzed, I dragged my soporific body out of bed, took a quick shower, which didn't manage to enliven me any, pulled on a Depends, and secured all my surveillance equipment. This time it included a long-billed baseball cap and hooded sweat jacket. At 5:30 A.M. the Civic was parked at the Camino del Pueblo side of the Walgreen's Pharmacy, at the intersection of Rt. 550 and Camino del Pueblo, a block from his house. The view was relatively unobstructed. Fortunately, there were other cars in the parking lot so my car didn't stand out.

Six o'clock arrived without incident. Then 6:30. Everything was still quiet. By seven o'clock the neighborhood was coming alive with students walking to the high school and commuters heading to work, making it harder to watch for the silver-colored Dodge truck.

At 7:15 A.M. someone left by the front door to enter the vehicle. Turning over my engine, I sank down in my seat so he would be unlikely to spot me though I could still see him. As he passed, I pulled out behind him. The light turned green and he turned left onto Rt. 550. As the light was turning yellow, I scooted in behind him. When I had a chance, I let another car squeeze between us so the Civic wouldn't be so obvious. He took the exit onto I-25 South. It looked as if he were going to Albuquerque … and work.

While he tended to exceed the seventy-five-mph speed limit, I did my best to keep him in view from the middle lane and not allow too many cars between us. Traffic on I-25 South at commuter time was often like the Indy 500. No signals and lots of weaving in and out between cars at ninety mph. One dirty white pickup with its bed loaded with metal tool cabinets quickly glided left from the right lane directly in front of me, nearly creasing my right front quarter panel. My honking was to no avail, except for prompting the driver to give me the finger.

As we approached the exit to Paseo del Norte, the east-west corridor, the traffic began to slow, cars kissing each other's bumpers (as if cars still had real "bumpers"). Fortunately, there were fewer horns blaring than expected. Already being tense, I didn't need any more stressors, especially noise. From there to the exit for Montgomery and Montaño, as well as access to the Albuquerque malls and Lovelace Women's Hospital, everything moved intermittently from five-to-ten miles per hour. But traffic began to speed up as we approached Route 40, the primary east-west State road. The Dodge Ram thankfully didn't take either the east or west exit for it but continued to the exit for Lomas.

He turned left on Lomas, left on Yale, and right on Camino de Salud. He was going to the hospital. Maybe this meant he was the hotline tip's orderly after all. As he pulled into the several-story parking garage, I slowed and pulled in after him. He parked on Level 3. I slid into a parking slot up around the curve, keeping him in view. Wearing his scrubs, he had put a baseball cap on.

Disguised with my ball cap and hoodie, I followed him at a distance, hunkered over, to the elevators. It was there I bypassed him after he had entered and the door had shut, then hurriedly took the stairs. Leaping down two stairs at a time, I arrived just short of the elevator door sliding open. I hung out on the landing until he strolled by.

After buying a take-out cup of coffee at the hospital café, he walked outside slowly toward the Neurosciences Clinic. Surprisingly, his face was still obscured. With my hair tucked under the cap, the hood of my jacket raised well over it, I pulled the bill of my cap down as I also lowered my face into the jacket. Slouching to hide my height even more, I pretended to limp along so I'd fit in with many of the nerve-impaired patients at the clinic. As he pressed the door release at the Neurosciences Clinic, I sped up my tottering. I couldn't afford to lose him now.

He walked through the foyer, where patients sat in vertical rows waiting for their names to be called for their appointment confirmation. There he said something to one of the receptionists lined up in horizontal cubicles facing the door. Then he turned left. To the very left was a set of automatic doors requiring medical personnel to slide a key card to open it. If he passed through those doors, I couldn't follow him. Instead, he moved up the hallway between the automatic door and the receptionists. I limped after him but he disappeared into a room and closed the door. What the ...?

I pulled myself up short as if hit by a freight train. What, I asked myself, in the world was I doing chasing after him like that? Amazed by my utter carelessness, I shivered. I could have caught up with him! And I didn't exactly have an invisibility cloak. Then what would I have done? But by the dint of sheer dumb luck, I hadn't caught up with him. As I stood in the corridor, shaking my head, grateful he hadn't turned around, someone spoke to me. My heart stopped. It was a Native American-appearing nurse with glossy jet-black hair in a long braid down the back of her peach-colored, cotton cardigan sweater.

She startled me, asking, "Do you need help finding your way?"

"No, I'm fine." Scrambling for something to explain my location, I added, "I thought I had left my keys in the exam room but I found them." I pulled them out of my hoodie pocket to show her. "Thank you."

Stunned for a moment by how close I'd come to meeting Moore face to face, I slowly limped back to the petite Hispanic patient-admittance person with whom he had spoken. She had beautiful long-lashed, nutmeg-colored eyes that were exquisitely lined, enhanced by what looked like professionally-applied makeup. She was just finishing with checking in a patient. I approached her, stooping over further. My mouth was so dry I wasn't sure I could speak.

"I hope you can help me." Wishing I had worn a wig and glasses to help disguise me, I asked, "I'm looking for an orderly named something like Catron Marr?"

"You mean, Clayton Moore?"

"Yes, I guess so. That sounds like it."

She eyed me suspiciously. "Why do you ask?"

It immediately occurred to me that what I was about to say might not sound credible if he treated patients the way he treated Carrie and dogs. But he wouldn't be working there with patients if he were totally devoid of interpersonal skills.

"I believe it was Mr. Moore my brother talked to a several weeks ago. My brother wanted to get in touch with him. I have no idea what it's about. Is he here most of the time? I mean, is this where my brother could find him or even send him a note?"

She raised a perfect L'Oreal eyebrow. "That was Mr. Moore who just left and went up the hall. I can call him back here for you if you'd like."

My heart dropped. "Oh, no, thanks," I said too hurriedly. "He wouldn't know who I am and I couldn't really tell him anything. It was just that my brother knew I'd be in the clinic area and asked if I check for him."

She squinted at me, destroying her fashion model image, as if memorizing my by-comparison bland features. I felt a little dizzy, wishing I had put on a pair of joke glasses with a false nose and bushy eyebrows.

"Well, he generally works 8-to-5 Monday through Friday but that schedule can change at any time. You can have your brother call ahead before stopping by or address a note to him in care of the Neurosciences Clinic and he should get it."

Knowing she'd probably tell him what I'd asked, I dismissed the idea that he'd make the connection to me as the witness to his Albertson's act of abuse.

With my heart cannonading in my throat and my tongue sticking to the roof of my mouth, I thanked her, turned on heel, and limped back out the automatic glass doors. As soon as I was out of sight of the clinic, I stood up and raced to the garage and my car. "Gotcha!" I whooped and jumped with my arms flapping, like a mating sandhill crane. People stared. I couldn't wait to get back home and start executing my soon-to-be revenge program.

After correcting the social psychology students' exams and their papers on their observations of people responding to someone pretending to be lost in public, I retrieved my news print pad. It was finally time to figure out what to do that would "strike fear in Moore's heart." That, however, was assuming a lot about someone who seemed to have no compunction about attacking animals in public. But even a soulless creep must not want those who associate with him to be put off by his socially-unflattering notoriety, if not his sadistic behavior. It might reflect badly on them as well, unless they were likewise so inclined. Surely it wouldn't do his reputation at the Neurosciences Clinic any good where "first do no harm" was the by-word.

Sending him an ambiguous, vaguely threatening letter might get him to respond so I could view its effect. As a first attempt, it was worth a try. Back home, wearing vinyl examination gloves, I cut words out of the *Albuquerque Journal* and pasted them onto fresh, common typewriter paper. It was an anonymous letter which stated, "I saw what you did!" No more, no less. It was reminiscent of the 1965 William Castle film, of the same name, starring Joan Crawford, except that in the film the anonymous letter was a prank phone call.

With considerable delight, I slipped the note into a cheap Walgreen's business-size envelope, wrote Moore's address on it with my slightly illegible left-handed scrawl, and stuck on a self-adhering stamp. Out of habit, however, I added a return address sticker I'd received from the ASPCA. Fortunately, when my cognitive functions snapped to attention, the rough place from where I had removed it didn't leave a hole. That suggested slowing down and being more careful next time, if there were a next time.

Immediately posted at the Bernalillo post office, it would be delivered the next day. The problem then was how to be nearby to observe his reaction when he received it and hopefully read it in public. That was going to involve risk. Maybe his face would be contorted with fear. Maybe he'd look anxious. Or maybe he'd look puzzled. The goal was to discomfort him which could give me a clue as to how to proceed.

The next day at 5:30 P.M. with my car parked in the partially-occupied high school parking lot across from his home, I sat looking out the side window awaiting his arrival. By 6:30 there was still no sign of him. Disappointed, I left.

The next letter read in cut-outs, "I know what you did and others will too." This would be posted the next day. In the meantime, the problem to solve was how I'd discover his reaction if he didn't show up again.

The day after I sent the second letter, I was again going to park at five-thirty but this time in the Walgreen's side parking lot. However, when I arrived at Walgreen's, the only open slots were in front of the building, on the Rt. 550 side. His house wasn't visible from that vantage point. That meant getting out of the car and making my way to the trees and shrubs that lined the driveway which opened onto Camino del Pueblo. Unfortunately, there was no hoodie or baseball cap with me to hide my face.

Circling around Walgreen's large stucco building on foot, passing the bank drive-in, I came out a distance from Moore's house then crept back along the driveway tree line to the road. Even with my additional hiking, I'd timed it correctly. His Dodge Ram was just pulling in beside the house. He alighted and headed for the post box. But as he reached it and I was readying my cell phone, a voice called out to me.

"Can I help you with something?" It was a woman who was entering the Walgreen's driveway, leaning out her open red Mini Cooper window.

Startled, I looked up from my crouching position at the end of the driveway where I was partially obscured by a shrub.

"No, thanks. I was looking for my car keys which I had dropped."

"If you're sure you don't need help."

"No, here, I've found them," I said, hiding my cell phone and pretending to pick up my key ring, which was already in my hand. I jingled it in front of my face to show her. "Thanks anyway." I smiled, stood, and quickly glanced at Moore's house. He was already entering his front door. Outpoured a stream of scatological comments barely under my breath before I started to walk back to my car, following my previous looping path.

The next day was back-to-back classes so there wasn't anything to do about Moore until I arrived home. I expected the semi-threatening missives to make him wonder and wrack his brain for what they could relate to. In his thirties, he wasn't likely to have viewed the 1965 movie. It was hard to know if he had seen or heard the phrase used as a prank or if it had become commonplace with his social group. Then I had an aha! That crummy movie had been remade in 1988.

Consequently, it was remotely possible he might have heard it on late-night nostalgia TV. Perhaps it didn't matter. However, the next logical step really depended upon what his reaction to what he had already received was.

Options for phrasing in another anonymous letter skittered through my mind, such as, "What would they say at work if they knew what you like to do to animals?" That was too specific too soon. It had to be more ambiguous. Maybe, instead, it could say something like, "What would they say at work if they knew what you did?" Then in the following letter his actions would likewise be vague but emphasize the reaction of his fellow workers to his "unacceptable" behavior. It had to sound fear-inspiring but would it? Without that feedback my campaign was stuck in a frustrating limbo.

Carrie arrived at my office door as I was leaving for my social psychology class being held across the street.

"I gave some thought to what you said about animal abusers. I once saw a large dried blood stain in the back of my former-boyfriend's truck. I asked him about it but he said it was from a deer hunting trip. Maybe it was. I don't know. What I know is that after he hit his dog with a flashlight, I never saw the dog again. I couldn't believe that the poor dog could have survived that injury with or without medical care. When I asked him, he dismissively said that he gave it to his cousin because it barked too much. Barked too much? That sweet dog never barked, not once. It was too afraid to utter a sound. I let that go. Now I wonder."

"Would his name be 'Clay' by any chance?"

"Why, yes. How did you know?"

"Someone who left a tip on the Animal Abuse Hotline said she thought the abuser worked as an orderly at one of the UNM medical clinics. Then," I fibbed, "I asked a friend of mine who works with staff records at the hospital if she knew an orderly who was fond of cowboy dress. She said she had gone out for drinks once with an orderly named 'Clay Moore.' What amazed her about him was how he was dressed for the bar. You know, he looked and acted like he was some well-known western movie star in a tight light blue outfit."

"Yeah, that was his favorite outfit. So, he finally left Walmart. But I can't imagine him working with patients. He's not exactly someone I'd called humane, caring, or over-flowing with compassion."

"As long as he doesn't treat them like his dog," I sadly chuckled, picturing him carrying a heavy metal flashlight on his hip with his Lone Ranger black leather, double drop, silver-studded gun belt and side holsters over his scrubs.

"That's gross!"

Just as Carrie and I were about to part company outside the classroom, it occurred to me that she might know how he was likely to respond to different situations, like my letters.

"One more thing about him. People who abuse animals may tend to express less happiness about positive things, true sadness about tragedies, and fearfulness in risky situations. Mostly they show anger, indifference, or coldness. I was wondering if you've ever seen Clay sad or fearful?"

"Sad? No, I can't think of anything. He certainly wasn't sad about his badly injured dog. He didn't seem sad about my leaving. Fearful? Well, maybe he was a little anxious when I tried to take the dog to the animal hospital. But mostly he was angry with me for suggesting it and angry with the dog for making a bloody mess."

"Thanks. See you in class tomorrow."

If he had been anxious, maybe it was because he didn't want veterinarians to know what he had done because they might report him to Animal Control if Carrie told them the truth about how the injury had happened. Being honest might have been a dangerous thing for her to do. If he could experience anxiety in that situation, maybe he could experience some from the letters. But without actually seeing his reaction there was no way to know. Until then, I had no idea what would work for me to anonymously insinuate myself into his life, to set him up for fear of exposure and its accompanying social and financial pain.

Since I hadn't seen any evidence that he still had the dog Carrie described, I could send the third letter asking, "What happened to your dog?" But that would be too specific. Besides, he could relate it to Carrie. Irrespective of whatever I might send to him, I would have to set up surveillance again. This was becoming increasingly awkward because I didn't want him to spot my car with any regularity, especially when he received these letters.

After the third letter, "What would they say at work if they knew what you did?" at 5:30 P.M. I once again parked around front of Walgreens on Rt. 550, circled around to approach the same stand of trees on Camino del Pueblo as before. I settled myself in a crouching position between two Siberian elms and waited. Time passed slowly. My thighs were beginning to cramp. By the time his truck finally passed forty-five minutes later, I worried my legs might fight my rising to observe his actions. After he had parked beside his house, I was more or less upright and focused on his postbox with my cell phone.

When he looked at his mail and saw the plain envelope with my scribble, he didn't seem surprised. He sliced it open with his thumb nail, pulled out the eight and a half by eleven sheet. After scanning it, he quickly looked around. Then he waved it in the air, grinning, and headed for his front door.

I was taken aback. A shiver ran down my spine. What did that mean? Did he think it was a prank and his friends might be watching to see what he'd do? Or could he possibly think the person who had filmed him at Albertson's had sent it and was watching? While the latter seemed highly improbable, he could still choose to believe it.

Since his reaction was anything but what I had expected, I debated about sending another, more specific letter. This would be something his friends would be unlikely to joke about, like, "How many animals have you abused?" Getting that personal could make him angry. I didn't want to make him any angrier than he already was. But I wanted a reaction. I felt conflicted. Yes or no? After mulling it over for an hour as I checked my e-mail and paid some bills, I decided reluctantly to do it. It was a risk but my cell phone pictures never captured a good full face. I'd include the poster with the photo of Teddy's injured body with the letter. It was only after I had dropped the fourth letter into the post box that I seriously worried it might pinpoint me as the sender.

The next several days moved along smoothly, quietly. Classes were going as expected. Nothing out of the ordinary attracted my notice. The clinical psych. students were getting together to do their observations and experiments with conditioning behavior. This was to demonstrate that the behaviors of animals and people could be shaped to create new, positive behaviors. They would do this shaping individually with animals first and volunteers second as part of learning in depth about aspects of cognitive-behavioral therapy.

To start them off, I showed them a documentary wherein Cambodians were training giant African pouched rats to detect landmines because they were less expensive to train than dogs and, furthermore, they have an impeccable sense of smell for detecting TNT. They let the rodent, which is about the size of a cat, smell TNT then use a clicker and give the rat a treat. Every time a rat sniffed a landmine, it would scratch the soil above it. The handler would then click a clicker and give the rat a treat. The rat could cover two thousand square feet in twenty minutes whereas a human with a metal detector could take four days to cover the same area. Considering that Cambodia is littered with landmines, this behavioral training of rats could help reduce the number of future people wounded and killed by these still-hidden bombs.

However, what the students were to do as a team was less socially impactful. It was only to demonstrate for themselves how shaping behavior worked. First, they were to pick a local homeless animal rescue shelter to visit three times a week and focus on getting one dog to do a particular behavior. The behavior they chose would be based upon something the dog already did that would be the first step in the formation of another, more complex behavior.

Carrie's team found a Pit Bull-mix named "Little Bingo" which would lie on its side when they approached. Consequently, they decided to try to condition the pooch to roll over multiple times on cue. As one member of the team with a treat in hand made roll movements over the dog's abdomen, saying "Roll over," other members observed and recorded the results. For every small movement toward a roll over the dog was praised, petted, and rewarded with a dog treat. Team members changed places so everyone had the chance to observe, practice, and record.

After Clay received his last letter, he did precisely what I worried he would. He contacted Carrie to ask to whom she had spoken about his dog. She cornered me after class.

"I said, 'No one, why would I?' But I don't think he believed me at first. But then when I reminded him that he'd told me he had given his dog to his cousin in Algodones, he changed the subject. That was when he stated something totally off-the-wall. He said he wanted us to get back together."

I raised my eyebrows but didn't say anything.

"I nearly freaked out. I mean, he always sounded on the verge of anger before but now he sounded unhinged. I didn't know what to say. I finally told him I was engaged. But he demanded to know who the guy was. Was he the guy who had made me pregnant? I know he'll be back in touch. Now I'm really afraid of what he might do. He'll do whatever it takes to get what he wants."

Carrie was in a tough spot. But maybe I was too. I could picture him receiving the picture of the injured puppy and starting to recall the person who filmed him at Albertson's. Even though it would have been unlikely that she would have known where he lived or anything about his having killed other animals, that didn't mean he might have decided that. That would likely spell out real danger for this Marvel Superhero as well.

10

Days later I had a call from Lydia who was taking Judy's place staffing the animal humane phone lines. She told me she had received a call from a reporter at the *Albuquerque Journal* who wanted to do a story on the person who filmed the abuser kicking the puppy. When I had submitted the original story and photo of Teddy to the papers, I had purposely conveyed it anonymously via the animal humane organization so there was no further information. Any other questions regarding the story were referred to the Animal Abuse Hotline.

"He asked me a lot of questions, such as, has there been any success in naming the abuser? Who's investigating this? Is Animal Control involved? What's being done to find this person other than putting up posters? He was very pushy. But I told him that I'd have to check to see if we had a record of who submitted the film to us and then, if we did, I'd have to call to see if that person wanted to speak with him about it."

"Did he give you his name?"

"No, he started asking questions right away and after that, I didn't think to ask him for it. Sorry. But he said he'd call back to get an answer."

"That's okay. If he calls again, please get his spelled-out name. Since the film and story were, to my knowledge, submitted anonymously, just tell him that."

I could only thing it was Moore. What Lydia would tell him probably wouldn't satisfy a real reporter but it might slow down Moore a little for the time being.

I was uncomfortable with this turn of events. The reporter initially contacted by snail mail was female. Of course, she could have a male assistant to further acquire info for her. While I wanted to get the word out again to remind the public, I didn't want personal contact with anyone, not even with a reporter. I filled Lydia in on what had been accomplished so far, which was nothing beyond a report to Animal Control. Of course, I was mum on what I was doing on my own. I suggested that she share the hotline tips to-date with the authorities but with no one else and not mention me to anyone as investigating it too.

The question that plagued me was could Moore discover my identity. I thought it must be tickling his psychopathic nerve endings that he could turn the tables and harass me. Only, of course, he wouldn't be so gentle about it.

Abruptly, I was on the defensive. That standing-tall Marvel Superhero with blazing red cape looked very small and vulnerable. I kept asking myself, "Is there any other way Moore could find out about me?" Nothing came to mind. "What about Coronado Pet Hospital where I took Teddy? Surely, they wouldn't give out that information. Clients were confidential."

A cold chill clutched my intestines. Was there anything I could do now … maybe along the lines of the letters I'd already sent … that could misdirect him? I grappled with this for a while but nothing resulted. I suspected it didn't matter. Once he'd pegged me in his mind as the perpetrator, he was not going to let that go. It would be too satisfying.

The rest of the afternoon after my karate practice, which felt unproductive because of my mood, I worked on reading the updated notes on the students' conditioning experiments. For the most part, they were coming along fine. A few on Carrie's team were a bit too enthusiastic in getting the dog to roll over, pushing the dog's legs to the other side. I'd have to go over the shaping nuances of what they needed to do and not do so they wouldn't confuse or panic the animal.

My cell phone rang around ten o'clock at night. I was just putting all my papers for the next day's classes in my briefcase. It was Lydia.

"The reporter called again. I told him what you said but he didn't seem happy. I asked for his name this time and he said something that sounded like, 'Nadie Puta' and that he was new at the paper. I've never heard of him. Anyway, he stated he needed some way to contact the filmmaker, you know like e-mail, Twitter, Facebook, Instagram, mailing address, phone number. He kept arguing with me, not listening to me. When I got a word in edge-wise, I stated that we had no record and there was nothing that I could do to help him. He hung up on me. I thought that was very strange and rude behavior for a reporter."

"Thanks, Lydia. Maybe he's new at journalism doesn't have the etiquette down yet." I did not think that was the case.

As soon as we hung up, I called the *Journal* to inquire of the night staff if a "Nadie Puta" actually worked for the paper. Frank Garcia, the city editor, wasn't there. I left a message and was told I'd get a call back by morning. I slept fitfully because the caller had to have been Moore. He *was* trying to hunt me down.

The next morning, I received a call at eight o'clock from the *Journal*. It was Frank, whom I'd known since I moved to New Mexico. I'd written a well-received series of articles on the homeless animal problem. Strangely, he was laughing.

"I apologize for laughing but I'm afraid someone's pulled a joke on you, and not a very nice one. 'Nadie' is Spanish for 'no one' and a 'Puta' means, well, 'whore.' Not exactly a love letter. If that's really what the person said, then it sounds like a warning, that someone is letting you know he, or she, is not happy with you."

"Terrific. That's just what I need. By the way, have you at the paper received any tips from the public about that Albertson's puppy abuse incident?"

"No, not a word. I suspect that anyone with information would prefer to leave an anonymous tip on the Animal Abuse Hotline. So, I take it, there's no luck on the hotline either?"

"No, not much," I lied. Then it occurred to me that Moore might try the paper directly to find me, if he hadn't tried already. "You know that the film was given to the animal humane organization anonymously and I directed it to you, *anonymously.*"

"Sure, kiddo. Of course, just because I know that filming that *el pendejo* and handing it over to animal humane is the sort of thing you'd do, doesn't mean I *know* you did it. Right?"

"*Moi*, Frank? If *anyone* calls, please just keep directing them to animal humane. And thanks. You're a good guy."

Frank replied, "I know," he laughed. "Stay safe. Gotta go," and hung up.

At a minimum that situation was covered with one less thread to worry about. I hadn't told anyone but Dr. Smith and Animal Control about my observing and filming the abuse. So, the places from which Moore could get my name were essentially non-existent. However, if he hadn't actually accepted Carrie's claim that she hadn't spoken to anyone, he would continue to browbeat her and scare or trick her into divulging my name. If she might then let on that I was someone involved in researching animal abusers, that would be even worse. Thank goodness I hadn't told her I was the one who filmed him kicking the puppy.

My revenge campaign was stirring up a hornet's nest. The next letters I had planned would make him even more determined to find me and deliver whatever revenge he considered appropriate. My superhero self now didn't feel so super or heroic. I knew he'd eventually find out who I was, where I worked and lived. It was only a matter of time. If I could find out about him, he could find out about me despite of all the measures I had taken to hide my identity. And he would come after me full of rage and unquenchable righteous indignation.

What bothered me most, after all this time and effort, was that I hadn't gotten any closer to avenging Teddy. All I'd done was antagonize someone for whom violence was, apparently, second nature. But, maybe, somehow, that was to the good. There was no way to connect the letters he had received to me. I had used sterile procedures. Using the Bernalillo post office wasn't a dead giveaway either. Whoever wrote the letters had seen him act, recognized him, and lived nearby.

As I sat in my office at UNM, I wondered whether I should continue the letters after all. I needed to do something. But to what end? Besides, the madder he became the more unhinged his behaviors could be in public. If I continued, I would mail them from different post offices so as not to target Bernalillo. My overall plan needed re-thinking. Things were beginning to feel haphazard.

Now I wished I hadn't gone to Animal Control. I could have sent them a copy of the film anonymously. But if I had, who's to say they wouldn't have dismissed it even more easily than they seemed to have dismissed it when I personally brought it to them. My head once again felt as if it were going to explode.

Students wandered in and out during my office hours. Some needed assistance with their projects; some wanted their exam grades changed for miscellaneous, unsupportable reasons (lots of luck); and Carrie showed up at the end of the hour, looking anxious.

"Clay has been calling me, bugging me because he is convinced that someone is trying to connect him with the puppy kicking at Albertson's. He's gotten unsigned letters suggesting it. He swears he's going to find out who it is and make them pay—and, believe me, he will, over and over again."

"Did he say what the letters said?"

"Just that the person knew he was guilty."

"So that suggests the person who sent them might have been a witness to the attack. Were they asking for hush money or anything like that?"

"He didn't say but if they had, I'm sure he would have mentioned it. He was furious, shouting about it."

"Has he gone to the police yet with these letters? They have all kinds of scientific ways to determine who sent them. If he thinks there's a plot against him, that would be the thing to do."

"Oh, no. He wouldn't do that because one of the letters talks about killing other animals as well as kicking that puppy."

"So, do you now think he's guilty of attacking that puppy ... and maybe killing his own dog too?"

"Yes. His dog was still alive when I left, barely, but, now, I don't see how it could have survived that assault. And I feel more and more panicky every time he calls."

"How do you think you should deal with it?"

"I think avoiding him would make him even more angry. I don't know what he'd do."

"It does sound safer to take his calls and visits. However, you might also consider keeping a diary of everything he does that scares you—you know, noting *what, when, where, how,* etc. When he tries to contact you online, print his messages to keep with your special Moore diary. You know, to document what he does in case you decide to go to the police."

"I'll think about it. I guess creating a diary could be useful ... *if* he couldn't find it. He's showing up at my house and at work. Heaven only knows what he'll do next." With that, Carrie slipped out my door and disappeared.

That evening, wearing my vinyl gloves, I put together another letter for Moore. It summed it all up. "You brutally attacked that puppy at Albertson's. Give yourself up to the police. Or else." When I finished, I held on to the envelope for an hour.

As I thought about Carrie's safety, I felt this letter could re-direct the conversation back to his public display of abuse. As far as she could tell, he seemed to have accepted her reminder about his dog's location. But whether he really had or not was still to be determined. It was possible he wanted her back in his life because he was comfortable using her as his sounding board, something he really needed right now. It was also possible he was spinning some sort of web by which to ensnare and punish her. Either way, his wanting them to get back together was worrisome. The more paranoid he became about the letters and me, the more danger she would be in.

Taking the chance, I drove nine miles north on Rt. 550 to Route 165 and the historic village of Placitas and dropped letter number five in their post office's outside mail box. It wasn't until I started back home that I realized how tight my chest had become. I needed to make him public. But in doing so I was really playing with fire and very probably going to get more than my fingertips singed.

Given the gravity of the likely scenario, the least I should do is write a letter for a lawyer to hold—that meant I'd have to find a lawyer first—stating that if something happened to me, it was because of Clayton Moore of Bernalillo who was stalking and terrorizing me. I'd lay out that I'd filmed him kicking and severely injuring a dog at Albertson's and he had seen me doing it, making a threatening gesture as a result. That I'd reported the incident to Animal Control and, later when I had discovered his name, passed that along too— something I hadn't as yet done but would have to be sure to do soon. With the letter I'd include the poster I had created, a copy of the video I'd recorded, the animal hospital's medical evaluation, and a full-face photo of Moore—assuming I could finally capture one in time for this letter to be useful.

In my imagination the police were scrutinizing Moore. He, of course, would deny that he had hurt the puppy or was stalking me. Instead, he'd claim that the person who filmed the attack had sent him "threatening notes." Since the police would be unable to track them back to me, I was in the clear unless Hardess passed my name along to Moore for fun. I wouldn't have put it past him.

If only a neighbor could complain about the "stench" in his yard that reminded her of "rotting flesh" and have the police bring in cadaver dogs to locate the multiple bodies of all his abused animals. Of course, if they found only one decomposed body, he could say it was his beloved pet which died and he buried it in his yard to be near it. If they examined it, the crushed skull might belie his claim that it had simply died, unless he said it had been hit by a car. That, however, might not be questioned.

Ten days later I was still trying to figure out how to photograph Moore without being detected when Carrie visited me in my office.

"It's getting worse. Clay is bothering me morning and night. I don't know what to do. He follows me and waylays me before and after work at awkward moments when it's not easy to get away. Since I won't tell him the name of the man that I'm 'engaged' to, he says he doesn't believe me. He's been asking about the baby I told him I was going to have. One minute he wants to know if he's the father. The next he says he doesn't believe I was pregnant, that I was lying. I'm really scared because he's acting so crazy."

"That sounds scary. He certainly seems serious about wanting you two to get back together."

"Back together? Never!"

"Please be careful about communicating that to him. You might also want to reconsider reporting him to the police and getting a protective order against him. Has he ever done any of this in front of witnesses who could testify for you?"

"No, he makes sure we're alone."

"Do investigate applying for protective custody. It could be helpful."

"If I did anything like that, he'd go ballistic. Right now, he's just a scary pain in the ass. But if I were to contact the police in any way ..." She shook her head and looked down at her feet.

Carrie left as I was getting my gear together. Five minutes later I followed on my way to the parking garage. No sooner had I turned the hall corner, past my last classroom, to take the flight of stairs down to the first floor, then I found myself within ten feet of Moore. He had Carrie trapped, pinning her against the yellow wall as he argued with her. As I approached all I could hear was, "No, you're *mine*. You belong to me. You can't be engaged to anyone else. That's it."

Hearing my footsteps, he turned. In a stunning moment of recognition, he smiled malevolently. "I know you!" he said, letting go of Carrie. She moved aside.

"Do you?" I said as casually as I could manage.

"Don't fuck with me. You're the one who filmed me at Albertson's. And you've been sending me letters, nasty, threatening letters. You're not going to get away with it."

"Yes, I filmed you at Albertson's but I haven't sent you any letters of any kind. I'd have no reason to do. I don't even know where you live."

"The hell you didn't, you bitch!" He moved toward me and grabbed my right arm, his fingers engraving his prints in my flesh. His other hand grasped my left wrist to twist it behind me.

"Let go of me ... now!" I dropped my briefcase on his foot, momentarily distracting him. "I'm going to have you arrested for assault."

He laughed, "Ha! I am so scared."

Trying to stand behind me, he let go of my right wrist to wrap his right arm around my throat in a choke hold. Carrie gasped. As she did, I lowered my center of gravity and quickly leaned into his arm, upsetting his balance. Then I kicked him hard in the knee cap with my left foot. He went down in a heap, screaming, clutching his dislocated patella.

Sputtering intermittently amid groans, he cried, "You bitch! ... I am going to get you for this ... and I'm going to enjoy it ... you better make out your will."

I grabbed my briefcase and Carrie and left immediately. I drove her home. As we neared her house, she looked at me somewhat hurt.

"You never said you were the one who filmed the attack on the puppy. You said you were doing research on abusers. That's why you were asking all those questions and why I told you what I did. You lied to us. I trusted you. You betrayed me."

As I rolled to a stop, I said, "I do research on animal abusers. I didn't want to bias what the class told me by saying I was involved in that incident."

"I don't care what you say now. How could you lie to me, to us?" Carrie opened the passenger door, got out, slammed it, and ran into her house.

As I pulled away, I wondered if she would still be a witness to Moore's attack on me. I went directly to the Animal Control where I'd made my original report to the police. Hardess was on the desk.

"Officer Hardess, I have some information on the man who kicked and seriously injured that puppy at Albertson's."

He glanced up at me, boredom masking his features, and waddled forward.

"The man's name is Clay Moore. He lives in Bernalillo on Camino del Pueblo. A hotline tip said he works at UNM Hospital as an orderly. He accosted me today at the university, claiming he knew I had filmed him and threatened to kill me. He was acting paranoid. He even tried to choke me. I have a witness."

"And where is he now?"

"I suspect he is on this way to the UNM Hospital ER. When he put his arm around my throat, I managed to kick him in the knee cap."

Hardess rolled his eyes as if he were watching a television re-run of *Wonder Woman*.

"I'm reporting him for physical assault and death threats."

"You said you have a witness? Who is that?"

"That's Carrie Baxley, one of my students. She lives on Dr. Martin Luther King Jr. Avenue NE. She was with me when Moore tried to choke me and she knows Moore. She had seen him smash his own dog's head in with a heavy flashlight. I want to get a protective order against him."

"The police can't give you a protective order. Only the court can. Have fun. It's a long process."

"What do I have to do to get it started?"

"Get an application and go to the appropriate court to file it. You can get the application online or at the court."

"What specific court would that be?"

"Look, lady, I'm not a lawyer. I don't even play one on television. Do your research. Look it up." With that, he turned on heel, and went back to his desk.

"What about the assault charge I want to file against Moore?"

"Fill out this report," he said to me over his shoulder before he brought some papers back to me. "And we'll look into it."

I found a table and chair, filled out the form, and returned it to him.

"We'll be in touch," he replied and went back to his desk. I wondered if he were going to pursue this assault as diligently as he seemingly had pursued the puppy attack.

11

On the way home I stopped at Coronado to check on Teddy. He was beginning to move around a little and looked at me in a way I couldn't fully comprehend. I wondered if he recognized me after all he'd been through. Sarah joined me, enthusiastic.

"He looks wonderful doesn't he."

I nodded but I didn't think he looked that great. I was just glad he was alive.

"He's such a little sweetheart. He keeps working his way back more and more each day. He's like a little miracle. We've become very close. He will be discharged soon. I don't know what plans you had for him but I'd really like to have him if that's okay with you."

I was startled. I hadn't even considered his recovering to the point of someone adopting him. While I suddenly felt possessive, I also knew he belonged with Sarah who had been attending to him and would continue to care for him and love him. Besides, it might help her get through Delilah's sooner than later departure.

"Of course, he belongs to you."

My lack of enthusiasm seemed to sail past her. She hugged me. I opened Teddy's cage, gave him a pet for which he seemed pleased. He cocked his head to the right and looked me in the eye.

Back home I found myself in a funny mood, suspended somewhere between happiness at his recovery and sadness at his loss. Snowpaws' death came back in a flash. Trying to put it all aside, I turned on my computer to find the New Mexico Justice Court forms for protective custody and printed them out. Looking them over, it occurred to me this would take some time. "If I'm lucky," I said aloud, "Moore won't kill me before I finish with them."

What the instructions for the forms indicated was that I could be granted a temporary restraining order which could later become a preliminary injunction and, then later, a permanent injunction. It was obvious I needed a good law dictionary or inexpensive lawyer to get through this morass. I needed a lawyer anyway for that "In case of my death by other than natural causes" letter I should write soon.

What a protective order could do, if the court sanctioned it, was keep Moore from threatening, harming, alarming, and annoying me and any family I might have. It could prohibit him from coming within some specified number of feet of my residence and workplace. Moreover, it could punish him for calling, texting, e-mailing, mailing, or in any way contacting me. He couldn't follow me or block me in public places or on roads. And if I had to bring a court case against him, he would have to pay me back for any costs and expenses I had incurred in taking him to court. That sounded positive enough.

However, as I continued reading the paperwork, my mood dampened. It looked as if my case for protection was as starkly skeletal as Georgia O'Keeffe's desert-bleached cow skulls. What he had done so far was threaten and assault me. But so far, I had no documentation or evidence that he had already been stalking or harassing me. I put the papers aside for the moment. Now that he knew who I was, he would no doubt start his own revenge campaign on steroids. I'd have to always keep my cell phone and notebook with me and be super-alert to my surroundings. But, I lightheartedly pouted, my lower lip protruding, "I was *supposed* to be a Superhero. It wasn't supposed to turn out this way."

Now that I had reported him to the police for both assault and animal abuse, I felt unsure about what I could do next. There was no longer a need for anonymous letters which didn't scare him anyway. It was demoralizing that all I could do now was wait ... wait until the police did something ... or Moore did. While I had cavalierly determined that I'd be ready for him if he tried anything, the potential physical and emotional consequences were just starting to seep into my consciousness.

The next morning after I had gathered together what I'd need for my four classes, I spotted something partially under my front door. It looked like an envelope. As I reached down to pull it out, I stopped. Instead, I walked to the kitchen to get a pair of vinyl gloves and returned. Carefully, I dislodged it. The face was blank. It was sealed so I went back to the kitchen to get a knife to open it. Inside was a folded slip of paper which I unfolded by holding the corners. Before me was a bullseye with cross hairs and a splotch of red, which looked like real blood. There certainly was no question that he had discovered where I lived.

Carrying them both, I retrieved an unused plastic food bag from the pantry, dropped the envelope and paper inside, sealed it with a twist-em, then wrote the date on the bag with a Sharpie pen. I made an entry in my notebook with the date, what I'd received, and how I'd handled it. As Sherlock Holmes would have said, "The game is on." And, alarmingly, it was.

As I drove I-25, I tended to keep looking in my rearview mirror for Moore's truck. For a second, I thought I had spotted him. My heart started doing a three-minute mile. But, no. When I gained a better look at the pickup, I saw it wasn't his. Being alert was the goal, not this stress-imbued hypervigilance.

My first class was introductory psychology. We discussed the attributions people make, how the attributions, or assignment of causes to things, one makes depend upon whether they're the one doing the action/behavior or the one viewing it. The example that started the discussion was when a car in traffic makes an unexpected swerving movement. The driver knows she swerved a little out of her lane because a squirrel ran into the road and she attempted to miss it. The cause is situational, something out of her control.

However, drivers in other cars will tend to think that she did it because she was texting, talking, tuning the radio, or momentarily fell asleep. Their explanation of the cause is dispositional, that she did it because of some internal characteristic, like personality, motives, or beliefs. The students' homework assignment was to first observe how they responded to what others did and what explanations they gave, then consider what situational explanations might also apply. Second, they were to consider how others might view the causes of what they themselves had done and were doing.

Even though I kept looking around as I walked to my next class, I knew that Moore was likely still on his 8-to-5 shift. The second class was also introductory psych. We were looking at action potentials of nerves to demonstrate how electrical signals via neurotransmitters are passed on from one neuron to another. Many students were obviously not thrilled about the physiology of neurons. They didn't seem to care about how and when different ions, such as sodium and potassium, crossed the semi-permeable membrane of the neuron and what happened when they did. I could tell they thought it was gobbledygook and going to be incredibly boring. That is, until I used "sexual stimulation" as an example. Faces lit up. "No kidding!" someone commented. Everyone then began asking questions and participating in the discussion afterward.

After class, I walked from the Logan Hall Psychology, crossed Redondo S., covered the length of Sara Raynolds Hall parking lot, and stopped on the other side of Central Street SE—old U.S. Route 66—at a vegetarian restaurant to see if I could get some sort of interesting salad to go. Traffic was always bad on six-lane Central near the university. My other nearby options were a burger joint, a brew house, and Dunkin' Donuts. I settled for a veggie-filled pita bread sandwich and trotted back to my office, dodging and weaving as vehicles sped by. That gave me about twenty minutes in which to eat before my office hours.

Carrie stopped by to tell me Clay was still pestering her to come back.

"Mostly he's calling and stopping by to interrogate me about you. He said for me to tell you that he knows where you live and you will be seeing more of him, so 'Beware.' He was smiling his demonic smile when he said it. I know that smile all too well. He had it on his face when he smashed his dog's head in. He really means it. You had better be very careful."

"How are you feeling now about my not having told you about filming the puppy attack?"

"I'm still a little mad at you ... but can understand why you didn't want to tell anyone. So, what's going on with the puppy abuse investigation?"

"I have no idea. After our encounter with Clay, I went to the police. I reported his assault and his name for my earlier animal abuse report. I'll have to give them some time before I inquire again. However, I don't feel encouraged."

"I'm thinking of leaving school, moving to someplace where Clay can't find me."

"Oh, Carrie, I hope you don't have to do that. You're so close to getting your counseling degree. It's only a few more classes and your internship. You're sure you won't go for a protective order? I can be your witness on this."

"I'm just tired of being scared all the time. I'm tired of him trying to control me. Still I'd hate to leave my apartment, which was a real find. And I like my job working with the elderly. I don't know. It's all so depressing and frustrating right now."

"If you can, hang in for a while longer. Maybe things will change for the better."

"I don't know why they would. All he talks about, besides me coming back to him, is you. I've never seen him so agitated. He has a real vendetta against you. Maybe you should move as well."

"I'd prefer not to give in to malignant narcissists like Clay."

"Yeah. But he's one seriously dangerous guy."

Carrie left and it was time for my third class. This was about organizational behavior, primarily for business majors. Later would be my last class of the day, social psychology. It was the most fun because it looked at how people and the environment and situations interacted, affecting and influencing people's behavior, attitudes, and beliefs. Everyone could readily identify with its impact, concepts, and theories.

It had been a tiring day. I had parked on the unnamed street that ran between Redondo and Clark Hall. As I approached my car, I was greeted with a delightful surprise. All my tires were still inflated. No one had keyed the length of the car's body or tattooed an obscene word on any of my doors. Moreover, there were no notes on my intact windshield. Feeling momentarily free, I took Central to Campus to Lomas to I-25 and back home.

Since I no longer had to spend hours cyber-searching for names that sounded like 'Marr,' Barbara Bayer and I decided to go out to eat at one of Santa Ana Pueblo's restaurants, Prairie Star. Barbara, who ran CARMA, the no-kill, all-volunteer, non-profit "companion animal rescue and medical assistance" shelter in Corrales, was someone I had met my first week in New Mexico. As usual, she had a handful of eight and a half by eleven picture posters with her with details about all the great dogs she thought I should adopt. I did miss having a furry companion around, someone to love and love me back. Because I still mourned for Snowpaws, I felt I wasn't ready for a new canine best bud.

Over Caesar salad, she showed me one in particular that almost made me cry. It was a young German Shepherd named "Phoenix," which had been seriously abused. He had burns all over his body from having been doused with gasoline and set on fire as a puppy. Consequently, he was missing hair in a number of places and the naked skin was still bright pink. His wounds looked as if they were still healing. There was glint in its sensitive, intelligent eyes that made it impossible for me to look away.

Something familiar stirred in me over which I had no control. I was such a patsy for members of the down-and-out of the animal world. It was manifest that he needed me ... as Teddy had needed me. More to the point, a creeping realization gripped me: I needed him too.

"You are such a sneaky devil. Yes, Barbara, you've done it. You knew I'd want to meet this poor, sweet baby." Barbara smiled mischievously.

"He's almost fourteen months old and not all that comfortable with strangers, especially men, but I really think you and he would get along famously. I've had him ever since he was released from the emergency clinic. He's a real sweetheart but no one has wanted him because of how he looks. By the way, he was found in the Bernalillo area, just off Rt. 550 and Camino del Pueblo, near you."

"Okay, if it's convenient for you, I'll come over tomorrow, around ten? And we'll see how things go. Don't get your hopes up. You never can tell about these things."

But, of course, Barbara could tell, especially with me. Nothing like my being such an open book where animals were concerned.

When I arrived home at 6:30 P.M., I found someone had spray-painted the words "DIE BITCH!" in red on my front door. This was doubly troubling since the Spanish-style door had originally been artistically stained to look weathered with minute touches of teal and maroon delicately wrapped in a silvery patina. Upon inspection, everything seemed to be locked with no other exterior damage. I snapped the picture with my cell phone then recorded the vandalism in my notebook. I called John, the owner of the house, to report it in the context of Moore's threats, and asked what he wanted to do. I offered to try cleaning the door, repaint it, or do whatever he wanted. Sounding discouraged, he said he'd come by the next day on his lunch hour to assess it.

Inside I went from room to room, checking to see if anyone had gained entrance. As far as I could tell, everything was fine. I checked for breaks in the electricity, water, cable/Internet, and gas. Everything there seemed to be in working order as well. Perhaps after meeting Phoenix, I'd purchase additional locks for the house and the garage and look into having a security system installed. Maybe, John would pay for it or go halfsies with me.

It was a restless night. Every little sound awakened me. I knew I was being paranoid. But each time I snapped to attention, I felt compelled to traipse around the house to investigate. In the morning I looked as if I'd been on a bender with my eyelids at half-mast and purple circles forming under my eyes. My hair appeared to have been fashioned by a grunge musician. If my skin had been a little paler, I would have been a shoe-in for a part as an extra in a vampire movie.

At ten I met Barbara at her dog kennel. Just in case, I had bought a large bag of dog chow, cans of soft food, food and water dishes, large doggy bed, and a collar and leash. If it didn't work out, which seemed doubtful, I could donate those items to Barbara for her animals.

Lying in a corner all by himself was a pink polka-dot-looking adolescent German Shepherd with a peach-fuzz-covered bony tail. I called out to him.

"Phoenix. Come here, baby. I want to meet you."

He looked at me, his gaze slightly sad but even more intelligent than in the photo of him. He moved his eyes around, seeming to be unsure of what was going on and how to respond.

"Come see me. Come on. I want to get to know you." I tried to sound as encouraging as I could.

He stood and slowly walked toward me. Suddenly, an impulse overwhelmed me. I wanted to hug him and shower his with all the affection he could tolerate. But I held back. I knew I'd have to let him make the first big move. He'd been through so much and needed to feel in control of the interaction. I could be the alpha dog in this relationship later. As he approached, he raised his head slightly to look directly at me.

"Come on, baby," I enthused. "Would you be interested in coming home with me?"

His eyes brightened. I swear he made his mouth into what I can only describe as a tentative doggy smile. I carefully petted and scratched him under his chin. Fortunately, most of his face had been spared third-degree burns. He stared deeply into my eyes and rubbed his muzzle against my hands.

"I brought you some special puppy biscuits. They're just for you. Wouldn't you like to have a couple?"

He gently took one biscuit after another from my hand. When my hand was free, I stroked his back, gingerly avoiding the multiple one-inch-diameter bald spots. After ten minutes, he flopped over on his side, his tongue hanging down toward the floor. He was begging me to rub his tummy. And when I did, he wriggled on his back, even with his wounds, in a state of pure bliss. Like Barbara, he had my number. I whispered in his ear what Christopher Robin said.

After doing all the paperwork, including getting all his health information and licenses, I attached his new collar and leash and directed Phoenix toward my car. He stopped and dug all four paws into the sandy dirt. I coaxed him but he again seemed uncertain. But once I opened the front and back doors and took a seat inside, he jumped in onto the front passenger seat. His whole demeanor changed. Now he was all eagerness and confidence. That tickled me.

"Okay, Phoenix, we're going to your new home. If you're ready, I'm closing the doors and turning on the engine."

He settled down on the passenger seat then, quickly changing his mind, he rose to try to stick his nose out the four-inch window opening. For the sake of his eyes, I wasn't going to let him hang his head outside the car.

New Mexico's grit-glutted winds acted like sandpaper on delicate mucous membranes, potentially harming both his eyes and his upright ears.

On the way back to Bernalillo, Phoenix was alert, panting, taking in all the countryside. Workers were pulling weeds in a tree farm. Horses were happily playing in a corral. And llamas were aristocratically strolling the expanse of a fenced enclosure. When we arrived at the house, before I could fully open the car door, he pulled his leash out of my hand and bounded out of the car. He raced for the front step, waiting for me to open the door. I noticed he hadn't volunteered to fetch and carry his food and dishes or bedding. Once inside, without a moment's notice, he turned right into the living room where he jumped onto the autumn-leaf print foam-cushioned sofa and sprawled on it, taking up three-quarters of its space. I could hear him claiming, "This is mine!"

This dog was still in his puppy-hood, not physically maturing for another year or so and not mentally maturing until he was around three years old. It was apparent that he needed to have some fun as a puppy. Since he had spent most of his first year constantly being manhandled by medical professionals who were trying to keep him alive and comfortable in spite of his intermittent infections and chronic pain, he was well over-due.

Without his supervisory help, I set up his food and water dishes in the kitchen, on copies of the newspaper on the beige linoleum floor near the pantry where his food would be stored. Initially, I put his large dog bed in the kitchen too, near the utility room, so he could comfortably keep me company while I cooked or ate. I suspected, however, that if Phoenix were anything like Snowpaws or Mr. Rogers, that when I was in the kitchen, he'd park himself beside me, behind me, or in front of me, awaiting some expected tasty morsel of human food to drop onto the floor, or, when he was really lucky, directly into his mouth. I had learned early on the dog credo: "What falls on the floor is mine." On second thought, a better location for the dog bed was in the bedroom in case he chose not to sleep with me.

That first night Phoenix stayed close to me most of the evening. Even when I used the bathroom, he was at my side. When I tried to close the door for a little privacy, he whined and whimpered. Quickly, I threw open the door. He aimed for me, trying to stick his nose in my crotch as I attempted to settle on the toilet seat. As I gently disengaged him, I knew I would have to continue to leave the bathroom door ajar so he could see me and know I was still there. It might take him a while to become less concerned about my abandoning him.

After correcting exam papers and checking on the students' intermittent behavior-conditioning reports, I carried Phoenix's dog bed into the bedroom. I washed my face and brushed my teeth, leaving the bathroom door open. He sat in the doorway, waiting, as I moved around. Sitting in the doorway to my bedroom, he watched as I changed and slid into bed. The moment my feet left the floor, he cocked his head to the right, looking unhappy and confused.

Because of having had Mr. Rogers, I knew when I finally went out on my own, I would have to have a double bed. Mr. Rogers used to take up the lower two-thirds of my twin bed in my parent's house. Sleeping around him, especially as he changed sleeping positions, was making me into a contortionist. And a tired one at that. As a result, in his later years, and during Snowpaws' time with me as well, I had a double bed so we both had our sleep territory. Not surprisingly, though, my dogs frequently trespassed. They no doubt assumed the entire bed was really theirs—and if possession were nine points of the law, it was. Due to their inherent canine sense of altruism, however, they offered me a claim to a small portion of it so I could sleep too. I had to appreciate their charity.

"Do you want to get on the bed?" Phoenix began to slap the floor with his skeletal tail. "You can if you want, you know." His head and upper body bobbed as if he wanted to but wasn't sure he was interpreting me correctly. "Okay, you silly thing, come on up." I slapped the bed as I said it. With that, he made a giant leap, almost landing on top of me. Looking happy but cautious, he tried to bury his face under my side. He gazed at me again as if asking it that were all right to do. I patted his head to show he was a good boy. That was all he needed. Within minutes he was snaking into the covers and dozing off. As usual, Barbara had done a whizz-bang job socializing him, helping counteract his early trauma.

12

Early the next morning, Saturday, I heard Phoenix's nails loudly telegraphing something on the Saltillo tiles at the front door.

"I'll take you out as soon as I get dressed."

Then I heard what sounded like growling. I wrapped a robe around me and raced to the foyer to see what was going on. I hoped a skink, scorpion, or black widow spider hadn't somehow gotten inside to tempt him.

When I reached the front door, Phoenix had what looked like a chewed white envelope in his mouth. I quickly looked out the dining room window to my right and saw dust rising in the wake of a vehicle rapidly departing. I couldn't see the vehicle but I could envision a Dodge pickup.

Phoenix was no longer growling but hadn't dropped the envelope. I kneeled beside him, gave him a head pat, put out my open hand palm up, and asked if I could see his prize. He seemed unsure at first if he should let me borrow it.

"Give it to me, Phoenix. I want the envelope." He placed it in my hand and received another head pat.

It looked like the one I had already received from Moore. I transported it into the kitchen and placed it on the butcher block island. There I put on my vinyl gloves to remove the tooth-perforated, soggy contents. It read, "You called the police. You're a liar. You're not going to get away with this. I'm not letting some stupid bitch interfere with my life. You've sealed your fate." I located my notebook, recorded the incident, and slipped the letter and envelop into another food baggy, sealed it, and scribbled the date and time on it.

By now it was obvious I wasn't going to get a chance to sleep in. Phoenix was tapping out a boogie rhythm, à la Fred Astaire, by the front door. I tossed on some jeans, a sweatshirt, and loafers without socks and attached his leash to his collar. We literally flew out the door. There was a fifty-foot tall Siberian elm in the grit-covered front yard which he would soon joyfully claim as his own. We started to walk down a dirt path toward the Rio Grande. A young hare, or as Mark Twain called them "jackass rabbits" (which became "jackrabbits" because of their donkey-like, erect ears), crossed in front of us. With its angular, un-bunny-like head, and long body, it was only vaguely reminiscent of the cuddly Easter creature. Phoenix became excited, straining to run after it but seemed uncertain if he should.

"You want to run? Then let's go!"

We started galloping down the path but not after the hare. Phoenix assumed his doggy smile again and took off at full speed. Since I was not trying to qualify for the Olympics, I wasn't about to do a one hundred-meter sprint in ten point twenty-two seconds, as had a teenager done in Houston in 2019. When I really ran, instead of my general jogging, at times I could maintain an eight-minute-mile pace for most of my entire six-mile run. But beyond that, I'd slump over, face scarlet, gasping for breath, hearing my Amtrak-like heart derailing and leaping out of my chest. It left me afraid I was going to expire then and there. German Shepherds have been clocked at thirty mph. At zero point five miles per minute, he'd have to slow way down for a slowpoke like me if we were going to, euphemistically, "run" together.

After an exhausting run-jog-walk, in other than my running shoes, we returned home so I could shower, feed Phoenix and me, and go for groceries. Of course, he wanted to come with me. I couldn't take him into Albertson's and it was too warm for him to stay in the car, even with the windows partially down. I promised I'd get him a treat if he'd stay home and not de-weave the throw rugs or gnaw on the wood furniture. After he calmed down enough for me to slip out the kitchen door to the garage, I was at the grocery store in ten minutes. I had a full list and headed for the produce area first.

After exploring several aisles, I was in the back of the store, nearly finished, wheeling my full cart to the left to inspect the canned foods aisle for vegetable broth. There I nearly ran into someone standing just around the turn.

"I'm sorry." I said, not looking up right away. "I didn't ..." And halted. It was Clayton Moore. He was in his nostalgic regalia. "Excuse me," I breathed as my mouth became arid. I moved my cart to the right to go around him but he grabbed my left wrist. "Let go of my arm. You don't want to make a scene, do you?"

"I've been hoping I'd run into you. You've accused me of injuring that dog and trying to strangle you. I don't like the police questioning me."

"That's too bad. Then, don't do those things. Now, let go of me ... or else."

"Or else what? You're going to try to kick me again? One lucky shot doesn't make you a black belt. You're coming with me." He took a step forward as if to drag me toward the front of the store.

"I don't think so."

As I was about to stomp on Moore's embroidered leather instep, transfer my weight toward him, and shove the heel of my hand into his solar plexus, a tall man wearing Levi's and a navy-blue t-shirt pushing a full grocery cart was approaching from the front of the store, about fifteen feet away. He had a medium brown crew cut and appeared athletically built. I stared at him. Should I follow through with my defensive karate moves or not? I was so tempted but didn't want to give the impression that I was the one assaulting him. I decided to connect with the stranger instead.

"Thank goodness you're here," I said, looking at the stranger, half-calling. Plaintively I begged, "Would you please help me." I managed to raise my left arm which was still being held tightly by Moore. "This man grabbed my arm as I entered this aisle and he won't let me go."

Moore looked around him. He couldn't seem to decide what to do. As the man abandoned his own cart and hurriedly approached in only a couple of strides, Moore let go of my wrist. He backed up, twisted around, nearly tripping over his embroidered boots, and disappeared, heading toward the next aisle over.

"Thanks so much. You really helped. That man has been stalking me. I keep seeing him wherever I go and he has grabbed me once before. I've made a police report but that hasn't stopped him. He said he was going to make me go with him. Your presence was serendipitous."

"That's a scary situation. You're welcome. What's with that getup he was wearing? Look, I'm all finished so do you want me to escort you as you finish shopping, just in case he's waiting for you?"

"That is very thoughtful of you. I am concerned he may still be lurking. Do you live around here?"

"Currently. I work with the Army Corps of Engineers."

"So, you're not *in* the Army?"

"I was but now I'm a civilian, a civil engineer, who's working with them on some projects in the Albuquerque District. I'm Brad. And your name is?"

"I'm Kiri."

"Is that an Irish name?"

I laughed. "No, I was named after the Australian opera singer Kiri Te Kanawa. Look, I have only a few more items to pick up and then I'll be ready to check out. After that incident, I just want to get back home. I have a new dog who's undoubtedly anxious for me to return."

"I love dogs. What breed is he?"

"He's a fourteen-month-old rescue, an abused German Shepherd."

"Is he okay now?"

"Yes, now, but as a puppy, he was doused with gasoline, set on fire, and badly burned. As a result, he's sprinkled with spots of fuchsia skin where his missing hair should be. He's been with me only two days but he's doing well."

"Considering your stalker problem, having a dog sounds like a good idea." He smiled with a captivating smile, "Which reminds me, would you like me to follow you home in the eventuality this guy is still waiting for you outside?"

I smiled back. Well played, Brad, I thought. "If you'll let me 'buy' you a cup of coffee when we get there. You can also meet Phoenix."

"Phoenix? That's an interesting name for a dog. I once adopted a dog named 'Royal Ratter of Kerry Country,' a Kerry Blue Terrier. A purebred, at one time he had been a show dog but his owner wanted to get rid of him. Lord knows why. He was a wonderful dog, strong-headed and highly spirited, but fun and sweet."

"Weren't they bred to hunt small game and birds, kill rodents, and herd sheep? But 'Royal Ratter'?"

"Yeah, his moniker wasn't too appealing, not something I thought a dog should be burdened with so I re-named him 'Ballou'. You know, after Sullivan Ballou, the Union Army officer. He's the one who wrote that eloquent letter to his wife before he was killed at the First Battle of Bull Run. Maybe you saw that. It was highlighted in Ken Burns' *Civil War*."

"Burns' *Civil War* was brilliant. But that letter nearly broke my heart, especially against the background of the musical strains of the 'Ashokan Farewell.' Anyway, Phoenix was the name assigned to him when he was found near death by a local rescuer. Apparently, she was determined to help him rise from his literal ashes, to live again, healthy and happy.

Sounds appropriate for a puppy who overcame such an incredible trauma. So, what about that coffee?"

"Sounds good."

I picked up a few of the remaining items on my list and we navigated our shopping carts to the registers. As soon as I was finished, I waited for him close by. I wondered if Moore were hiding, ready to attack again. We'd find out soon enough. As I rolled my cart to my car, I kept expecting Moore to jump out at me. If he was around, maybe he had decided not to do anything with Brad hovering as my temporary body guard.

Brad followed me in his metallic-tan Range Rover. Phoenix was jubilant to see me after having been alone for the last forty-five minutes. But he gave Brad the eyeball. Circling him at a distance at first, he watched him warily, cautiously approaching him. Barbara had said that Phoenix tended not to like men, probably because his abuser had been a man. Unbeknownst to me, Brad had picked up a bag of dog treats before checking out which he had secreted in his pants pocket. Phoenix began moving closer, sniffing the air. Suddenly his muzzle was in Brad's front pocket, ignoring his crotch for the time being. When Brad managed to produce the cellophane bag and tore it open, Phoenix went mad. He practically mauled Brad to get hold of the dog yummies.

Shaking my head, I laughed. "You really know the way to a dog's heart."

"It's knowing what the customer wants."

After putting my groceries away, I made coffee. We chatted in the living room about our histories and whatever else occurred to us. Phoenix tried to crawl onto the lap of his new best friend. I told myself he was simply looking for more dog treats and not that he was obviously so fickle. That immediately reminded me of the Broadway musical *Finian's Rainbow* where "Og," the leprechaun, sings, "When I'm Not Near the Girl I Love, I Love the Girl I'm Near."

Before Brad left, he asked if he could examine the kinds of locks I had. I had installed deadbolts on the front and back doors as well as the door from the house to the garage. Fortunately, the garage door operated by remote so that I didn't have to get out of the car to manually open or close it. He recommended that I get an alarm system for the windows. Either that or put up wrought-iron grating on each, which many people in New Mexico did. Maybe my landlord would consider one or the other. When he left, with his jeans and t-shirt coated in Phoenix's hair, the dog gazed after him with a dispirited expression.

"Okay, no moping. Let's go for a walk."

The sight of his leash restored his good mood. As we pursued the path to the river, I wished I had decked Moore instead of relying on the "seeking another's assistance" routine, getting a male to intercede. Given the circumstances, it was probably the right way to go. Moore would have stumbled backward into the rows of canned green beans and peas, making a loud clattering mess which would have brought other shoppers and store security around. That would also have given him the opportunity to claim that I attacked him, totally without cause. Still, using a little karate on him would have been very satisfying. Although, meeting Brad was pretty satisfying in and of itself. Of course, it didn't hurt to have Brad as another witness to Moore's aggressive behavior toward me.

After our walk, Phoenix pulled away from me to run toward the front door, growling. The newly-sanded and tinted door now had a bullseye on it in red. Damn that Moore! I called the landlord, explained about my stalker, and sadly shared the news that all his woodwork had been in vain. John wasn't happy. I worried he might want to evict me to have someone renting who wasn't the target of a vandalizing nut-job.

"Go back to the police before this gets even worse! And tell them I'm a witness." His parting words.

It was Sunday afternoon when after I'd photographed the door, I reluctantly drove back to my old standby, Animal Control, and the cop there. With me I had my untouched threatening letters in plastic bags, photographs of the two door paint jobs, and my up-dated diary of the stalking incidents. I presented the evidence to Hardess.

"I want Clayton Moore arrested for stalking and assault. His second assault was yesterday, inside Albertson's, where he grabbed hold of me and tried to drag me out of the store. This was witnessed by another shopper who intervened."

"We've already talked to him once. He claims you threatened him. You sent him threatening letters."

"That's ridiculous! I never sent him anything! I didn't even know where he lived until just recently. After he had kicked the puppy, he got a good look at me. I certainly wasn't going to do anything to make him even more likely to come after me. Someone who abuses animals is violent and likely to take out his anger on others, especially someone who films his abuse."

As I filled out the report form, something occurred to me. I couldn't wait to get back to the house to fix it.

Once I was home, I deleted all my computer files on my results from InstantVerification and cancelled my account. Unfortunately, I knew that deleting them wouldn't totally erase them from my hard drive. It was unnecessary but I didn't want there to be any record of my having done research to locate Moore. I'd felt compelled to lie to the police about searching for him. I didn't trust Hardess. I could just picture him turning it all around, that I deserved what had happened to me because I was the one pursuing Moore. I probably had even written those "threatening letters" to him. Consequently, I was the one who provoked the situation and poor guy, Moore, was only defending himself the only way he knew how.

I went to the gym to lift weights and then to my dojo on Rt. 528 to practice my karate. Jerry, the sensei, was always around to provide lessons and help, even on Sundays. I shared with him my two encounters.

"The side kick to the knee works wonders. The second time I almost went for his solar plexus. I just wish I could have."

He laughed. "Now, if you had had both hands available, you could have used one hand to force back his head, making him off-balance, and the other to strike his solar plexus. Something to keep in mind next time."

"I hope there won't be a next time, thanks."

"And I hope you have the police on this and are not trying to take care of it all yourself."

"Yeah, I've made two assault reports and stalking and vandalism reports with hard evidence—you know, pictures of the vandalism, the harassing letters, and a list of witnesses—but I have a bad feeling about their taking it seriously, much less really doing anything about it. I've been talking with Hardess who doesn't seem to like me or believe me."

"Hardess? You mean Lard Ass. He's a lazy, stupid jerk. I don't think he likes anybody, but especially women who stand up for themselves. Tried and true misogynist. Most of the cops there are conscientious. Rodriguez, who is a friend of mine, is a well-thought of, serious cop who believes in adhering to the law, not just taking up space, eating donuts, and waiting for his pension to kick in. Connect with him next time. Hardess won't like it but you'll be more likely to get some real police action. In the meantime, get a big dog."

"Just got one. Thanks for Rodriguez. I can always count on you!" I gave him a quick hug.

13

Monday morning, I had an eight o'clock class. I always had to allow at least an hour to arrive at one of UNM's parking lots near Redondo and find a vacant space not too far from the psych. department building. Monday's traffic always seemed more congested with reckless maneuvering.

I was in the right lane and had just passed the exit for Alameda and CarMax on my right. Suddenly, my car lunged ahead. My rearview mirror revealed a silver Dodge truck trying to shove me into other cars. My intestines turned to slush. It was Clayton Moore! My car jumped forward again! I braked, just enough to avoid crashing into the car in front of me. But that inadvertently let Moore stay magnetized to my rear. He continued to ram me as we passed the Coronado Village Manufactured Home and RV Community, just before the on-ramp for Paseo del Norte. I hit my horn over and over.

As we were about to slide past the exit, I slipped onto the on-ramp. But as I reached the top of the rise where I'd turn left onto Paseo going east, the traffic light turned red. Behind me was Moore. Gunning his motor, he jostled me again, undoubtedly denting the Civic's hatchback door because of our mismatched bumper heights. Even with my foot on the brake, I inched toward the cross traffic. I hit my horn again. With my right hand I pulled on my emergency brake with all my strength. His truck hit me again, harder. My car leapt inches forward. He was going to get me splattered all over the highway. One more good jolt would do it. I'd be struck on the driver's side by vehicles going forty-five mph. I'd be instant road kill!

The blaring of my horn alerted drivers stopped around me that something was wrong. I could see everyone look around. Then out of an old, battered, mud-covered red Ford pickup truck to my right and two vehicles behind stepped a burly sixtyish man with a graying beard and balding head, dressed in overalls. In his hand was a shotgun. My doom was sealed. I released my emergency brake in case I could somehow turn a hard right, barely in front of the other cars waiting for the light to turn green. Maybe I could escape both him and Moore.

If I could do it, it likely meant being struck in the rear instead of being totally side-swiped. To my surprise, instead of arriving at the front of my car, the man with the gun parked himself in the front side of Moore's truck. He aimed his weapon at Moore. Moore cut his engine. In my rearview mirror, I could see his jaw drop.

After words were exchanged, the rescuer eased on back to his truck. The light turned green. Moore followed me closely as I turned left on Paseo then right on San Pedro so I could take Ellison to get back on I-25. I knew he was going to start doing it again. Unthinkingly, I had put my cell phone in my briefcase before I left the house. I couldn't easily reach it to call the police. Bad news. I knew better than to do that again.

Then the old red truck appeared behind Moore. I assumed I now had two tails ready to kill me if they could. But the red truck began nudging Moore's vehicle. I could see Moore pull over to the side of the narrow street. The red truck parked behind him. After that, I didn't care what happened although I was sure Moore would tell my savior some wild-ass tale about how I was the Devil incarnate and he was the hapless, tormented victim that had been driven to do something dire. Because I had not only harmed him but also discredited him, I deserved his retribution. On I-25 again, I arrived at UNM with mere minutes to spare.

I had three classes and saw Carrie after the second one. She looked haggard as if she hadn't been eating or sleeping. I asked her into my office and closed the door.

"What's going on? You look as if you need help."

"It's Clay. He's punishing me for not moving in with him. Well, that's one thing. He's decided that you're the one preventing me from moving in with him. In other words, it's you who has ruined his life and you need to be punished, unrelentingly. Whatever works for him to believe becomes an irrefutable fact."

"Tell me what has been going on. What has he been doing?"

"In the evenings he comes by and stays until all hours, not letting me go to bed. He raves about being accused of hurting the puppy, you filming the abuser and claiming *he's* the one who did it, and the letters."

"But you heard him admit to the puppy."

"Of course, he's ignoring that. It's all making him deranged. His anger and negativity are giving me palpitations. And when I finally get to bed, I can't sleep." She breathlessly rattled on. "He says the police have talked to him several times. He's trying his damnedest to persuade me that I 'belong to him, that we were destined to always be one,' that we should move back in together ... now. He won't keep his hands off me. He tries to bully me into having sex with him. And when I won't, he takes me by force, like he used to. I'm afraid to call the police."

"So, what are you going to do? Are you still considering moving?"

"I can't stay here any longer under these circumstances. He's so full of rage and demands. I know if I don't go back to him, he'll kill me for sure."

"It's so unfair for you to have to leave. But I understand your situation. What about your mother or your aunt and uncle?"

"I couldn't put my mother at risk like that. Aunt and uncle? Oh, you mean the 'aunt and uncle' I was supposedly going to live with when I was supposedly pregnant? They don't exist. I do have godparents in Jemez Springs but I couldn't stay with them. They already have a full house."

"What about good friends that Moore doesn't know about?"

"He knows about them all. He used to rummage around my place, looking in drawers, checking my purse and the pockets in my coats. I had no privacy at all. One time when he was there, he found my address book in my bureau and wouldn't give it back to me. As a result, he'd know where to look for me. One by one he'd track me down and put my friends in danger too."

"I'd invite you to stay with me until you could move but he's already stalking me and vandalizing my place. Besides, he might go bonkers if he discovered that *I*, of all people, was hiding you from him. It wouldn't be safe for either of us. But I can get you in touch with people who may be able to assist you in finding safer quarters until you move."

"My life is such a frightening mess. I want to blame this on the poor puppy getting attacked at Albertson's. I want to blame it on you for filming it and caring about finding the abuser. But mostly I'm blaming myself for not doing something right away when I discovered what a headcase he was. It was easier to hang around and put up with his domineering treatment." Carrie wrinkled up her face and began to cry.

I got her a tissue and putting my arm around her.

"Don't blame yourself. In intimate relationships it's very hard to know what to do especially when conflict is laced with fear. Just be thankful that when he smashed in his dog's head, you knew that he also had a very dangerous, violent side ... and that you, like his dog, weren't safe."

I called the domestic abuse hotline. When I spoke with Elizabeth, a friend and colleague, I told her the story and that we needed help. She spoke with Carrie who wrote down an address and cell phone number.

"Okay. I'm to go where she directed and after I arrive, someone will go to my home and get my possessions and we'll go from there."

I gave Carrie a big hug and wished her all the best. As she was about to close my office door behind her, she turned. Her look was still one of desperation but, perhaps, accompanied now by an atom of hope. I did a double thumbs up. She smiled and disappeared. I knew Elizabeth would let me know if Carrie and her personal property had arrived safely. God, I hated that bastard Clayton Moore! And I disliked myself a little for feeling even a part of making it worse for Carrie.

On the way home I stopped at Lowes to pick up some rebar and to see their exterior video cameras I had researched online. They had a package of two digital, wired security video cameras that captured a one hundred and thirty-degree wide-angle view with night vision capability. When the camera detected movement of any kind—unfortunately, that included animals—it would signal my designated phone. The question I had was how to wire it into the house circuit and my cell phone. Easy. My landlord, John, was a licensed electrician so I was sure he'd be happy to do it for nothing since I was paying $298 for the cameras and trying to save him from further costs of repairing vandalism damage. I gave him a call just to make sure. No problem.

That evening John arrived to install the cameras: One between the garage and front doors and one at the back door, under the portale, like a porch overhang. Phoenix was not happy about any of it. He sat in the room nearest where John was working, staring in his direction, baring his teeth ever so slightly. Whenever John moved, Phoenix moved with him, his muscles taut, a growl just barely within human hearing. John tried to look unperturbed but I could see the hairs on the back of his neck were erect. I gave Phoenix his peanut-butter-filled chew toy, but he ignored it.

Because of his steely gaze, I hoped he wouldn't misunderstand some innocent gesture made by John and attack. At the same time, I hoped he'd be as vigilant and ready if Moore came around ... again.

While John worked on the cameras, I worked on the windows. The primary windows in my one-story home, in the living room and dining room, were seventy inches wide, consisting of two thirty-five-inch glass panels on metal runners with a central bronzed pot metal lock. When unlocked, the right panel slid left in front of the other panel to open. Only the right panel had a screen. In the runner on the left side of each such window, I inserted a thirty-one-inch piece of rebar I'd had trimmed at Lowes. This allowed the window to open only four inches for air. In an emergency, I could quickly remove the rebar, open the window all the way, and disengage the spring levers holding the screen in place.

On the smaller vertical windows in the kitchen, my office, master bedroom, bathroom, and utility room, I placed rebar above the lower sash that moved upward, holding it in place with a large magnet. If a home invader were intent upon getting in through a window, these measures might not stop him. But they might require him to smash the glass, alert us, and slow him down enough for Phoenix and me to either escape or retaliate. I suspected Phoenix would not have welcomed his presence.

When we both were finished, I invited John for dinner. I seasoned a salmon fillet with lemon juice, soy sauce, and garlic and ginger powders then broiled it, made rice pilaf flavored with rosemary and Irish herbed butter, and steamed asparagus for a Hollandaise sauce. Phoenix stood in the large entrance between the living room and dining room, on guard. Even when I offered him some salmon, he never moved or took his eyes off John. Poor John. Good Phoenix.

Since I knew John liked brownies, I had made some chewy ones when I returned from the university, cut them large and slathered them with a thick layer of semi-sweet chocolate frosting. Just before serving them, I decorated each with a dollop of premier Dutch chocolate ice cream. It was a true "death by chocolate" that I nearly groaned over. John obliged me by having two helpings and might have had more except that his face was starting to sweat.

As he was leaving at seven-thirty, with a plastic bag of extra brownies and Phoenix following him closely to the door, we tested the camera system once again. It was still working in the twilight. And, yes, my cell phone rang and there he was in high definition video, waving at me as he walked twenty feet to his car. As soon as I closed the door, Phoenix immediately relaxed and went for his peanut butter chew toy, pretending to be a predator in the underbrush. He had been a super-good boy for which I praised him. As a result, he received a long brushing and petting session. That night he slept very close to me.

My cell phone which I kept by my bed rang at 6:30 the next morning. I looked out and could see Moore pulling in toward the house. Phoenix was already at the front door growling, creating hieroglyphs on the wood door with his front paw nails. I saw Moore creep toward the stoop with something in his hands. I couldn't make out what it was. I had to know what it was in case it was a bomb. But if I flung open the door as he was in the act of arming an incendiary, Phoenix would have been on Moore like a bad smell, going for his throat or his crotch, anything he could tear apart, and maybe inadvertently set off the device. I couldn't allow that. It was becoming increasingly evident that I was one pathetic Superhero "Animal Abuse Avenger."

As soon as Moore started back to his truck, I called the police. I asked specifically for Rodriguez. I explained I had Moore on video this time, as I had when he attacked the puppy. As I talked, I checked the front door to see what he had done. This time he hadn't done anything to the front door. But, oh my god!

Lying on the stoop on its side was a recently-gutted young puppy that looked like a cross between a Schnauzer and a Cocker Spaniel. Its longish hair was tan with heavy moustache and eyebrows, black on its folded ears, and angry wounds on its back and neck and a ragged, nearly chewed-off left ear. It looked to me as if it had been used as a bait dog for dog fighting. Upon closer inspection, I could see its intestines were still intact as opposed to being outside its body and draped all over the concrete step. Its fur was dripping with metallic-smelling blood, forming red rivulets around its back legs. The smell was heavy, almost sweet, in the early morning air. Flies were beginning to do touch downs in its abdominal cavity. Saliva was collecting in my mouth as I was hypnotized by the horror.

Phoenix went wild, jumping, growling, and barking. I had to grab him by his collar and attempt to haul him back in. He had no intention of going anywhere. However, when the police car arrived, he acquiesced. That seemed odd. I wondered if he had encountered a police car before or it was the men.

As I reflected upon his behavior, I had expected him to sniff the bloody carcass and maybe nudge it. That's what Mr. Rogers and Snowpaws did when they detected a dead or exsanguinated animal on our walks in fields or along roadways. But maybe it was because it was a dog ... or, more likely, that he could smell Moore on the deceased animal. Even with three hundred million olfactory receptors in his nose—as compared to a mere six million in inadequate human noses—and with forty times greater smell analysis in his brain, was it possible he could detect Moore's touch?

As his partner looked around, I tried to staunch the blood flow with a hand towel and check for any life signs. I apprised Rodriguez about the recent traffic incident and how close I'd come to being killed, as well as my reports of Moore's reported assaults, stalking, and vandalism since I'd filmed him at Albertson's.

"He's violent and dangerous. I've added locks and cameras but he still comes after me. I'm afraid he'll kill me too. Why won't the police do more than talk to him?"

As I gently pressed the towel a little harder, trying to close the wound and keep out the flies, I petted the once-lively body lying on my stoop.

"That's a good question. I'll go over your file reports and all the evidence you've provided." He took a copy of the video and said, "I will be back to you."

"Please do. I ... Wait!" I sensed something.

"What?"

I grabbed his arm as he put on rubber gloves to scoop up the puppy's body to put it into a black garbage bag.

"It's still alive! I can feel a faint pulse. We need to try to save it. Please take it immediately to Coronado Pet Hospital. I'll pay for it. They know me."

Rodriguez nodded, carefully placed the puppy on top of the black bag, tightened the towel around it's middle, then he and his partner left for the animal hospital.

While Phoenix was having his breakfast, I slipped outside to clean the front stoop. Wearing my vinyl gloves and armed with a Clorox spray cleaner and a roll of paper towel, I endeavored to remove every sign of the nearly-slaughtered puppy. Fortunately, the chlorine had no deleterious effect on the concrete surface. I couldn't say the same for my lungs. Even being outside, I started to cough from the chlorine molecules rising and curdling my airways. My eyes were burning too.

As I stood back to take in the front of the house, I needed to do something, something to take away from the image and lingering smell of an almost-deceased body. It occurred to me that two large terra cotta pots, one on either side of the door, overflowing with aromatic lavender could be just the thing. I could likely get the pots at Home Depot just north on Rt. 550 and the lavender plants from Santa Ana Garden Center, next door to the Santa Ana Pueblo's casino and hotel. Originally called Tamaya, the Santa Ana Pueblo held reservation lands which included a fertile strip along the Rio Grande. Maybe I could look for those items on the way home from class. In the meantime, I needed to take a shower and drive to Albuquerque. My first class was at ten o'clock.

While the introductory students took their exam on the psychology of aggression, I tried to conceptualize what I could do to bring this situation with Moore to an end. I had no personal control any longer. While I had caused him a modicum of emotional discomfort, it wasn't the haunting fear I had hoped for. To the contrary, it was only anger and vindictiveness. At the rate I was going, all the social pain I had planned to cause him for his abuse would never come to fruition either. I felt I should have known that the likelihood of my scaring him was wishful thinking. Anyone who could blithely harm animals, and forcibly control Carrie, wasn't psychological-terror-victim material. So far, I'd mucked this up.

Unless, I thought, everyone had some internal conflict, or flaw, where he or she felt vulnerable. Perhaps there was some personal life problem which could be tapped to trigger an intense moment or a panic state. How could I create an unsettling atmosphere or mood, a sense of foreboding that the letters didn't? What could I do to make Moore feel that something bad, twisted, surreal, and overwhelming was waiting just around the corner? What evil could lurk and befall him?

After my third class, I decided to visit Barbara again. Socializing with her and the animals always calmed me and de-cluttered my mind. Right then my brain felt like a hoarder's abode, filled to the rafters with junk I had to climb over to wade through to get to the living area. At CARMA she was in back finishing in one of the feline houses, this one designated for feline-leukemia-positive cats. It never ceased to amaze me how so many of her FeLV felines were leading relatively quality lives in spite of their viral infections which typically killed about eighty-five percent of the persistently infected animals within three years of diagnosis. FeLV was the second leading cause of death in cats after trauma.

There was one cat she had rescued as a ten-month-old kitten that had an upper-respiratory problem that no medication, anti-viral or anti-bacterial, touched. "Foxy" had been on everything that was potentially helpful and available. With her history, she should have lived no longer than a couple of years. But now she was eleven, still had the chronic respiratory condition, but played, snuggled, and enjoyed herself.

While the various cats, slept, played, or tried to entice us to continue to pet them as we were sanitizing ourselves before leaving, I told Barbara all that had happened since the Albertson's puppy attack. She laughed about my "I saw what you did" missives.

"Those are so old school. For a turnabout, you need something innovative. You need to regain the upper hand. You can't let him continue to reduce you to victimhood."

"I agree. But I seem to have run out of ideas. How do I turn the tables? The police are involved so I have to be careful I'm not seen as provoking him."

"You know, I was watching the old 1940 film *Angel Street* last night, made four years before Charles Boyer starred in it with Ingrid Bergman. I can't help thinking the story line might provide you with some ideas."

"While I love the whole premise of *Gaslight,* I don't know how I could successfully psychologically manipulate a psychopath like Clayton Moore into not trusting his own perceptions and interpretations, to doubt his own sanity."

"Think about it. What about some of the nasty things you thought you might do to him but decided you couldn't ethically do them. That was then, before he started to terrorize you. Could you reconsider them now as something you could expand upon to see if they might fit into a gaslighting plan? Let your imagination fly free. You know that I'm only half-joking."

"You're a terrible influence on me," I laughed and hugged Barbara.

My brain was abuzz with crazy thoughts. Maybe, I perked up, it was too soon to put away my white Superhero bodysuit. When my cell phone buzzed, it was Dr. Smith.

"We've done surgery, given a transfusion, and all we can to save the puppy but it had lost a lot of blood. It's still alive however I have my doubts about it making it. I'm so sorry. We'll keep working on it and I'll keep you apprised."

14

Driving home, I rolled the potential of what Barbara suggested over in my mind. I knew everyone was susceptible to gaslighting. A form of negative social influence through manipulation, it is aimed at changing another person's discernment of what is going on around them and their behaviors through deceptive, exploitive, and indirect tactics. Moreover, it is a common technique used by cult leaders, narcissists, dictators, and ... abusers. Whatever I chose to do, I'd have to do it slowly, over time. It would be like that grotesque psychological experiment with the poor frog in a pot of water. It demonstrated that if you very slowly increased the temperature, the frog would not realize it was being cooked to death. With gaslighting you have to gradually change the environment so that it creeps up on the victim. As a result, the victim doesn't realize he or she is being brainwashed until it's done.

By the time I arrived home again, it was transparently clear that gaslighting couldn't work with Moore. To influence and manipulate him I would be required to be close to him, even an intimate, so I could set up scenarios to make him doubt himself. Moreover, it would take time, lots of time, to create the result. There was absolutely no way to do it. That was too bad. Immediately thereafter, I realized that stopping at Barbara's had totally erased my intention to stop to look for decorative pots and plants to put in them.

Phoenix and I went jogging down toward the Rio Grande. He needed exercise and I needed to further clear my brain which felt all gunked up, something like the transmission of my dad's second-hand classic, a canary-yellow with white upholstery, 1955 Nash Rambler Custom Convertible. Between him and that car was a love-hate relationship. Because he had worked on it since his teens, he agonized over finally parting with it when he could no longer turn over the engine, no matter what he did. It was a sad day for him when he had to buy a more modern car. The nostalgic stories he would tell about that old vehicle. The one I remembered best was about his working to flush out the transmission's grime. The gunk somehow gotten into other engine areas. He decided to use a pressure wash, which weakened the valves. But, worst of all, the flushing dislodged the plugs of sludge which had filled in previously undiscovered holes in its ancient transmission.

After our run, Phoenix had a snack while I showered. Showers were problematic for me. I loved them. I never took baths unless medically required to do so because I always felt I was still covered in soap and dirt. Showers were cleansing but also provided to me an instantaneous way to relax. Unfortunately, in drought-plagued New Mexico water was particularly precious. This required that I spend no more than five minutes being pelted by these muscle-unwinding, aquatic flesh tenderizers. As I turned off the shower and gathered a bath towel around me, I had an aha! Beaming, I asked myself, "What about a con game?"

As the perpetrator, I wouldn't have to be close to Moore to arrange to have something taken away from him, in a "sting," without his knowing what happened. It could be done easily, simply, and not take much time. The great thing about doing a con game would be that Moore could be made a mark as a result of something he wanted.

The overarching principle of the game is "confidence" or trust. The con artist, who appears to be innocent, compassionate, altruistic, or helpful, offers *his or her trust and confidence* to the victim, in this case, Moore. The victim in return offers his or her trust and confidence to the con artist.

In David Mamet's Pulitzer Prize-winning play, *House of Games*, which is all about confidence games, Mike, the confidence man, shows Dr. Ford, a young psychiatrist, how a confidence game works. They go to a Western Union office where he asks if money has arrived yet for Martin Howard, Mike's alias for the moment. He sits beside an anxious young man who is also waiting for his money that's supposed to arrive there by nine o'clock. They begin talking. Mike tells how that afternoon at three o'clock his car and wallet were stolen, his child is waiting at the hotel, and they haven't eaten. The young man has to make a bus. Mike asks where he's going. The answer is Pendleton. Mike says, "You're in the Corps. I was in the Corps." They shake hands and Mike asks how much the young man needs for his bus. Then Mike says if his money comes in first, he'll give the young man the money he needs. Making an understandable error of judgment, the young man replies that if *his* money comes in first, he'll share it with Mike. Since Mike isn't waiting for any money, the young man's money will come in first. By giving the young man his confidence, Mike created confidence in the young man in him and, thus, would have conned him out of his money. What the young man would have gotten in this fake transaction was feeling good about himself for helping a fellow Corps member.

I've always been fascinated by the psychology of confidence games. There is no need for coercion. It is merely applying the elements of trust, sympathy, and persuasion to manipulate the other's belief. The basic plan is to create empathy and rapport through contrived similarity and familiarity, followed by the logic of the presented situation, and then to persuade the victim by showing what benefits are at hand if he, or she, gives their trust.

This works best when the victim is naïve, credulous, compassionate, vain, irresponsible, or greedy. If the victim is in transition or in a state of unease, so much the better. By then the victim has an emotional investment and commits to the scheme. The perceived benefits to the victim could be anything from reputation, trust, money, saving face, status, legitimacy to support.

That reminded me of research done by Claremont Graduate University psychology professor Dr. Paul J. Zak on how the levels of oxytocin in our bodies help us all relate to and empathize with someone offering to help. Oxytocin is a neuropeptide produced by the hypothalamus, and released by the pituitary, which plays a role in all social bonding, sexual reproduction, and childbirth. He said that oxytocin, which helps us attach to family and friends and cooperate with strangers, acts as a "potent stimulus" to make us respond positively when someone needs help. So, unless Moore had low levels of oxytocin in his brain, he was likely to be vulnerable to being a victim of a helping-related con.

That sounded like a good possibility. I knew his areas of vulnerability were likely his aggression, impulsiveness, lacking empathy, need for power, and a need to defy the law and social mores. However, it would be useful to know what his hobbies were, in addition to killing animals. Like, does he participate in any sports or competitions? Does he collect anything that's not connected with animals and violence? Does he have any voiced personal or professional goals? Carrie had said something to that effect but I didn't remember it off-hand.

Maybe I could get in touch with Carrie if she hadn't already moved. Then it would be a matter of thinking of a good con to pull on him, knowing precisely what I wanted to achieve as a result of it, without the risky use of confederates.

Through Elizabeth, I heard from Carrie. In response she indicated Moore didn't have any outstanding hobbies.

"I know he wants jobs that recognize his special abilities and have some status. He has often talked about being seen as a professional and all the bennies that go with that. From comments he's made, he's seemed particularly interested in the medical and related fields but said he couldn't see spending all that time and money to get the impressive degree, despite what it would give him. He was always looking for short cuts."

Carrie said she was doing okay and would be moving to Arizona to stay with a friend in Prescott temporarily until she found an apartment.

"Prescott College also has a Master's degree in Counseling so I could finish up there. By the way, can I use you as a reference?"

"Absolutely, Carrie. You're a fine student and will make a fine counselor. Much success."

Of course. I shook my head. I remembered that Moore wanted to be considered a professional—more "professional" than an orderly—a person with status making more money to meet his elevated conception of himself. Since Carrie had already told me he was very controlling, he would more likely want a profession wherein he was calling all the shots, like a "Lone Ranger," a lone entrepreneur, as opposed to working for or closely with someone else.

I wondered if I could set up an online "school" just for him, one that would be legitimate as far as the law was concerned. Furthermore, it would assess, recognize, and give him credit for his prior learning: his competencies, work history, current standing in a profession, academic achievement, performance management, and volunteer work. It would provide real lessons, tests, reading assignments, and a Master's-like thesis project to do. All in an intensive series of months. It would provide him with an appropriate professional label. There was no federal U.S. law that would prohibit my creating what in essence might be called a non-academic "diploma mill."

This would be especially true if the credential he achieved were an honorary title, part of ordination, and conferred by a church as well. Like "Doctor of Divinity in Pastoral Counseling." And the money he paid for the course, its texts, other fees, etc. would be donated to one or more of the local non-profit animal rescue organizations in Teddy's name. I didn't want it for myself even though he had terrorized me and I had spent a lot of time, money, effort, and cortisol on him.

Then suddenly it occurred to me. Making his degree related to a church was iffy. I had no idea about his religious inclinations, if he had any. Moreover, the church would have to be the Universal Life Church or the Universal Life Monastery, which ordained people for a donation. He might already have heard of them and their degrees. That could be a problem.

Phoenix indicated I should play with him for a while. With a wide-eyed look of anticipation, he dropped the thick braided cotton rope I had bought him at my feet. We reached for it at the same time. For twenty minutes we stumbled around the house, from room to room, as he shook his head, yanking it this way and that, pretending to growl. But when his back feet shifted the throw rug in the living room into a lump, nearly toppling the coffee table, I let go. He fell back onto the balled-up Navajo-woven "Two Gray Hills" wool rug and looked triumphant.

I had a coruscation! From what Carrie had said it crossed my mind that it might be better if I could provide Moore with something like a "Professional Problem-Solving Coaching Certificate" from an online "university." That had real possibilities. "Certification" had some prestige and "university" was not a legally protected term. And it wasn't even slightly unethical if I set up a business under a university name which actually provided those services for money.

Furthermore, I was a professional from an accredited university, a coach, and instructor. I'd truly be providing a real education in coaching. Of course, his "professional certificate" would not be an academic degree or a state-issued certificate. But it still would be legitimate. It would indicate he had gone through a training course. What was even better was that he really didn't need any academic degree in order to coach. As long as he used that term. If he made the mistake of calling himself a "counselor," that would be problematic for him. He wasn't one. "Counseling" required state certification or licensing as well as accredited academic courses whereas "coaching" didn't.

As someone with a "professional" label, he could get the approval he wanted as long as he didn't stray from "coaching." His clients, if he ever had any, would be paying him for his knowledge and skills, not his accreditation or his alma mater. His knowledge and skills would include asking the right questions, listening to what was being said and left unsaid, compassion, and people skills—which might be a stretch for Moore—creativity, problem solving, decision making, goal setting, progress management, and marketing.

Most people knew nothing about this type of coaching. And problem-solving coaches were really just people who had skills and knowledge to share with others to help them meet their challenges, solve their problems, and accomplish their goals in their personal and work lives. It all revolved around asking key questions that would provide clarity to both the client and coach about the nature of the problem, and the client taking responsibility for both the problem and its solution. It would entail what had been done, what were alternative approaches, and what worked best for each client to meet his or her goal.

As I worked on it in my mind, it was bothering me less and less. This looked like a way I could finally do something as a Marvel Superhero to achieve some retribution for Teddy.

If I were really lucky, he'd go to jail for a while after paying for his "professional title." By the time he was released, my "university" would be long gone ... or ... well ... maybe not, if I thought I could provide others with the essentials of practicing problem-solving coaching. It wouldn't really be a con because Moore wouldn't be out anything. I'd have provided him with what he needed to start a coaching business and perhaps even succeed. Then it would be up to him to see what he could do with his coaching training. For the first time in a long time I felt uplifted. I was going to be able to do something—though not what I originally had in mind—in my fight to impact animal abuse. I wondered if this sort of coaching approach could be worked on other animal abusers. I'd have to see first if it would work on Moore.

I had to work fast in case Rodriguez acted on my reports. If Moore were arrested and jailed before I could entice him into my coach training, it would ruin everything. Jail was good but not enough, not for Teddy and all the other "Teddies" Moore had abused.

15

I visited the Bernalillo Town Clerk to set up a DBA, "doing business as," for "International Professional Coaching University." I left "problem solving" out of the title to be emphasized in the course description. The rest of the day was taken up by creating a professional-looking letterhead, marketing presentation, and a diploma-like certificate. As the marigold-yellow sun dipped into the splashy peach and lavender-striated horizon, I realized I needed a website ASAP. A computer-savvy friend said he could make a general template from university sites and then let me fill in the particulars. Because he had been one of my coaching clients who had been trying to resolve a burdensome business problem and had happily accomplished it, he offered to do the website work for free.

I had been doing life coaching for a decade, on the side of my clinical work, even before some national coaching associations had begun teaching it and requiring their own certification in order for coaches to practice it. Consequently, I had a file cabinet full of readings, exercises, problem-solving maps, and projects to use to help others meet their challenges. I could use these to teach the ins and outs of life coaching and the problem-solving skills as well. For some reason I had never before gotten around to putting it all together to develop this training.

As I did another flowchart on news print of how I'd structure the program, I discovered a problem with introducing Moore to it. Once the initial program was a go on my end, how would I make sure he was the *only* one to see the advertisement prompting him to go to the website and fill out the application form? The only thing that came to mind was to have that ad on a separate sheet which was slipped into his newspaper alone. That meant that I'd have to convince or "hire" the newspaper delivery person to do it.

I would explain to that person that "Moore had signed up for this experimental introductory program. If the program works well, it would then be made available to the public. But at the moment, only those who had volunteered for the project could participate. That was why it was on a separate sheet. Some volunteers received the sheet in the mail and some in the newspaper. That was to see which method worked best for reminding and motivating those who'd signed up." It sounded a little flaky but could work.

Without Carrie in my UNM classes, things were less interesting but also less stressful. Any time I had a free moment, I worked on the problem-solving coaching program. It would start as a nine-month intensive training with a personal on-call mentor to be paid in total up front. The total charge for all nine months would be $10,000. Not a bad price for guided, specialized psychological training that *could* change his life and career financially for the better.

In two-days' time, my International Professional Coaching University website and associated e-mail, with an appropriate "university" signature, were ready for me to add what I needed. My computer-whiz had incorporated licensed photos of individuals "suffering from their inability to handle their problems" as well as those who were "delighted to have worked through their problems" as a result of "professional problem-solving coaching" taught by the university.

The site quickly described all the ways that professional problem-solving coaching was the upcoming entrepreneurial trend for providing services to individuals and business people. It also demonstrated its many benefits: How it was a boon to making money because there always would be problems that people felt inadequate to solve on their own ... or solve well. Furthermore, the coach didn't solve the problems for anyone but guided the problem-stymied clients through a process wherein the clients could and would do it themselves. The clients were responsible for their problems and for solving them. Moore would like that.

Now to see if I could actually get him to sign up. But first I needed a burner phone—a cheap, prepaid, anonymous mobile intended for temporary use—for him to call. I didn't have a landline, which he could trace. And I didn't want to use my personal cell which had an unlisted number. Although, there supposedly were apps that you could use on your regular cell phone to act as a separate phone. The more I read about the apps, installing them on your mobile, and what came next, the more I was sure I just wanted a separate burner phone.

Around midnight my cell phone, which was lying on my night table, rang. It woke me and disturbed Phoenix. I saw an ID number but I didn't recognize it. Sleepily I said, "Hello."

The low-register voice stated, "You influenced my Carrie to leave. She was mine. You've messed up my life. Your days are numbered. And this is not an idle threat." Then it clicked off.

There was no doubt that was Moore. He had traced my unlisted number which irked me no end. So much for ensuring privacy. Now I'd have to leave the cell phone off at night. I had to let Rodriguez know about this new wrinkle. I tried to get back to sleep but my mind was humming like the thunderous hydroelectric power turbines at Hoover Dam. Exhaustion took over about 4:30. My alarm shattered the stillness at 7 A.M. Dark circles looked back at me in the mirror as I brushed my teeth. I had no desire to do anything, much less go teach. I could hear my bed calling to me, "Kiri, come on back. It's so comfy here and you know you want to slip under the covers for just a few more moments. You need it. You deserve it. What difference can a few more minutes of sleep make with what you have to do today?"

Temptation was pulling me. My eyelids were barely open. My brain was stuck in neutral. Hoping to dilute that, I took a quick shower. While it rendered me spanking clean, it had no effect on my somnolence. Dressed, I staggered into the kitchen. Phoenix was doing a jig, demanding attention, breakfast, and a much-needed walk. When he started to whine, his priority was clear. I clipped on his leash. In an instant he ran out the front door and decorated the elm. It was becoming obvious that I'd have to spray the tree bark with water to neutralize the accumulating nitrogenous waste. This was mostly for the smell because this tree was tolerant of almost everything, except heavy winds.

Originating in Asia, the Siberian elm was like a large, invasive, aggressively-spreading weed that could rapidly grow to fifty feet in height with root access to water. It spread its seedlings near and far with a high-rate of germination. If you weren't vigilant about pulling out the seedlings as soon as they appeared, you could be living in a Siberian elm forest in only a few years. While I liked a treed ambiance, that would have been a dark, claustrophobic scenario.

After walking Phoenix and practically inhaling a glass of fresh-squeezed orange juice and a lemon zest Luna Bar, I threw my briefcase into the Civic and made it to UNM in forty minutes—a record for me. Fortunately, each of my classes was having exams today so I didn't have to be at my brilliant best. Lunch was a brown-bagged left-over kale salad, apple, and granola bar in my office. On the way home I stopped to see Rodriguez to tell him about the call. He wasn't available so I left him a note. Hardess wasn't in sight so I lucked out there. I was in no mood to hear his bitching and moaning about my disrespectful switching to Rodriguez or his stale harangue about witness statements.

On the way back to my house, I stopped at the dojo for karate practice. Jerry inquired about the Moore situation again. I had been keeping him intermittently updated on what had happened and what I was doing about it When I told him about the call, he furrowed his brow.

"You know that turning off your cell phone at night is a problem."

"What do you mean?"

"You said your exterior cameras are linked to your cell phone, to warn you when someone is there."

"Oh, shoot! That's right. I forgot about that."

"You could get another cell phone or use a landline and have the cameras linked to it. That way you could turn off your old cell phone to get some sleep."

"This situation keeps getting more complicated by the day. Thanks, Jerry."

At the house I left a message for John then uncoiled the two hoses coupled together creating one long hose that was attached to the faucet in the rear of the house that could be used anywhere on the property. I wanted to spray the elm's trunk. Phoenix, on a long lead line attached to a low elm branch while I was outside, was delighted with my activity. He pounced on the hose until I turned on the water. Then he went crazy, attacking and biting the water stream, getting soaked, reveling in his play. When I finally turned it off, he looked crestfallen. Seizing the hose in his teeth and shaking it, he signaled he wanted it back on.

"Sorry, Phoenix," I said as I recoiled the hose, "wait until next time." I grabbed the towel I'd brought out with me to soak up his coat's excess water.

Back in the house I tossed Phoenix's peanut butter ball to him to play with while I began research on a second phone. I had already decided on a burner phone for my initial "university" discussion with Moore. It now was just a matter of picking one. T-Mobile was offering a pre-paid cell with no contract for three dollars per month plus ten cents per minute or messages over thirty. That sounded good. I made my excuses to Phoenix and headed to the nearest T-Mobile store.

After purchasing the burner phone and service, it occurred to me to use this phone for the exterior camera only instead of for the "university" call too. Maybe I didn't need to talk with Moore on the phone. Besides, it would be better if I didn't. He might possibly recognize my voice from our in-person encounters.

John came by to change the camera signaling over to the new prepaid phone. Furthermore, if Moore called again to leave another midnight message, my cell phone, which I would leave on vibration, would take the message. I would have a record of it but it would not awaken me. Now, though still fatigued, I felt much better.

The rest of the day was spent preparing the "university" paperwork. It was taking longer than I had imagined it would. Looking legitimate was necessary and not that easy. I had to check out numerous academic institutions online to make sure I had everything that was needed. The logo was tough because it had to be slightly different from others but close enough that it looked as one would expect.

After reviewing Ivy League universities, I settled on a double circle—one within the other—wherein the school's title, "International Professional Coaching University," was written around the circumference between the two circles. In the center was an eagle holding arrows in its clenched claws against a maroon background. Above it was written, "Veritas et Integritas" (Latin for "truth and integrity"). The lettering was in gold

211

with a black drop shadow. I'd have my website designer add the logo to the website. The school's location was listed as Harvard Square in Cambridge, Massachusetts, with no specific street address given, just a number of a building on the Square. All communication would be by e-mail and post. Sending mail to Harvard Square was a bit more complex. But it was possible I could work that out too.

Harvard Square was occupied by the Massachusetts Bay Transportation Authority, MBTA transit station, and "International News." I had known the manager of this world-wide newspaper establishment, Harry Bostwick, for years and felt I could arrange with him to handle mail receipt and re-transmission. Exactly how we'd handle the exchange would be a collaboration. But first, I had to call him as soon as possible to make sure he'd be willing to do it.

"Hey, Kiri, love, great to hear from you! We've missed you. You want me to do what? Sure. Why not," he said and then added, "It sounds like *Mad Magazine*'s 'Spy vs. Spy.' Too bad I won't have to wear a trench coat and hide messages in crumpled, empty, discarded cigarette packs." He laughed. We chatted a while then we both had to get back to business. "Don't be such a stranger."

With heavy-weight stationery, envelopes, and my university logo I went to UPS across from Albertson's to have the printing done. It was surprising how professional and academic the correspondence would look. What I planned to do was respond to Moore's e-mail inquiry with this stationery then direct him to use e-mail for future contact, for *his* convenience. I was feeling very proud of myself as I drove home. Then it struck me. I hadn't as yet set up a bank account for the university.

The Bernalillo Wells Fargo informed me that I needed documents showing my ownership of the business and its structure as well as my state or federal ID: social security number (SS) or employer identification number (EIN). I also needed a local address. Since this was an online course, the only reason to have an account was to have a legitimate place to accept payment for the course. I took bank account forms and returned home.

Fortunately, the university stationery didn't need a local address for Moore. But for the bank I would have to create special copies of it with a local address. Since no one else would see it, I could use a post office box. As I had to keep reminding myself, while a post office box in Bernalillo, Placitas, or Rio Rancho didn't have the gravitas of an Albuquerque or Santa Fe address, no one of any importance in this con would care. Consequently, it likely wasn't a problem.

After an hour fretting, and giving myself the beginning of what I was sure would become a peptic ulcer, about how to handle the coaching fee, it occurred to me he could pay online using PayPal. I could set up an account for the "International Professional Coaching University" which would require money transfer. That seemed like the answer ... until I thought about his possibly not wanting to use PayPal, but, more importantly, the problems with credit cards, transaction fees, and needing a credit card processing function on my website. Setting up a card processing function was a complex, time-consuming, and expensive task that would require computer help. No, not at this juncture. What made more sense was to have him pay by certified check, which he would send to the "university" at the Harvard Square number. I was beginning to feel as if I were trying to juggle well-honed butcher knives one-handed.

While this was a more complex process, it was more desirable. Harry would send it back Priority Mail and I'd deposit it in the bank account here under the university name. Of course, the local account would have my name and address, but I didn't foresee any problem. After all, there was no reason to expect I'd have to pay Moore anything out of that local account. I'd be sure to set up the contract such that there would be no refunds.

I filled out the bank papers and drove back to Wells Fargo. Would I need anything else? Like a rubber stamp with the university name? I wasn't sure. What about for Priority envelopes? I'd have them printed. I wanted to be prepared for everything. I was getting closer. Above all else, I had to snag Moore before the police did.

16

As soon as I arrived, Phoenix began doing a frantic four-legged version of the Continental schottisch to remind me that the outdoors was calling him, *now*! Once again, he bolted out the front door, nearly tearing my rotator cuff. I'd have to work on obedience training while he was still young ... and before I had any serious shoulder injuries. After he re-claimed his tree, we jogged down to the river. Little lizards with long claws were everywhere along the bank, some sunning, others skittering, but all tantalizing Phoenix to chase them. Instead, he swung his head around and nearly caught one in his mouth, which could have made him ill. As he did, however, he almost rubbed his jaw against some golden foxtails waving beguilingly on the breeze. Touching this grass-like weed was potentially even worse than ingesting lizard guts.

Foxtails have barbed seed-heads which can work their way into any part of an animal, from nose to between the toes, and become embedded. These tough seeds don't break down in the body's digestive process so they can migrate. A foxtail in the hard palate can migrate to the eye causing blindness. I'd rescued a kitten with that problem. One in the nose can migrate to the lung. If not addressed right away, it can cause serious infections, even death. To my great chagrin I discovered this area was covered with foxtails, something to which I had been oblivious before. We'd have to walk or jog someplace else for Phoenix's safety.

Before we arrived back at the house Phoenix began to growl. I hoped other dogs weren't trespassing. To my surprise it was a "dog" of a different kind. Moore was coming around from the back of my house. White cowboy hat perched low on his forehead and his metal-toed cowboy boots covered in dust. I didn't think he'd be back from work so early. What had he been doing? What would he try? This could be awkward and difficult.

Phoenix was pulling hard on his leash, barking, rising up. His front legs suspended in the air. I dug my Nike running shoe heels into the dirt and leaned back to keep my balance. With his teeth bared, Phoenix was desperately trying to reach Moore. He wasn't just unhappy with this stranger's presence. He was primed to charge, strike, assassinate, and totally extinguish.

"Keep that dog away from me!" he blurted, looking anxious.

"What are you doing here, prowling around my house?" Phoenix and I moved inches closer.

"I'll kill that son of a bitch if he gets too close."

"Not if he kills you first. What are you doing here?"

"I was going to leave you a message."

"I'm here now. You can give it to me. You can put it on the ground and leave."

"On second thought I don't think I will."

"Then just leave. This leash is cutting off the circulation in my hand so I can't hold him much longer."

"Fine." He strode toward his truck which was partially hidden behind the flowering silver lace vine which oozed over a six-foot, wide-pale, unpainted picket fence on the other side of my driveway, facing my front door. Opening the truck door, he turned and spat, "Just you wait. You haven't heard the last of this." It was then I noticed he was wearing surgical latex gloves.

His truck backed up, made a circle, and supplied sufficient torque to his rear wheels to raise his front wheels in a wheelie veil of dust. I mumbled, "What a jerk!" He was gone. Phoenix had relaxed and was ready to go inside to get his snack.

"Just a couple of minutes," I whispered to him. "First, we need to inspect the exterior of the house."

I knew he hadn't been in the backyard to bless the nesting yellow grosbeaks in the oak tree. We started our circumnavigation to see if Moore had done any damage. As it turned out, yes. The Schlage lock on the rear door looked scraped as if someone had tried to jimmy it with a screwdriver. I took a picture of it and called John to ask what he wanted to do about it.

"Nothing," he stated, annoyed, "unless the lock no longer works."

I tried it. It worked fine. I relayed that to John who was making snorting sounds. I was thankful Moore apparently hadn't acquired a set of lock picks online. Who knew what he might have done on the inside of the house if he had actually been able to gain access to it? I had to take the photo of the lock and that from the backyard exterior camera to the police. Hopping about and ready to play, Phoenix led the way to the front door where he placed his paws on it and looked back at me with expectation.

After a late lunch, I sat at the dining room table with Phoenix curled on my feet, double-checking that I had everything ready for Moore's con. I had located the paper delivery person for Moore's paper and arranged for him to add the flyer to that newspaper for twenty dollars. I ran it over to him after lunch. As I handed the twenty-dollar bill to this tall, thin, bewhiskered middle-aged man who was finishing one cigarette and lighting another, he snickered as smoke curled around his face. It was clear he thought what I was doing was likely more than what I had described. I gave him my most innocent yet professional look, to which he shook his head, rolled his eyes, and smiled.

This venture was becoming more expensive and time-consuming than I had imagined, especially if I included my effort and gas and the wear and tear on my aging Civic. All I had wanted to do was shame him psychologically, socially, publicly, and financially for being such wart on the backside of humanity but it wasn't working out that way. Maybe lightening his bank account to support animal humane organizations wasn't such a bad goal. But what, I wondered, was happening to my Superhero revenge plan?

The next week went by uneventfully. Students were finishing their dog-behavior-shaping projects. In all four classes we watched the 1957 Reginald Rose film classic, *Twelve Angry Men*. It is about a jury deliberating the conviction or acquittal of an accused inner-city teenager for allegedly stabbing his father to death. The film deals with leadership, consensus-building, group decision making, interpretation of evidence, and how individuals' personalities, morals, values, biases, histories, and experiences come into play in producing a unanimous verdict. Because of how brilliantly it was written, directed, and acted, it fitted into discussions of many psychological issues. Classes always became animated by it, with students practically falling all over themselves and their classmates to contribute. There was never enough time to fully discuss its many dimensions.

The following week Harry sent me an e-mail with a jpg scan of the contents of Moore's letter which accompanied his printed online application. He wanted more particulars. By sending the university's e-mail in response, I re-iterated the professional and financial benefits of the nine-month intensive training with a personal mentor, how the training was tailored to each individual's experience and competencies, and the cost. That evening Moore e-mailed me back. He stated that he could see benefits to the training but he was not interested in paying that much money for it.

The next morning, I replied, "Just so you'll know, you are unlikely to encounter such an offer anywhere else, one that has been prepared by expert and experienced professional coaches from accredited universities. You might wish to reconsider your rejection of it given that the deadline for registering for the July through February training is in ten days. Furthermore, thirteen of the fifteen available slots have already been filled." I emphasized, "You need to keep in mind that this professional coaching training with a full-time mentor, who receives well in excess of $20,000 offline for these services, will prepare you to make money from the get-go whereas coaching without it often results in struggling and having to wing it for months, maybe even a year or more. Please let us know at your earliest convenience if you change your mind."

"Oh, Damn!" I groused aloud, grimacing. "What if no matter what I do he doesn't sign up? All this work will have been for nothing."

Phoenix was all over me to play. I just didn't feel like it. As soon as I sat on the sofa, he was in my lap, snuggling, stretching his upper body to try to lick my neck and face. My first impulse was to shoo him away, but I didn't. He didn't deserve that just because my plan was in the root cellar. In the root cellar today and maybe in the septic tank tomorrow. When he wasn't licking, he was grinning, overjoyed at having his body stroked and scratched. While he was treated well at Barbara's animal rescue shelter, he was in competition with so many other dogs for attention. Extended periods of hugging and petting just weren't available to him, or to any of them, there. Nothing could compete with having one's own home and *all* the attention.

I knew I needed exercise. Snapping on Phoenix's leash, we went for our run in the opposite direction of the foxtail-glutted path. When we returned, he blithely adorned the Siberian elm. I needed to do some weight-training, where I was focusing on strengthening my legs, and my karate practice. After kissing him good-bye on the top of his head, I left to push harder on both. When I was finished, I felt exhausted.

My new e-mail revealed a message from Moore. He was asking to be made an exception.

"Since I don't know much about coaching, I'd like to take a session or two before deciding."

"Fat chance," I chided his e-mail.

"Also," he wrote, "if I decide to take the training, I'd like to make my payments in installments."

I spoke back to my monitor, "As if I'd trust a manipulator like you to make the multiple payments?" If he didn't pay, there would be nothing I could do since I didn't want him to know I was the one behind the training.

I wrote him back, "There is no opportunity for any of our trainees to experience this intense special coaching instruction without paying our professional coach/mentors for it. Moreover, our coaches who have committed to this nine-month period of time will teach only when paid in advance, as it is with their actual offline individual and corporate coaching clients. In re-reading your application, I can see that you have had a lot of experience with clients so I suspect you are likely to whizz through the nine-month course and get so much more out of it than, perhaps, our average participant. Because I believe you may have great promise, I will, however, share with you one short exercise that will be expanded in the training to give you an idea."

If that didn't do it, I'd go to the next step. I attached an exercise pdf, which I thought he would like, to the e-mail and crossed my fingers.

It was several hours before he replied with the results of his simple exercise. His responses to it were only adequate. But his eagerness was showing.

I wrote back, "From your exercise, it's obvious you would be a credit to the program and the field. So, I've spoken to a few of our coaches to see if there, perhaps, were something we could do to assist you. Let me emphasize that this is highly unusual and not something we've ever done before or are likely to ever do again. A couple of coaches said they might be willing to provide you with a four-and-one-half-month training for only $6,750. Since they are currently finishing setting up their lesson plans and schedules, they'd have to know right away. It would be a real shame for you, of all people, to miss this extraordinary opportunity. By the way, this likewise would have to be paid in full in advance. Please let me know your decision at your earliest convenience."

Phoenix and I snuggled on the sofa binge-watching *Law and Order* on cable's WETV. After a while, the only sounds that got his attention were the police car sirens and the famous thunk-thunk from mixed sounds, including Japanese monks stomping on the floor, that occurred during the show. It seemed to resemble a prison door slamming. After four hours, we unfolded ourselves from the sofa. Turning off the TV, I surveyed my e-mail. There was nothing from Moore. We both needed a brisk walk outside. When we returned, I checked that the external cameras had recorded us, and no one else. They were working well.

After brushing my teeth, I gave Phoenix's teeth a going over with a soft bristle toothbrush all his own. It was in addition to the dental chew stick I'd bought at PetSmart. Since I left the burner phone, that was attached to the cameras, on, I turned my regular cell phone to buzzer, placed it on the night table, and slid under the covers. Phoenix no longer needed an invitation to assume his carved-out territory on my bed so he jumped over my now-supine body. Dragging a paw across my belly, he insinuated himself beside me. Given the body heat he threw off, it was a good thing that the air-conditioner was available if necessary.

By the amount of hair that flew around him as he soared over me—enough to fill a small throw pillow—it was clear that I had to groom him more frequently. I thought how hot and itchy all that loose hair must be. As I started to apologize to him, one levitating hair slipped past my lips ... and I almost swallowed it. Coughing and clearing my throat to try to extricate the filament, I tearfully gave up my intended apology. A quick drink of water loosened it enough for me to use my index finger and thumb to grab hold before it caught between my molars or slid down my throat. After rinsing my mouth with Listerine and spitting several times, I retrenched myself in bed and turned out the light.

Despite the nightly concert of crickets, sleeping through the night was glorious. I almost felt fully rested the next morning. Before taking Phoenix out for his bathroom break, I scanned the exterior cameras' videos from the night before. There had been a dog sniffing around the elm, a raccoon looking for the cat chow I had put out, and a shadow I didn't recognize. Outside, Phoenix gave special treatment to the elm which had apparently been trifled with. He lifted his leg at several spots, saving enough to cover other scents around it. Then we took off. It was a retina-destroying bright, sunny morning, already getting hot. I really needed another good pair of sunglasses. My last ones had become pitted as a result of grit-infused high winds, making everything appear to be veiled in fireworks and stars. We jogged to Sheriff Posse and back. Thinking about the unrecognizable shadow, I had us circle the house when we returned but didn't spot anything of significance.

After our breakfast, out back under the portale I spent forty-five minutes brushing and combing Phoenix. Well, I tried. He was so delighted with the procedure that he kept wiggling and jiggling his hind end doing a fox trot. When I finished, I quickly swept up the hair before he threw himself onto his back and shimmied in the lingering hairs on the brick floor. I put the hair in a cardboard box on a bench under a forty-foot, densely-leafed oak which resided near the left corner of the back of the house. A rock placed in the center would hold it down when the winds blew. Birds of all kinds in Central New Mexico could use it for their nests. Unlike clothes dryer lint, the hair was safe and had no harmful chemicals or dust in it.

I whisked away the additional loose hair from Phoenix's back and we went in. He immediately went for his cotton rope toy, rubbing it against me to get me in the mood to play with him. I wanted to survey my e-mail to see if Moore had replied so we played for about ten minutes before I tossed his peanut butter ball that sent him skidding across the dining room floor after it.

There it was, right on schedule. He was still finagling to get what he wanted for bargain-basement prices. "Your course sounds very interesting. I will pay you the $6,750 in two installments, of $3,375 when I register and $3,375 after the first two months, half-way through."

"I'm glad to hear that you're so interested in our program. But, as I mentioned earlier, our coaches expect to receive their full fees in advance. We have no available multiple-payment plan for this special intensive training. As I said before, it would be such a shame for you to miss out on this since you obviously have the talent and drive for professional problem-solving coaching. Let me know if I can be of further assistance." That should give him something to think about.

I had late classes today. We were finishing up on course material since final exams were approaching. In all the classes we also talked about critical thinking. How one had to be skeptical of information presented as reality and fact without supporting empirical evidence. One needed to be objective and analyze what was presented instead of passively accepting it as truth. How to tell education from propaganda and fact from advertising hype or political spin.

The classes became boisterous and disagreements broke out, individuals spouting one belief over another. I challenged them to support their beliefs with empirical evidence, not cherry-picked anecdotes or someone else's opinion. Over and over again, they became defensive when they couldn't defend their attitudes and beliefs with facts.

It was affirming to see students jolted into an awareness that they weren't ready to support most everything they believed as gospel to be true, perhaps only somewhat true, or simply taken on faith. The goal wasn't for them to reconstruct their entire belief systems. It was for them to reconsider the sources they used to reinforce their beliefs and be a little more discerning and circumspect with accepting whatever came down the pike that seemed to support their beliefs.

On the way home I went to the gym, lifted weights, concentrating on my lower body, and stopped at the dojo to practice my karate. After picking up a few items at Albertson's, I made a quick stop at Coronado to check on the "gutted" puppy's recovery. "Benji," as Karen, a part-time receptionist, had named him, was doing better than holding his own. I hugged everyone in sight. Maybe he would recover after all. If so, he would then need a good place to recover, hopefully being fostered but preferably being adopted. He deserved to live a happy, healthy, protected life, though not necessarily with me.

I hadn't seen Moore. Hopefully he was fighting traffic on I-25, on his way home from the Neurosciences Clinic. I hadn't heard anything about his having been carted off to the pokey so I guessed he was still free, somehow. I was beginning to think he had a Teflon coating, some kind if talisman, or he lived under the protection of a Harry Potter *Patronus* charm.

17

Phoenix and I ran again before I checked my e-mail. This dog needed lots of exercise ... and so did I. When I pulled up my e-mail, there was he was. Frustration was exuding from his reply to my earlier note.

"If you feel I am such a good candidate, it seems to me you would try harder to get me into this program. Money should not be your first consideration. Graduating talent and professionalism representing your university should be more important. I'm sure you can work something out for me to make this a go."

"Whoa!" I exclaimed, laughing. "When God passed out brass ones ..."

I couldn't wait to reply. "I'm sure this must be a frustrating situation for you and I empathize. Of the two professional coaches who said they might be able to tag-team to help with a four-and-a-half-month training, in addition to their nine-month scheduled training, only one said he might possibly consider creating a special course for you. This would, however, require his totally remaking the course so it covered all the essentials but in a much shorter, more intensive period of time, with less of his personal input.

"But, he said, he was so impressed with you that he'd try to work something out. Given the time involved in his totally reconstructing this super-packed course for you alone, and all that entails, he thinks he can do it as a two-month training, June through July. Since this would be his project alone and, as such, he would be receiving no co-training with the other coaches, the cost would be $4,700. He has indicated you have until the day after tomorrow, Wednesday at 8 P.M. Eastern time—that's 6 P.M. Rocky Mountain time—to decide on this because if he's going to do this for you, he needs to start right away to get ready. This will be no easy task. Believe me, you'll never have an offer like this ever again. This is truly the offer of a lifetime by a well-known, highly-respected professional. I urge you to decide quickly." Let's see what you do with that, sweetheart.

I didn't hear anything from him the rest of the day. The next day he was silent as well. Phoenix seemed to sense my concern and stayed close to me to be available. The magical hot goldenrod sun slipped behind Cabazon Peak, a large volcanic plug, rising to an elevation of 7,785 feet in northwestern New Mexico, and set the sky aflame with halos of tangerine interspersed with carmine which as it deepened into magenta was pierced by lingering rays of pink gold. Once again, I checked the e-mail. Nothing from Moore. Tomorrow was Wednesday. He was cutting it close if he was going to do something. I felt conflicted. I wanted his money for the animal homeless shelters but I didn't want to do anything positive for him in exchange, like actually provide the course to him. Revenge was still motivating me. There must be something I could do to make his life miserable while the police took their time finally catching up to him.

Wednesday didn't start well. Phoenix pushed the front door fully open before I had his leash snapped onto his collar. Calling, I raced after him. He looked at me, mouth open, smiling, and ran on ahead, back toward the foxtails' path. Moving out at full speed, he was luxuriating in total freedom, untethered from his tortoise-like human, doing what he wanted wherever he wanted. Half a mile along the Rio Grande he slowed to inspect some gulls swooping over him. They were looking for fish. The most abundant non-native fish in the Rio Grande were channel catfish. However, I had my doubts that where the river was shallower here that many of these were thriving.

I finally caught up with him as he reared on his back legs to swipe at the gulls. While he had a few foxtails snugged in on his front legs, he had managed to avoid any in more sensitive places. I'd have to use pliers and scissors to carefully disengage those barbs. And I'd have to do that before leaving for class.

For the eight o'clock class I provided optical illusions, "find the kitty" object searches, and fun memory exercises which would be useful in preparing for their final exams, and in general. I decided to do the same in each of the other classes as well. As I finished the last class, Carrie appeared at my office door. I was shocked to see her. I thought she would have already left.

"What are you doing here? Why aren't you already in Prescott."

"There was a hang-up. I was supposed to leave yesterday but I can't leave until today. So, I decided to see you one more time. Clay hasn't found me yet. I'm grateful for all your help."

"But aren't you taking a chance coming here that he might see you?"

"Yeah, I guess. Well, I really hadn't thought about it. It's been wonderful not jumping whenever the phone rang or there was a knock on the door." She gave me a big hug.

Something occurred to me. "This may sound off the wall, but I have one more quick question for you about him. You mentioned he wore latex gloves at the Walmart warehouse because he didn't like getting his hands dirty. Would you say Clay is afraid of dirt or germs? Does he seem even a little obsessive about them?"

"Oh, yes. He's definitely obsessive-compulsive about germs. I had to scrub his place all the time. And he was never satisfied I had done a good enough job. I figured he could do it himself if he didn't like what I did but knowing his temper, I was reluctant to make such a foolish suggestion."

"Anything else about dirt and germs, perhaps of a more personal nature?"

"That's a funny question. I don't want to know why you're asking. Well … and I don't really know if I should tell you this because, well, it's embarrassing. But … he made me wear surgical gloves or clean white cotton gloves when he demanded I give him a hand job. That was odd enough. But that wasn't his only obsessive behavior about sex. When he wanted oral sex, he had to wear a condom during it and I also had to use Listerine before. I had the distinct impression that he thought I—

or maybe it was all women—was a dirty, germy creature, likely to give him a disease if he didn't use a prophylaxis. So, when he asked me if *he* could have been the father of the make-believe child I had, I wanted to laugh. That made no sense given his constant use of condoms, unless, of course, there had been a pin prick hole and one of the little swimmers had gotten loose."

"That must have been very awkward for you but thanks for sharing it. Actually, it tells me a lot about Moore. However, your being here right now is too risky. I think you should leave."

"Yeah, you're right, I guess I shouldn't take any more chances. I'm too close to getting out of here. I'm going. Just wanted to stop by to say, 'Adios.' You be really careful yourself. He's dangerous ... and he's persistent. More OCD?" She grimly laughed. "See you!"

With that she was gone. Just to make sure, I hoisted my briefcase, locked my office door, and followed her to the station wagon in the parking lot where her friend was waiting. Suitcases, boxes of books, clothes, and miscellany clogged the back area of the tarnished-pewter 1980's Buick Skyhawk V6 wagon. As they drove off, I breathed a sigh of soul-lightening relief. There was no sign of Moore or his silver truck as I scurried back to my car and quickly blended with the commuter traffic.

Heading toward home, I stopped one last time at Coronado to see Benji. He was all set to be picked up by one of CARMA's dog fosters. Soon he would be in a loving home to await adoption. As I approached the house, I could hear Phoenix start barking. I pulled into the garage. Fortunately, his noise-making was from happiness at my return rather than readying himself to go for the carotid of someone who had invaded his inner sanctum. He nearly knocked me down with excitement at my return. The smell of another dog, despite its clinical overtones, briefly confused and unnerved him. But with a front-paws-on-shoulders sloppy kiss, he waited patiently for the leash to connect with his collar before racing to the elm tree.

By 4:30 P.M. there was still no e-mail from Moore. "Oh, crap!" I muttered aloud, "Don't tell me I've lost him. I've put so much time, money, and effort into this project that to have it fall apart now isn't acceptable." I had no idea what I'd do next. My brain felt weary from thinking about it.

Phoenix and I had an early dinner. PBS was re-running Ken Burns' 2009 incredible mini-series *The National Parks: America's Best Idea* as part of their pledge drive. In 2010 it had won two Emmys. I'd been to Yosemite, Grand Canyon, and Yellowstone but was salivating to go to as many others as possible. I'd have to devise a plan for Phoenix and me to do so ... and then actually execute it. It would be our own version of Steinbeck's *Travels with Charley* adventure.

As I settled onto the sofa with a dog in my lap, my desktop computer in my office chimed. It was 5:55 P.M. I lifted Phoenix onto the cushion beside me and jogged to check my e-mail. I had a bunch of demands for donating to charities and political causes all coming in at the same time. But at the bottom was one from Moore. I didn't feel like bothering but needed closure on everything I'd done.

"I have decided ..." it began.

I wanted to say, "Who cares."

"... to take you up on your two-month offer." I nearly collapsed on the floor. "Thank that coach for me. And tell me how to make the payment."

I replied, "Congratulations on what I believe is a wise decision. I will send you the contract, spelling everything out in detail, including how to make the payment. Please read it carefully and sign it. Much success in your new career endeavor."

Now I had to create a contract with time limits on taking the training, etc. It had to specify: *This would be a one-time training, June through July of this year only. It would not be repeated. It would be conducted by e-mail only, instead of Skype and phone, so there would be a record for both parties of everything that was presented and done. This would be unlike the nine-month course which would be conducted via recordings and transcripts. Passage of exercises back and forth would be by e-mail attachments.*

This two-month course would be condensed from the nine-month course, given July to February, by psychologist and professional coach, Dr. Robert Stoddard, PhD, who was simultaneously preparing the nine-month training. This short, intensive course would be specifically and only for Clayton Moore. Consequently, the other coaches in the nine-month course who were not involved in this special project would not be available to provide mentoring to Moore.

The fee of $4,700 would be paid in advance by certified check and sent along within ten days' time with the signed contract. The cost would cover the coach's time and effort creating the course for Moore, his time away from his other scheduled clients in order to do this individual project, and providing the actual training to

Moore. Therefore, if for any reason Moore did not participate in this training on the assigned days at the assigned times, there would be no make-up time available. The arrangement would be that instruction on week days began at 6 P.M. Mountain time for two hours—which would accommodate Moore's work schedule—and on weekends, Saturday and Sunday, at noon Mountain time, each for four hours. Since this was a training course, and not coaching, counseling, or therapy, Moore's participation would not be considered "confidential."

Certification of Moore as a "professional problem-solving coach" would be dependent upon his satisfactory completion of all classes, exercises, tests, and the final practicum. The practicum would be designed to give Moore the opportunity to apply the coaching theory he was studying. Furthermore, Moore's registration fee for the course would be non-refundable.

I figured that I could have the contract ready in an hour or so. I'd put two copies, one for him and one to sign for me, in a letter-size Priority Mail envelope addressed to Moore from the Harvard Square "International Professional Coaching University" address. This I'd place in a larger Priority Mail envelope to Harry along with another letter of confirmation to be sent out to Moore as soon as I'd received the signed contract and check. In the meantime, Harry would receive Moore's contract and check and re-send the unopened envelope to me.

Once that was out of the way, I had to get to work gathering all my coaching materials—lessons, exercises, examples, articles, and bibliography—together to make up this two-month intensive training.

To keep from becoming depressed I had to keep assuring myself that the primary result of my effort was that one, likely CARMA, or possibly more, of the non-profit, no-kill homeless animal shelters would be getting some needed financial assistance. And, secondarily, I could design the course to be used for seminars for other clients in the future if I chose to go that route.

As I worked on the contract's formal nomenclature, something was intruding, stimulating my little gray cells. It was that old overshadowing desire for revenge. Collecting $4,700 was not enough. Sure, it was a financial burden on Moore, but it wasn't publicly revealing his bad behavior as it affected his finances. Even worse, what I'd done through offering this training didn't negatively affect him socially or psychologically.

Could I still engineer some way to add misery to Moore's life? Not just misery, but a whole lot of misery. So far as I could tell, the police weren't doing it ... yet. Which made me wonder why Rodriguez apparently hadn't acted on my accusations. I'd have to check that out.

Carrie's comments about Moore's overriding desire for cleanliness and his fear of germs might hold some possibilities. That thought created a cheek spasm of a small smile. I wasn't going to be posting the Priority Mail envelopes until the next morning so I had a little time to huddle with my "dark side" on this.

Hours passed as my fertile brain vomited malicious possibilities. The first was rubbing poison ivy on the contract margins so he would develop a blistery, intensely burning rash that he would want to scratch until his hands bled. But there was no way of knowing if the oily resin, urushiol, found in the leaves, stems, and roots, would darken and look like grease or dirt on the contract. That would be too tacky, unprofessional, and not worth the risk. But what about finding his truck in the UNM hospital parking garage and smearing his driver's side door handle with poison ivy. That wouldn't be noticeable ... but, there was no way of knowing if he were sensitive to it. Surprisingly, not everyone was. But if he were, his allergic reaction would develop twelve to forty-eight hours after exposure—so it would be unlikely to be associated with the contract or door handle—and last for two to three weeks. However, if he washed his hands well right away, he would significantly reduce the reaction if there were one.

Then again, if he were that afraid of germs, he might open the envelope and handle the contract wearing his surgical gloves and the same with his truck door. I couldn't remember if I had seen him wearing gloves when he alighted from his truck in the UNM hospital parking garage. But whether he wore gloves or not, the oil would be on him to be spread on anything and everything he touched.

"Bloody hell!" I exclaimed. Phoenix jumped off the sofa, looked around, and galloped into the office to my side to make sure everything was copacetic. I gave him a pet. "I can't do that! He could give allergic reactions to almost everyone—medical staff and patients—and leave the allergen everywhere else." I had no idea how long the oil remained potent once it left the plant. Phoenix put his head on my lap and looked up at me wistfully.

"You want to go for a walk, don't you?" He raised his head as his tail repeatedly slapped my chair. "Okay, let's do it."

As we walked toward Sheriff Posse, I considered sending Moore a health alert ostensibly from the Sandoval Country Health Department to try to convince him that he was probably infected with Lyme Disease or even Black Plague if he had handled any animals in the Bernalillo area. I bounced that around for a while, inspecting it from all directions, until it petered out with disgust. He wouldn't believe it and could check it easily enough.

Exercise was promoting oxygenated blood flow to my brain cells. Soon I discovered I didn't like what I was contemplating. It was a far cry from originally wanting to make him face deserved psychological discomfort and social and public ridicule for his animal abuse. By the time Phoenix had taken his last partial-leak to spread the wealth and mark as much of his territory as possible, we were home. I hoped he had *finally* emptied his urinary bladder for the evening. Back in my office I was disappointed with myself and once again frustrated.

While Phoenix watched me brush my teeth, something just out of reach was bubbling to the surface of my consciousness. It was like seeing a shadowy figure in my peripheral vision. Foaming at the mouth, I looked in the mirror, and smiled. I had something. This time I *really* had something. It was brilliant … if it worked. Nodding and looking toward the heavens, I murmured, "By the pricking of my thumbs, something 'just wicked enough' this way comes."

The next morning on my way to class I mailed the Priority envelope to Harry to pass on to Moore. So far so good. As far as I could tell, Moore had been pre-occupied with setting up his coaching course so he hadn't bothered to stalk or harass me. Maybe by having this other focus, he was finished with his campaign against me, or, at least, less interested in pursuing it at the moment.

Students were completing their behavior-shaping projects with shelter dogs. Carrie's group, without benefit of Carrie's input, had gotten their dog to roll over repeatedly on cue then get to its feet. One group had their dog sitting and offering one paw than the other to shake. Another had their dog standing up on its hind legs and hopping toward them on a signal. They all demonstrated how working with a pre-existing, initial behavior, and using lots of patience and positive reinforcement to slowly add to the behavior, they could influence the dog to behave as they desired. Something the dogs enjoyed doing as well. Their final exams were next week so I gave them a general sense of what the test would cover. I emphasized that they had better be ready for mostly short answer and essay questions.

When the expected groans accompanied my indicating the dreaded "essays," I outlined on the blackboard how I wanted them to answer these questions: stating *what*, *why*, and *how*, and then providing supporting evidence for it with examples. I also gave them a gift.

"I'm going to ask you to define 'critical thinking.' I expect you to describe it fully plus provide five solid examples of it, explaining each of the examples." Then I reminded them, as you may recall, this is definitely a no-fluff course. Filling an essay with hot air, inconsequential verbiage, is insulting to me and to you. As in the past," I raised an index finger in the air and cocked my head toward it for emphasis. "I'll take off points for BS. I kid you not."

More groans and sighs.

On the way home I stopped at Albertson's and nearly plowed my shopping cart into a second-degree sunburned Brad in the bread aisle. I was the first to speak.

"Ooh." Looking at his swollen face, "You're looking like you could use some burn unguent, an ice bath, and maybe a little morphine. Is it as uncomfortable as it appears?"

"Funny you should ask. Yeah." He hardly moved his mouth as he spoke. "I'd be happy if I didn't have to flex my body at all. Every little movement wrinkles some inflamed piece of sun-scorched flesh."

"It's not just your face then? I hope you weren't wearing shorts."

"In fact, I was. I'd also run out of sun screen and didn't take the time away from the job to replace it because we were dealing with some dicey problems."

I started to laugh, picturing blistered scarlet knee caps and swollen, crinkled, puce skin behind his knees. He looked at me with mock shock and began to laugh too. Then he grimaced, his hand touching his dark-pink peeling cheek.

"Ooh, don't make me do that."

"If it would help, I could buy you a Starbucks' *venti* Caramel Frappuccino with a straw to make up for inflicting the torture of making you laugh. You could even stretch out on their padded bench to get comfortable."

"I guess I could take you up on that since I don't have anything frozen or requiring immediate refrigeration." He carefully shifted his position and leaned on his shopping cart. "I've been wanting to call you since we met but we've been helping out on a project south in Las Cruces. I had no idea when we'd return. Just got back last night."

"Welcome back. I understand how that can be. Like you, I've been mobbed with all kinds of work. Are you sure you don't want to get checked out at Urgent Care? They could slather you with antibiotic ointment or cortisone, maybe even wrap you in gauze like a mummy and add an opiate patch."

He tried to smile again but his cheeks wouldn't cooperate.

"On second thought, maybe I should just let you go home to soak in a cool tub before you keel over. You look just this side of crispy bacon."

His face began to look relieved. "Yeah. Maybe you're right." His words fell out between sun-blistered lips, sounding muffled. "Actually, I don't feel so great."

"Getting around must be difficult. Give me a call if you need any help. And don't forget to get paper straws to use in the meantime. We'll have that Frappuccino when you've recovered."

Brad touched my arm, nodded, and waddled like a toddler with a full diaper toward the cashiers. He looked a lot sicker than he was letting on. What was he doing out shopping in that condition? Then, I watched as he headed for his vehicle and wondered not only how he could drive but also if he really might call now that he was back.

From experience I tended to be somewhat skeptical about men's promises to call and their excuses for not calling. But my rule of thumb was that if they made an excuse once, many things could have intervened so I'd give them the benefit of the doubt. Not a real problem. If it happened twice, and they didn't work for the police, fire department, FBI, or as an OB/Gyn or paramedic, my antennae would begin to twitch, telegraphing "pay attention," but I'd still give them the benefit of the doubt. However, if it happened a third time, there was no benefit of the doubt in the offing. This looked like a behavioral pattern that suggested I wasn't high on their priority list or they were more disorganized or forgetful than I wanted to deal with. My response? What Douglas Adams had entitled the fourth book of his *Hitchhiker's Guide to the Galaxy*'s so-called "trilogy," *So Long and Thanks for All the Fish.*

18

Still wondering why nothing had apparently happened to Moore as a result of all my reports, I called Animal Control office.

"May I speak with Officer Rodriguez?"

"Officer Rodriguez was in a bad auto accident and is currently hospitalized. How may I help you?"

"When did this happen?"

"Several weeks ago."

"Who has taken over his caseload in his absence?"

"No one I know of. What case are you specifically asking about?"

"That's okay. Thanks for your help." I hung up.

Any moment the cop who answered was likely to give me to Hardess. I could picture Hardess, self-satisfied, smiling with glee when he saw my name from my caller ID, planning on hiding my file as he rooted for Moore to retaliate against me, "To the moon, Alice."

When I returned home, I entered by way of the front door to check the grounds for the morning paper which didn't always arrive. The moment I entered the house,

Phoenix crawled on his belly toward me, looking petrified. He nearly knocked me over as he tried to get as close as possible for reassurance. This was puzzling. What could have happened to have this effect on him? Sitting on the cool clay tiles beside him in our tiny foyer, I petted him and spoke softly to him, telling him it was okay now. But was it? When I rose, he stood up with me, still looking afraid and shivering. Together we walked cautiously from room to room, starting in the living room at my right then to the hall where I listened at the partially open doors. No sounds from my office, the bathroom, or the master bedroom. Phoenix began whining. In the kitchen, however, I found glass from the backdoor window on the floor. There was a little bit of blood on the ragged edges of what was left in the door near the lock and on the scattered shards on the floor.

Now I ran into my office to see if anything there had been disturbed. Papers obviously had been moved. The drawers had been rifled. My desktop computer was partially unplugged but still on the desk. I always kept my laptop with me. My mouth went dry. It must have been Moore. What if he had discovered my documents for the International Professional Coaching University? Everything would have been lost. The money for the animal homeless shelter and my embryonic revenge plan would have disappeared in a puff of acrid smoke. Not to mention that he'd likely sue me for fraud.

I searched the interiors of all the rooms. They too had been torn apart. In my bedroom bureau drawers were pulled out. Clothing flung about. In the bathroom the medicine cabinet was open and the few vials of pills I'd had on the shelves were spilled into the sink. From a quick glance I couldn't tell what, if anything, was missing. Back in the kitchen, where cabinets and drawers had been opened, I thought a small glass of wine could settle my frayed nerves. It was then that I discovered something even odder. An unopened bottle of Argentinian Pino Grigio, with its punchy flavors of lemon, lime, green apple, and honeysuckle, had vanished from the refrigerator door.

Just as I was about to call the police, I noticed the burner phone was blinking red. I turned on the video, knowing full well it was going to be Moore. But, to my immense surprise, it wasn't! WTF? Who the hell was that? It was a shabby-looking teenager wearing a worn red ball cap, soiled gray hoodie, and low-slung pants, trying to jimmy the backdoor with a small crowbar. When it wouldn't accede to his demands, he smashed the glass with his bare hand. His head was constantly twitching to the left and his hands were shaking. I heard a horrible yelp then nothing. A little while later he left through the backdoor holding the wine bottle and a pill vial.

The recorded sound sent me immediately to Phoenix. Very carefully I examined his body. Everything thing seemed okay until I reached his lower jaw. It was untouchable and covered in dried blood. It looked as if the intruder had caught Phoenix with an upward swing of the crowbar. I called Coronado Pet Hospital, left everything as I had found it, and raced to their facility. I'd call the police later. First things first.

Fortunately, an x-ray revealed his jaw wasn't shattered but the upward force had broken off two tall canines as his jaws slammed together. Dr. Smith shaved the bloody fur from under his chin, cleaned and sutured the two-inch gash.

"His broken teeth will probably be okay. They look as though they broke off at the tips. But you should monitor him for mouth pain, like his not eating or drinking or rubbing his mouth with a paw. I'm giving you a prescription for the antibiotic Clavamox by oral suspension drops to address any possible bacterial infection of his jaw. He gets it twice a day."

She began to shave clean a spot on his left rear leg. "This is for a 50-mcg. fentanyl patch for pain. It will last about three days. But since it won't kick in for about twelve hours, I've given him some oral buprenorphine in his cheek pouch. You'll need to bring him back to have the patch removed and his recovery evaluated."

Dr. Smith's soothing attention and addition of the pain med temporarily lifted my spirits a little. Phoenix still looked abashed.

On the way back home, I stopped at PetSmart to fit Phoenix in a harness. I didn't want his regular collar to chafe his wound. As soon as we were in the house, I called the police who said they'd be right over.

Back in the kitchen where it all had occurred, poor Phoenix looked even more distressed. His head down, he stared at the floor. He appeared embarrassed, ashamed he hadn't protected his home from the burglar. That would have been his centuries-old sacred duty as a watch dog and protector. By not keeping the intruder out or at bay, he had failed not only me but also himself and his ancestors. We'd have to work together to get his confidence back. It had been only ten minutes before the police arrived. I didn't recognize either one of them.

After taking them on tour, pointing out the pill vials and the blood on what was left of the glass pane, I showed them the video. One officer recognized the teen as one of the drug-addicted Doersicki brothers from Algodones, about nine miles away, who were always in and out of trouble, breaking and entering and stealing, trying to feed their habits. When they left, I called John to report the need for a new backdoor glass pane then swept up the shards and vacuumed the linoleum floor for slivers and microscopic particles.

This incident screamed at me to make sure nothing—absolutely nothing— about the university and the coaching course Moore was to participate in was available in either hard copy or digital file in the house. I didn't have a safe so I'd have to put everything in my safe deposit box at Wells Fargo. However, I'd have to keep my coaching materials close at hand. What this meant was that after each session, I'd put them into a plastic bag and tape it with a strong adhesive to the back of my bed's headboard. Just in case. Before taking Phoenix out for his walk, I checked my e-mail.

Harry had left me a message. He had received the Priority package and mailed the inner envelope with the contracts to Moore.

"As soon as I receive his response, I'll let you know before mailing it back to you. Hope this all works out for you. Double-Oh-Seven signing off."

When I received Moore's signed contract and his certified check, I would send Harry a personal check for several thousand dollars from my savings account, not from Moore's check, that I had put aside for his daughter, my god-daughter's college fund. I'd known Marcy since she was a baby and reveled in all she did. She was a prodigy and I loved her as if she were my own. Her sites were set on attending Massachusetts Institute of Technology to become a chemist or chemical engineer. Her heroes were Marie Curie who pioneered radioactivity research and Jacqueline Barton who probed DNA with electrons. If given a chance, she would conquer the world of chemistry and make remarkable contributions. I could see her being awarded the Nobel Prize for Chemistry, only the second women to have been awarded such an honor since her idol Marie Curie had in 1911.

I hoped for Harry and Marcy's sake that she could get a scholarship based on financial need. I was surprised that M.I.T. didn't give scholarships based on merit, despite how incredibly bright Marcy was. Attending was not inexpensive. Even without room and board, the yearly bill would be roughly $52,000. That topped even Harvard University which was roughly $46,000 without room and board. That was going to be a real challenge for them without financial aid. I'd help out as best I could.

With his new harness, Phoenix's sutured upper neck presumably would heal faster. If he had a problem with wearing it, he didn't indicate it. As we made our way to Sheriff Posse, he plodded along. His shoulders were slumped. His mood, despondent. Even when a roadrunner with a small lizard in its mouth scuttled across the dirt path in front of him, he hardly looked after it. I'd have to give him some special attention when we returned home.

Maybe as soon as classes ended and before Moore's course began, we could take a day trip, to drive to northern New Mexico to take a ride on the Cumbres and Toltec Railroad. I had done that when I first arrived in New Mexico. This train with its coal-fired steam engine was a National Historic Landmark. The sixty-four-mile journey began in Chama, New Mexico, and ended in Antonito, Colorado. Traveling at twelve-miles an hour, it zig-zagged along the narrow ledge above the Rio de los Pinos through steep, spired mountain canyons. One gorge it passed plunged eight hundred feet. There were lush alpine meadows dotted with wildflowers and white-bark aspens. And high-desert elk, deer, and bears could be spotted everywhere. Cumbres Pass reached 1,015 feet which was the highest point reached by rail in the U.S. We would have the option of riding in a closed coach or standing on a railed open platform car where our clothes, exposed flesh, and lungs could gather all the carcinogenic flying coal dust the smoke stack could provide. Phoenix would love everything about it.

I scrutinized their website but didn't see anything about prohibiting non-humans. I strongly suspected that only service animals were allowed but called anyway. There were times when I didn't want to be right and this was one of them.

"Phoenix," I called to him in the kitchen where he was having a refrigerated dog snack, "Do you want to be a service dog for a day?" He didn't answer me, undoubtedly because he had more scruples than I did about what he was willing to do, even for me. I had to think of something else.

In the meantime, I worked on the two-month coaching course for Moore. I assumed he was going to sign the contract and send it to me with his certified check so I had to be ready. I expected to be hearing soon from Harry that he had received mail from Moore and was sending it on.

My outline listed all I needed to cover from the power and possibility of coaching to its mechanics, coaching skills, establishing rapport with clients, confidentiality, professional issues, marketing, websites, and getting clients. Of course, there were myriad sub-topics under each topic which would be covered in detail with exercises, questions and answers, and extensive readings. Working with clients' projects, goals, and transitions, Moore would learn to help others discover how to solve their obstacle-producing problems. He would learn to help them define their vision and learn what they wanted in life. Moreover, he would assist them to unlock their abilities and improve their overall effectiveness. He would facilitate their growth and their transformation to what they wanted themselves to do and become while fostering their accountability for it all.

When Moore finished this course, there was no way he could think of it as a con. He would have gotten more than his money's worth, no matter how much my evil-twin side still intermittently flirted with really scamming him somehow. The reality was that I *had* to do my best with the course if I were to pull off my newly-hatched, real revenge plan which would dramatically follow.

As I waded through these lessons, which was like trying to escape quicksand, Phoenix was getting antsy. I had been trying to ignore his hunkering under the desk, untying my running shoes' laces, and scrambling the pages of my lesson-relevant papers with his sweeping tail. But when his out-flung paws glanced my keyboard spelling out the equivalent of "etaoin shrdlu," I knew we had to take a break. It was after eleven o'clock at night. I grabbed a hefty flashlight, shining an impressive 32500 lumens, from the kitchen. With his leash attached to his harness, Phoenix exploded out the front door. Only to stop dead in his tracks.

Moore was about to exit his truck fifteen feet away. The moment Moore hit the ground Phoenix began to bark, straining to occupy more than Moore's personal space. My leash-wrapped right hand was in danger of being amputated from my wrist. Surprised, Moore stepped back toward the driver's door. I couldn't tell whether he was going to reach inside for a weapon or get back in. I fervently hoped he was going to get back in. I had no idea what I'd do if he pulled a gun. I wasn't close enough to use karate on him. While Phoenix was, I didn't want him hurt by this animal abuser.

Fortune and an additional full moon this season—a "blue moon"—were smiling on us this night. Moore climbed back in, started his truck, revving the engine more than was necessary, and peeled out. Phoenix and I were suitably impressed by this macho maneuver. Now hypervigilant, we took our walk.

Phoenix now strutted down the street to Sheriff Posse and back. I was pleased with his change of mood. When we arrived back home, we checked the outside of the house but found nothing awry. Once inside again, Phoenix brought his cotton rope toy to me, ready to shake it then happily abscond with it. When I checked the front camera, it showed Moore pulling up and alighting from his truck but did not reveal his face. I recorded the episode in my Moore diary and wondered when Rodriquez was getting out of the hospital.

It was surprising that Moore was still hung up on going after me. So much time had elapsed. Didn't he have anything else to occupy his mind? Hopefully, when he was finally engrossed in the coaching course, he'd be too busy to think about me. It might not be a bad idea for me to make doubly sure I kept him doing exercises or studying all the time. That meant I wasn't as close to being finished setting up his lessons as I had thought. No rest for the weary, the wicked, or those dealing with the wicked.

Harry sent me an e-mail. He had received the mail from Moore and had already sent it on to me Priority. As soon as I received the check, I'd deposit it and then have Harry send the confirmation to Moore to let him know everything was set. That meant I had better get myself into third gear to be ready for the first of June. Whether Moore would know it and appreciate it or not, this was going to be an excellent course. If I offered it to others, it would require more of my physical time in which to present it with my in-person mentoring— essentially how I'd described the nine-month course, except I'd probably parse it into thirds.

My psychology majors, both graduate and undergraduate, had had their final exams which I now had the indescribable joy of correcting. Since they had spent most of their time responding to essay questions, it was going to take me some time to do them justice. Those instructors who used mostly multiple-choice questions could correct their tests in a flash. But that begged the question of how sure they could be that their students had really learned the material so they could apply it and then build on it.

Of course, the academic bureaucracy demanded that I have the results in by the end of the week. As much as I enjoyed teaching, acceding to such demands, not to mention contending with the covert and overt politics in academia which too often raised its ugly head, was a royal pain. I wondered if I'd have been happier at a Summerhill-like school, similar to the one started in England in 1921, where education was not so regimented, restrictive, programmed, and test-evaluation-oriented. Maybe not. Students who might express a laissez-faire academic attitude through their behavior could be more than a little irksome with which to work. While I did let classes take their own course, to some degree, I was always providing direction and necessary control.

That night before Phoenix and I watched a PBS's Masterpiece Theater re-run of an episode of *Endeavor*, I added further experiential exercises to Moore's course. If he worked hard and did all that was required, he'd be in a good position to start a coaching business sooner than later. The only thing he would then need would be more actual experience and further assistance with making his coaching known. Smart marketing, especially education-based relationship marketing, was everything to building a coaching business, or any business.

The next morning early, after a restful night's sleep, I would begin correcting exams and continue until I was finished. Except, of course, for taking essential breaks for Phoenix. I wished for both our sakes that Phoenix could have had a large, fenced yard in which to run so he wouldn't have been so dependent upon me for exercise, of which he needed a lot more, and for his elimination. Too bad he hadn't been trained to use the toilet. Too bad he couldn't have been given a high-tech, bathtub-sized litter-like box, one which immediately absorbed the associated odors and was easy to clean.

When the mail arrived the next morning, there was the Priority from Harry. It contained the signed contract and a certified check for $4,700. Correcting exams could wait until I made the deposit in the "International University for Professional Coaching" account. Since there was no problem, I e-mailed Harry to send the university confirmation. I additionally e-mailed Moore to tell him that he'd receive his first e-mails from his coach the morning of June 1, a week away. I reminded him that the course would be intense so he should plan on devoting all his time to it to get the most out of it. Irrespective of what the course could do for me and my revenge plan, I wasn't looking forward to it. I had an inkling that the next two months would be like being fired in a crucible.

My cell phone rang. It was Carrie. She was in Prescott, Arizona, and had signed up at Prescott College for the advanced counseling course, because of what she had already achieved at UNM.

"Rentals here are very pricey. Eight-hundred to several thousand a month. I was very lucky to find another student who has a two-bedroom about four blocks from the college, on West Gurley. By splitting the rent, we'll each pay about four hundred."

"Paying only four hundred a month sounds like a gift."

"Now I have to find a job to pay for the next year of school and support me during my internship, but I have a couple of good behavioral possibilities. So far things seem to be working out okay. I miss you and your classes. You made the most difficult concepts easy to understand and fun. Loved our class discussions. Apparently, Clay hasn't found out about my location.

What a relief. I am so grateful. Are you still having problems with him?"

"So glad to hear from you and that things are working out. Please keep me apprised of how things are going. As for Moore, I hear from him now and then. No biggie. Contact me by e-mail when you're ready. In general, it would be safer for you not contact me often. Just in case. I'll remove your phone number from my cell as soon as we finish our conversation. Thanks. And stay well."

"You too."

At that moment I envied Carrie for being some place new, relatively unfettered, and starting afresh.

Since I'd finished working on the exams, I gathered them together and took them plus each student's calculated grades to the university. They had done better than average. Over the four years I had been at UNM I had worked to make the psychology topics entertaining, important, and individually identifiable. It was a no-brainer: Whatever worked to get the concepts, research, theories, and applications across and cemented into their skulls so it all was relevant to their lives. That's why I used essay questions to evaluate their understanding and their ability to use it. Multiple choice questions too often were merely a guessing-game about specific facts only. Isolated facts were useful only on quiz programs.

It was almost two o'clock. Phoenix had an appointment with Dr. Smith to check his under-jaw area and remove his fentanyl patch. He had been very accommodating taking his Clavamox but he was beginning to resist, shifting his head from right to left and clenching his jaw, to keep me from inserting the calibrated syringe into his mouth. Thank goodness for loose jowls. Fortunately, this was his seventh day so it was only one more after this morning's dose.

When we arrived at Coronado, Phoenix jumped from the front seat to the back. As I opened the back door to grab his harness, he leapt back into the front. He was whining. I crawled into the front again. As I reached for him from the driver's seat, he immediately stood up on his hind legs, one front paw braced on the back of the passenger seat and the other stretched onto the dashboard.

"Come on. No one will hurt you."

He whined even louder, making a gargling growl in his throat.

"I know you're afraid of animal hospitals but you have to go in. I'll protect you. I won't let anyone do anything nasty to you. You know Dr. Smith. She just wants to examine your jaw, that it's healed properly."

As I leaned closer, Phoenix moved back against the passenger door. He reminded me of the typical next-victim in a horror movie, panic-stricken, pinned against a wall as the villain armed with a sharpened axe malevolently reveals himself to him or her. I really needed to have a safety harness for him in the car.

"If you don't go willingly, I'll have to carry you in." As I closed the driver's side door and back doors, I added, "That will be embarrassing for a big, brave dog like you."

Hearing something else, Phoenix turned his head to catch a glimpse of another dog going by the car. As he did, I scurried around to the front passenger door, popped it open, and wrapped my arms around his abdomen. A look of shock followed by betrayal covered his face. Attaching his leash, I placed him on the pavement. He looked at me for a moment. Thinking that he was co-operating, I gave him a tasty treat to reinforce his relaxation and encourage him to walk under his own power to the hospital door. But, instead of truly relaxing, he again had locked all his muscles in place as he dug his paws into the heat-softening asphalt. That is, until he fully observed the other dog.

It was a female standard poodle that had sashayed by, her white pom-poms seductively swaying on her hips as she made her way to the hospital's glass door. He glanced at me then again at her. Instantly, he relaxed and quickly made a move forward, now pulling *me* along. His jowl-raised expression seemed to say, "Well, maybe I could tolerate just one more vet visit after all," as he strode after her.

Inside the hospital Phoenix sidled up to the poodle and sniffed her. Unperturbed, she looked him over. Without a sneer or growl, she seemed to accept his attention, despite his moth-eaten coat. He gave me a side-long, fleeting look then sat down on the ceramic-tiled floor with me on the only available wooden bench seat. The poodle was sitting serenely with her human companions across the room. Every time he shifted his position to eyeball her, he was enveloped in a tornado of loose fur. In the process he had covered my black slacks with hair. This reminded me of having read some time in my childhood that German Shepherds were notorious for shedding all the time. That was the reason I had been brushing him once a week. Undoubtedly, that was not often enough, especially in the increasingly warmer weather. Despite my frequent auto detailing, the front passenger's seat in the car was blanketed with his discards.

With his recovery now assured and the pain patch having been removed by Dr. Smith, to whom I confided his burgeoning interest in the poodle, I gathered Phoenix up again and parked him at home. From there I drove to the gym to lift weights and then to the dojo to practice my karate, both of which I sorely needed. The upcoming stress of the next two months was already plaguing my body with knotting muscles.

19

When I returned home and before I pulled the car into the garage, I spotted a twelve-inch by twelve-inch by twelve-inch UPS box waiting on my front stoop. I hadn't ordered anything. Phoenix inside was beside himself barking, nails clattering on the Saltillo tile floors as he raced around from room to room, peering out the windows. After parking in the garage, I walked around front to inspect it. It suddenly occurred to me review the camera video before picking up the package. Squeezing past Phoenix at the front door, I scanned it. But all the video told me was that a UPS driver had dropped it off. That didn't tell me if it were safe. Myriad frightening thoughts assailed me.

Fearing the worst, I isolated Phoenix in the bathroom and slipped out the front door to examine the box in the front yard, away from the house. Then, very carefully, I'd open it to check for explosive device leads. The shipping label didn't say "Moore" or "Camino del Pueblo." But it did say "Nadie Puta." I could feel myself start to sweat.

With the slim-bladed utility knife I always carried with me I tentatively sliced through the tape at the top sides, gently feeling and looking for trip wires as I did. I found none. Wedging the blade in at the side, I slowly sliced across the top and tenderly parted the top flaps.

"Oh my god!" I gasped. My blood pressure fell. My gut felt encased in ice. My breathing became rapid as my pulse roared. In the box was a tightly curled, four-foot rattle snake. But its rattle was silent. Furthermore, its mouth was open. It appeared heat prostrated. I pulled my cell phone from my slacks' pocket to shoot a picture.

I closed the box and gingerly carried it at arms' length down the dirt path to the river. Laying the box on its bottom in the water a foot out from the water's edge, I let the corrugated cardboard soak up some liquid to cool the snake. I opened the top flaps with a long, slim, spiny Russian olive branch which had undoubtedly been broken off by the wind. Like the Siberian elm, the Russian Olive was also an invasive plant which grew in riparian habitats and choked out native vegetation. The branch's long, narrow, pungent silver leaves were still intact, masking any aroma from the overheated snake. I waited. No question: Only the diabolical Clayton Moore could have done this. While I wasn't fond of rattlers, I didn't want one killed as a result of his attempt to terrorize me.

Time passed slowly. In about fifteen minutes the box moved only slightly as the snake began to stir. It was no longer totally unconscious but logy. Hopefully, the water soaking the cardboard underneath and up the sides was lowering its body temperature to around seventy degrees Fahrenheit so it would recover if it could. I didn't know how overheating actually affected its individual organs, if this would leave it damaged, but I knew that overheating caused by exposure to conditions above ninety-five degrees F. could prove fatal to it within a few minutes.

I waited at a distance, watching. Slowly the snake began to uncoil itself. When it appeared to have recouped some of its strength, it slid guardedly over the collapsing box side and into the water. As soon as it had swum off, I retrieved the box and ran back home with it. I wanted it for fingerprint evidence for the police. I'd make sure I recorded it in my Moore diary.

Entering the house from garage, I found Phoenix on his hind legs scratching the inside of the bathroom door. When I released him, he jumped out at me, nearly knocking me over, to race to the front door. I clutched his leash to take him for a run. However, when he leapt out the door, he stopped short the moment he landed on the front stoop, sending me nearly tumbling over him. For an instant he didn't move. It was as if he were glued to the front stoop. Then in a moment of manic agitation, he growled and barked, digging at the step with his front paws. I couldn't budge him. He was getting bigger and stronger as he matured. Over time my strength against his wasn't going to work. I'd have to start obedience training soon, once I finished with Moore. The more he barked and dug, the more furious he became.

The only thing I could think of was to wash off the concrete step. Unable to move him back into the house so I could retrieve some detergent, I unrolled the hose and sprayed it instead. In spite of my inadvertently soaking him in the process, he still wouldn't yield his ground. Initially, he didn't seem to be aware of the forceful spray dousing him. His adrenaline was pumping. The hair on his back was on end. His body was seething with aggression.

But gradually the submerged stoop seemed to have less olfactory pull. Moreover, shaking his paws one at a time, he finally appeared to recognize his dripping body. Now he became calmer, practically disinterested in the step itself, as if it hadn't held him in its grip only seconds ago.

It was only then he seemed ready to hear me and accede to my wishes. He dismounted the stoop. But before we could go for a run, he rolled his loose-skinned, soggy fur ninety degrees to the left and then ninety degrees to the right, sending water flying in all directions. Especially in mine. In no time he had bathed me from scalp to running shoes. I inspected my trickling self as my Nike's continued to fill with water. Wringing out my shirt and slacks wouldn't help. I shook my head. There was no need to bother changing into dry running gear. With so little humidity in the air, it was hot enough to dry me quickly, except for my shoes. Phoenix started to run. What the hell. I took off after him.

The week went by quickly. Tomorrow was June 1, the beginning of Moore's coaching course. First thing I did in preparation for that day was get all my materials together in sequence. It was only then that I discovered that Phoenix had tossed his cotton rope toy onto my desk. In trying to retrieve it, he had knocked all my lessons and resource sheets onto the floor. They were scattered all over the place, some under my desk but others in the hall bordering the bathroom and kitchen. Making it worse, some were punctured with tooth and nail marks and others were torn, requiring cellophane tape to put them together, assuming I could find all the right pieces. Twenty minutes later I had corralled everything, well, everything Phoenix hadn't swallowed, fastened what required it, and had begun typing the e-mails I would use to instruct Moore in his training. He would receive e-mails every day: Everything he needed.

Little did he know that he was going to have to reveal himself to his mentor in ways he hadn't anticipated as he worked on his required "self-survey." This was something I had contrived for him alone and confidentiality had never been asserted. I wanted it to make him divulge what he had done with animals. How I handled it needed to be subtle, so as not to make him recoil and somehow not connect it with me personally as the object of his inflamed lethal desire. I needed it for my revenge plan but wasn't sure exactly how quite yet. At the very least, if what I was formulating didn't work out, I could pass it along to Rodriguez.

Because of Moore's work hours, he would work on this in the evening as soon as he returned home, which would be around six o'clock. He would have to spend most of each Saturday and Sunday afternoons on it when I would provide him with multiple e-mail tasks. I had originally wanted to have the entire course laid out in unchanged e-mail form ahead of time so I could just ship off what he needed to do next. But that was unrealistic. I knew better from my other coaching, seminars, and class work. Humans had a way of poking their finger into the eye of another's agenda to instantly change everything. However, since I was the one mostly in control, I could and did have templates for the next lesson ready to go only to modify them according to what Moore had done and how I needed to address his responses.

Even with that, I hadn't recognized how consuming these two months would be for me as well, how they would totally occupy my life. As much as the vulture on my left shoulder still so badly wanted me to drop him flat and flee with the cash (and do whatever else came to my fertile mind at that moment), I couldn't, even with all he had done to me and the animals. This conflict plagued me. Sometimes having principles and feeling ethically obligated to abide by them could be such a hemorrhoidal pain. Even though I had originally thought this would be a cinch, it was going to be anything but.

While I was putting this course together, I had given short shrift to Phoenix. He was showing signs of wanting to chew on anything not encased in a plastic bubble. Boredom was settling in. All that energy needed dissipating. As a result, during my time providing the course, I really needed to make sure I devoted more attention to him through exercise and playtime.

I had heard about Pet Paradise, a dog spa on Northern NE in Rio Rancho. It offered three indoor heated swimming pools, multiple indoor play areas, and outdoor play areas. It also had spacious, climate-controlled indoor suites for boarding, grooming, and training classes which might possibly be of interest to me if they used *only* positive reinforcement. I couldn't imagine them using choke chains, shock collars, or punishment but I'd have to investigate this fully. For fun, Phoenix could be signed up for the spa for all day on one day, half a day (four hours), or weekly. Their website's virtual tour made it look pleasant, well-thought out, and clean.

The outstanding question for me was would he acclimate quickly to his new surroundings. If he demonstrated any fear, anxiety, or aggression, would that put the kibosh on his partaking of their doggy delights? I assumed he'd get along with the other dogs since he had managed at the shelter. It was male humans that might be a problem. He didn't like Moore and was leery of John. Dog-treat-sharing Brad was another story. I'd talk with the veterinary techs at Coronado to get their take on the place. They were knowledgeable about all the areas' facilities for dogs and what their clients had said about them. When I called, they told me Dr. Smith's Maiti was an enthusiastic regular customer, loving every minute of it. At least it was one possibility to pursue. Poor Phoenix desperately needed more activity and fun in his life. I'd scope it out the next day while Moore was at work.

The following day, after Phoenix went for his run, we immediately piled into the Civic so he could assess what possibilities Pet Paradise might hold for him. Hesitant about entering the building, Phoenix quickly did an about face once we were inside. He began leaping about, whining, trying to get to the fun side of the glass wall where dogs were playing and splashing. I could hear him thinking, "Come on, Mom! I want to join in. It's party time!"

We, however, were first taken on a physical tour. It nearly drove Phoenix crazy. Being tethered to me was unacceptable when he could be swimming, leapfrogging over ramps, or knocking a soccer ball around the artificial turf in competition with those already having their alpha-dog fun. There were sofas on which to lounge or snooze. Even though Pet Paradise required reservations for a play date, amazingly there had been two last-minute cancellations. We were in luck. As he tugged on the leash to be free to join in, I attempted to register. My resulting handwriting was barely legible as I signed him in for four hours that afternoon.

When I was signaled to release him, I slipped off his harness. Without a "Good-bye" or "Thanks, Mom," he dashed away. As he joined the others, he stole a yellow rubber ball from a tail-wagging Beagle which was batting it around. With it in his mouth, Phoenix made his way to a pool. He was already in the water, making circles, and splashing as I was about to leave. Despite his wet fur lying flat making his bare spots more noticeable, he raised his head and bounced the ball hard in the water. Watching it submerge and then re-emerge, he went for it with his mouth open. He seemed to smile, muttering in dog-ese, "Now this is more like it."

As glad as I was for him, I also felt a little guilty. I hadn't seen him this happy since I had first brought him home from Barbara's. He'd have to be scheduled for more frequent doggy spa time. We'd also have to find ways to play more creatively at home.

On the way home I stopped at Home Depot for the two twenty-two-inch-diameter clay pots and three forty-pound bags of potting soil. At Santa Ana Garden Center I corralled the two largest *lavendula augustifolia*—English Lavender—they had. Their long wispy floral spikes, silvery-green leaves, and pungent fragrance were overwhelming. The car was immediately awash with its scent as it refreshed the interior's doggy B.O., reminding me that Phoenix could use a shampoo and the car upholstery a cleaning.

Lavender had several benefits besides fragrance and beauty. While it was attractive to butterflies and bees, it would be shunned by deer and rabbits. I wasn't sure about the presence of deer in my area but I definitely knew I had rabbits around the house, aside from the hare. Sadly, one morning I discovered a white fluffy cotton tail sans bunny near the front door. It occurred to me that a coyote likely had partaken of the French delicacy, *Lapin a la Cocotte,* but hadn't bussed its table afterward.

With four hours to work on enhancing my course e-mails, I accomplished a great deal. Each finished lesson template was augmented with additional practical supplementary material as well as resources to read and be quizzed on. The busier he would be learning and practicing, the better for him, but especially for me.

When I went to pick up Phoenix, he was curled up on a sofa, the yellow ball beside him. Hearing me approach, he raised his head. He began to open his mouth to grin, then stopped before his jowls could wrinkle. His eyes riveted on his harness in my hand. He leaned back. His front legs pushed on the cushion to raise himself to a sitting position. His body stiffened.

Petting his head, I kneeled down on the floor beside him to avoid the wet surface of the water-proof cushion. In an enthusiastic voice, "You'd like to have dinner, wouldn't you?" He perked up at the word "dinner." "You had a good time, didn't you? I'll bet you went swimming and met a lot of other dogs. You want to come back, don't you?"

He eyed me quizzically and stepped down from the sofa to let me slip on his harness. I wished I could believe he truly understood my words rather than just my intonations. Before we left, I was able to schedule him for once more this week. That was pure unvarnished luck. They were generally booked well in advance. We'd go from there.

As we walked to the car, he turned around once, looking yearningly at the building. After I opened both back doors to roll down the windows about four inches, he hopped onto the front, waiting for me to roll down the passenger side window too. I called him into the back seat where I had set up his crash-tested safety harness I had purchased on the way over. It had taken me a while to find one that would work best for him. Luckily, it fit. Even though he seemed to furrow his doggy brow to show his disappointment and longing for riding in front, he reluctantly let me strap him in the back. He'd eventually adapt. Besides, at least he was going for a ride which he enjoyed.

Places for him to go with me were limited. Unfortunately, he couldn't go with me for most errands because he couldn't stay in the car. It was too dangerous with the temperature rising quickly. In the winter it would be somewhat different, especially on overcast days. Most stores were not accommodating about dogs wandering around on a leash. His look of regret indicated to me that if only he hadn't been so tethered, he could stick his head out the window as compensation.

It would have been pure doggy joy for him to feel the air ripple his facial fur and rush by his ears. With the contorting of his jowls, as the wind pushed them open and back, he would have looked as Lieutenant-Colonel John Stapp did as he reached peak acceleration riding a rocket sled at Holloman Air Force Base in 1954. Speed of four hundred and twenty-one miles per hour, making Stapp "The Fastest Man on Earth," broke many bones and blinded him temporarily. Phoenix, however, would have been content with a mere fifty-five miles per hour.

That evening Moore e-mailed me that he was having difficulty answering his self-survey. He didn't want to respond to the question: *What have you done that society in general might not approve of or that they might condemn?*

He wanted to answer in some neutral, trivial fashion, like he sometimes peeled out with his truck or played his music too loud. I explained that he had to look deeply into himself to reveal something embarrassing, something that showed him at his worst according to others.

I explained, "It's very important to do this because you have to be able to deal with your own underlying behaviors and/or problems. You have to accept yourself for what you've done. This is necessary to do before you can unconditionally accept your clients with whatever they have or haven't done. It helps clear the path to your helping them deal with their problems."

That didn't seem to cut any ice with him because he didn't respond. Time passed. When he still didn't respond, I wrote what his "coaching mentor" had revealed when answering this self-survey, something that Moore might find more identifiable. I stated, "I had been married and treated my wife very badly. I ordered her around. I even struck her when she didn't respond to my demands fast enough. I took her by force sexually whenever I pleased. She was my physical punching bag and verbal whipping boy for whatever had gone wrong that day. But, in fact, this was even if nothing had gone wrong that day, that I was just feeling like I wanted to punish her because I felt she deserved it. Occasionally that sent her to the hospital. She knew she didn't dare go to the police."

That got Moore's attention.

"Yeah, women are so stupid you have to hit them to get their attention."

"When answering this question," I continued, "I found that I had to explore and then confront my own unresolved problems with anger and fear. What I discovered was that I had to be the one in control. I needed others, like my wife, to recognize my status and power and constantly show how much they admired it, practically kissing my feet. They had to do whatever *I* wanted. I used violence, fear, and intimidation to get my point across. I felt that if I didn't do these things, she, and others, would see me as weak and unmanly. I *had* to do it. And doing it made me feel really good about myself, that I was the one in control, the master of my life. I was impacting my surroundings rather than letting them impact me."

Moore had to respond.

"You do what you have to. You can't let anyone take your manhood away. And certainly not some damned inferior woman."

"The self-survey required me to open up and admit it to myself and the world, like what I'm admitting to you. That was what initially pushed me into working through these issues. And, it was through this work that I became the professional, compassionate, *profitably-in-demand* coach that I am today. It was hard but I am very pleased I did it. I now require all my students and clients do it as well because it's not only revealing and helpful but also very liberating."

"Well, maybe I already know myself."

"There's always more to learn. I know the questions are asking a lot of you but, believe me, they're worth your effort. Now I don't fear others learning about my formerly unacceptable actions. I've accepted that I did them. And now, it's a matter of 'so what?' We'll be referring to the self-survey in some exercises. This means that continuing without answering it would be difficult."

Moore didn't reply immediately. As time moved by slowly, I thought I might have lost him right there. It was no longer just about his $4,700 which I had in my hand. No, I needed his abuse confession more than anything. He needed to expose himself now when he was most uncertain about the course and his instructor. If he didn't do it now, he was less likely to do it later.

Minutes passed. I was holding my breath. So much labor and so much time. It had to work. I had to believe I could make it work. The situation reminded me of Nelson Mandela's quotation, "It always seems impossible until it's done."

Finally, he began typing. I didn't dare breathe. What was he going to say? He couldn't fail me now. I couldn't ...and wouldn't ... fail myself ... and Teddy.

The words slowly spelled out what I'd been waiting for, "I've hurt animals."

I was so relieved I started hooting and yelling. Phoenix who was at my feet looked concerned and confused, moving out of my office to stand in the doorway, looking back at me, unsure what it all meant. I thought that was a good start for Moore, necessary but not sufficient. He had to share more, much more.

"Tell me how you've hurt animals."

"I've kicked them and beaten them to a bloody pulp."

"What was your purpose in doing that?"

"To rid the world of them."

"Tell me why you think the world needs to be rid of animals."

"Not *all* animals, just dogs. Their existence irritates the hell out of me. They're vermin. They're everywhere and constantly multiplying. They defile grass, trees, buildings, sidewalks, and roads with their piss and shit. You're always stepping in their crap. They carry fleas, lice, ticks, and mange. They give diseases to humans. They stink. They are disgusting. They lick their asses ... then try to lick people. They eat their own vomit and roll in dead animal carcasses. They're scavengers. As far as I'm concerned, they're God's biggest mistake. They don't have a right to exist in my world."

"What do you do after you hurt them?"

"Get rid of them, of course."

"I mean how do you do that exactly? Put their bodies in a dumpster?"

"No, I bury them in my yard."

"Don't rotting carcasses create a smell problem?"

"I use lime."

"How has hurting dogs been a social problem for you?"

"Generally, it's not. But recently I attacked a dog in public and I was filmed doing it by some fucking bitch I'm going to get."

"If you know that people don't approve of your abusing animals, why did you choose to attack the dog in public, in front of others?"

"It was arrogantly walking by as if it owned the world and had the right to use the same sidewalk I used. I had to show it that it didn't."

"Why do you want to go after this person if you did this in public where others could view you?"

"Because she had no damned right to film me doing what I did."

"You know that if she hadn't caught you on film, other people or security cameras would likely have. There may be multiple films out there of your action. Keep in mind that everyone is being filmed everywhere all the time these days."

"Maybe. But she's the only one I saw. And she needs to be punished for it."

"I think you might want to reconsider retaliating against that person since you are on your way to becoming a professional problem-solving coach. It would be a real shame to risk tarnishing your new professional public status by assaulting or harassing her and getting the police involved."

"Yeah, maybe."

"Moreover, as your mentor, I strongly suggest when you have finished this course that you consider having a little therapeutic assistance with your desire to harm dogs, or any animal. It could help you be an even more successful coach."

"Well, I'll think about it when the time comes."

"Are there any other questions you have for me about the self-survey or anything else?" I asked, changing the subject.

"No, not at the moment."

"Okay, I also have a self-acceptance exercise for you to do. It picks up where the self-survey leaves off, showing you how to get beyond any negative feelings or judgments you may have about what you have revealed. It shows you how important it is to love and accept yourself irrespective of anything negative you have done. This is an exercise you can use with your clients for their benefit too."

20

When I finished with Moore, it was eight o'clock. I located my flashlight and Phoenix's leash and we went off for our evening walk. Just before we reached Rt. 550, I observed something thrashing about in the tall-weed area which was blanketed by the illumination from a high-mast street light near the intersection. As we drew closer, I saw it was a slenderly-built, long-legged coyote with intelligent golden-brown eyes, a narrow naked snout, and dark tail. It had something white in its mouth. At first, I thought it was another rabbit. It tossed it in the air then batted it with its padded paws. Seizing it again, it shook it in a frenzied manner. Then dropping it, it pounced on it. To my great surprise, it was Phoenix's cotton rope toy that I'd initialed. I hadn't seen Phoenix take it outside. I'd have to be sure to get him another one.

By observing the coyote's antics alone, if I hadn't known it wasn't a domestic canine, I wouldn't have been able to tell. The behavior wasn't wild or domestic, it was just dog-like. When the youngster became cognizant of our presence, it stiffened. Circumspectly, it glanced at us then quietly turned tail and trotted off. Its prize was still firmly lodged between its teeth.

Because so much of their territory had been encroached upon by humans, and so many of their prey animals had been purposely exterminated, coyote's choice pickings were slim. While they would eat snakes, fish, frogs, insects, fruit, and grass, ninety percent of their diet was mammalian, when they could find it. Consequently, they often came into town looking for food scraps, cats, rodents, rabbits, and small livestock. However, despite the purpose of their expedition, a frolicsome romp along the way was certainly not out of the question.

Back at the house after I worked on the next few e-mail lessons, I put that aside to plan a raised vegetable garden in the backyard. I'd talked with John who okayed my having one but he had suggested I put some kind of protective fencing around it before planting anything. Not only as protection from rabbits, deer, raccoons, and coyotes, but also from an exuberant Phoenix.

After examining vegetable catalogues online, I decided on having one plant of "Sweet 100" cherry tomatoes and one "Cherokee Purple," large, sweet, dusky-pink tomatoes with a deep red interior. For peppers there would be one plant of "Lunchbox," which were red, yellow, and orange, sweet, and crunchy for snacking, and one "Sweet Banana," which was perfect for using in a wok. I read everything carefully so as to bypass the medium-hot peppers like "Big Jim." My intestines couldn't tolerate their capsaicin inferno. In order to make ratatouille, which I loved, I also needed two eggplant, specifically the "Ichiban," which were long, slender purple fruit, and one zucchini. One Armenian cucumber, which was long, sweet, and light green, would be good for salads.

It was too late in the season to plant cold-weather kale, endive, or broccoli so I'd skip greens this year. For culinary herbs I chose basil, flat-leaf parsley, chives, and lemon thyme. And, maybe, marjoram and an upright rosemary because I loved their fragrance with or without their contribution to my recipes.

The next morning when I mentioned to Phoenix that he had another spa day, he lifted his cheeks in a grin, leaped about, and began doing a Gregory Hines tap dancing routine on the tiles at the front door. He was so excited I could barely snap his leash on his harness. But to get to the garage we had to go out through the house. Phoenix stubbornly disagreed. We always exited by way of the front door ... unless we were going to the vet. He was not interested in going to the vet, even on the off-chance he'd see his e-Harmony-matched poodle again.

Much to his vexation, I picked him up and shuffled to the garage. He looked at me with his ears back until, in the garage, I opened the car's right back door. He scampered in where I secured him in his safety rigging, opened his windows four inches, strapped myself in, hit the remote, and slid us out into the front yard. The door down, we were off, Phoenix making yodeling sounds as soft breezes streamed in to ruffle his fur. After a sunny greeting from the female attendants, he immediately located the Beagle with the yellow ball, and absconded again with its possession.

Over the next few days while Moore was at work, I collected everything I'd need to create a raised bed. Because I was uncomfortable with the chemicals which could be used to process pressure-treated lumber, I chose cedar instead. While it was more expensive, its natural oil would prevent rotting of the wood with no need of any additional preservation. Since my father had made a raised bed for flowers for my mother when I was a child, I knew I was only building a frame with no bottom or top—of course, I could always add a hinged-lid frame covered with translucent plastic wrap later to use the bed as a cold frame too. That way I could start growing greens, broccoli, and other plants early next year.

I had had to decide if I wanted the bed to be four feet by eight or four feet by twelve. Eight seemed more reasonable since most of the plants would be primarily upright except for the zucchini which would need a little additional space to spread its large leaves on their ten-inch stalks. That size would also fit better with the lay of the land.

With Phoenix tied on a long lead attached to one of the columns of the portale at the rear of the house I spread out everything I needed. First, I placed a weed barrier where the garden bed would be and then arranged the wood for the frame on it. This location would receive between six and eight hours of sun a day. After digging a two-inch trench into which to place the frame, I struggled to drive the stakes about two feet into the clay soil at each inside corner. As sweat poured from me, the stakes inched their way vertically into the concrete-like ground, taking longer than seemed reasonable for the project. John had lent me a battery-powered drill so I could use galvanized screws to secure the frame's boards to the stakes.

Of course, everything required Phoenix to inspect it with nose, paws, and gleefully switching tail. Before the bags of soil, sand, and compost entered the bed, his lead would have to be shortened. Otherwise, he would have had the distinct pleasure of mixing the components himself by gamboling like a spring lamb and digging in them. He looked eager to oblige. Having the bed twelve inches deep to give the plants' roots a chance to gain purchase required opening and pouring a multitude of forty-pound bags which seemingly took forever. Hauling them from the car and hoisting them into the bed did not please my back, despite all my body work at the gym and with karate. After this, access to a jacuzzi, which I didn't have even at the gym, would have been a plus.

It would take another trip to Santa Ana Garden Center to fill my vegetable plant list. But, before purchasing and planting them some sort of fence, likely of either chicken- or dog wire, would have to be in place. John undoubtedly had some good ideas about how to construct it and from what.

It was barely six o'clock when there was an e-mail from Moore. In it he stated, "You've criticized my first attempt at coaching. That's unfair."

Wrinkling my forehead, I stared at his words without a clue as to what he was referring. The last exercise he was to do was about the mechanics of coaching. It explained that problem-solving coaching relies primarily on asking questions to get the clients considering the problem from different aspects and scrutinizing it to get a better understanding of what it means to them. The exercise had asked him to address a client who said "he was unhappy with how his life was working out and couldn't decide whether to 'change jobs or get a divorce or whatever.'"

Moore answered, "Neither choice is all that great unless you know what you want. But, getting a divorce could relieve a lot of stress since women can get in the way of achieving your goals. So that might be a good way to start."

I had responded, "It's useful to first find out what the client means by 'being unhappy with how his life was working out.' Furthermore, it's then necessary to determine whether the client is really considering 'changing jobs or getting a divorce' or if he is just expressing his confusion or anxiety that way. This means you need to *ask questions* to get the client expressing thoughts and feelings. Sharing your opinions about women shifts the focus from him to you. The client needs to remain the focus of the coaching session and on the two of you in figuring out what the problem really is."

Apparently, my not accepting his response was unreasonable. "Clay, the exercise was about 'asking questions.' You needed to ask a question of the client to start off the session. Perhaps there was a misunderstanding of what the exercise required of you?"

"What if it's obvious what the problem is? Why go through all that drawn-out interrogation instead of immediately getting to the point?"

"What the problem appears to be to the coach may not be what it is or appears to be to the client. That's why you have to ask questions to get the client's take on it as it exists in their life. As a coach, you can't *know* what the client thinks, feels, and is going through until he or she tells you through their being asked the right questions."

"If you say so."

From there the lesson proceeded haltingly. Every other of my statements was met with comments which began to express challenges. It was a difficult two hours. At the end I gave him another exercise about getting clients to talk about their problem to more concretely describe it to the coach and how they felt about it. Also attached to that e-mail was an article that detailed several initial coaching sessions with the coach's questions and the client's answers since Moore didn't seem to have tumbled to how it was supposed to work.

While he was embroiled in putting himself into the world of problem-solving coaching, no more packages or threats appeared. As the days passed, I was feeling more confident that his stalking, vandalism, and harassment were likely becoming a thing of the past. What that meant was that maybe I didn't have to be constantly on the alert any longer.

Phoenix enjoyed another half-day at the doggy spa. But he probably could not get another appointment for about ten days unless there were a cancellation. I'd have to find something fun for him to do until then. While the spa activities were taking the edge off his boredom, I didn't want him to revert to it in the meantime.

Brad was recovering. When he called, he suggested a tour of the J&R Vintage Auto Museum nearby. I was fond of lovingly restored and maintained cars and trucks from the 1920s and 1930s. When he appeared, his skin looked like the outer surface of a buttered, overbaked croissant: greasy, cracking, and flaking. Phoenix met him at the door, ready to bark, until he saw it was Brad. Without further ado, he stuck his snout into Brad's pants pocket. Being an engineer, Brad anticipated this and was ready with a treat. Phoenix made a yowling sound in his throat as he blissfully did a two-step. Brad picked up his new cotton rope toy from the floor and they tugged on it for a few minutes. Then busy munching on the treats Brad deposited in his food bowl, Phoenix ignored our departure.

When we arrived at the museum, we discovered that after twenty-five years it had closed a few months earlier, in March. That was a disappointment for both of us. We turned around and drove to Placitas to have an early dinner at Blades' Bistro. Nestled in the inner corner of the small Homestead Village Shopping Center, this neighborhood restaurant, which surrounded diners with beautiful original artwork, was noted for its "Creative Casual Cuisine," a mix of European and American influence in a classical bistro setting. I had been there before for dinner and had the most delicious "Forest Soup," made from all kinds of fragrant mushrooms. That and a spinach salad was for me a to-die-for meal, even without their Chili Chocolate Pot, a spicy crème brulé dessert.

While Brad had calamari with aioli and blue cheese and a spinach salad with sliced pears, candied pecans, blue cheese, and a raspberry vinaigrette, I had the roasted fresh beets with goat cheese and a Caesar salad with smoked salmon. We shared. Both were tasty and satisfying. The "dessert" was Brad's explaining that he was expecting to be around and wanted us to get together, often, and again very soon. That was followed with a soft, body-juices-stimulating kiss.

Back at the house, I began to work on finding additional instruction sheets on the process of coaching which used lots of examples. Moore needed to adapt and accommodate to this new way of thinking and interacting. As soon as he could make it a habit, he'd be okay. How long that would take, however, was up to him. Hopefully, he'd have an aha! sooner than later.

At six o'clock there was no Moore. Six-thirty passed without note. At 7:15 his e-mail appeared with no explanation. There was no attachment for the completed assigned exercise due tonight.

Before I began asking how he had fared using the examples as guides, I wanted to address this lapse of professional etiquette. "Clay, I have been waiting for you since your assigned class time. The next time you find you're going to be late I would appreciate your letting me know."

"I'm paying for your time whether we're communicating or not."

"That being the case, you need to remember that if you miss a session or part of one, you can't make that up, so that it's your loss."

Ignoring that, he stated, "I have a problem with the way the coach is supposed to approach the client's problem. It seems to me to be going around the bush when he could get to the heart of the problem and solve it much more quickly."

Again? I thought. "Maybe it would be helpful if you thought about coaching like this. The client and his or her problem exist in a circle. The coach is on the outside of the client's circle. As a result, the coach doesn't know about the client or his or her problem. A coach can't assume he knows. To open the door to get inside the client's circle, the coach has to ask the right questions, questions about the problem and about the client. As the client answers the coach's questions, the coach learns what the client's life situation is and what the problem is in that situation. The door opens. Once the coach discovers that, he can help the client determine how to proceed to unlocking the door to the next inner circle."

"Why can't the coach just give the client the different possibilities and let the client choose?"

"Because the coach would be the one deciding what the possibilities are as the coach sees it and not necessarily as the client sees it. There may be other factors that the coach hasn't as yet uncovered that are important things to be considered."

"Actually, a coach can do this anyway he chooses. He doesn't have to follow these guidelines, precisely or otherwise."

"Granted, once a person becomes a professional coach, he or she potentially could do whatever but that wouldn't necessarily be what was expected by potential clients. Clients would more likely expect you to *help them* figure out the problem rather than you telling them what the problem and solutions are from your perspective."

"There's nothing wrong with giving them *my* perspective on their problem."

"No, but that's once you have helped them express what the problem really is from *their* perspective."

"So, what if I don't see this constant questioning as the best approach to a problem? Who's to say I'm wrong?"

"What are you telling me?"

"Just asking questions."

Frowning again, I finished what was left the lesson time, gave him some reading assignments, and two more exercises, asking that he attach his responses to the exercises to an e-mail *before* class next time. Something was amiss.

Phoenix walked over and put his head on my lap. I took a moment to scan my e-mail for any other communications. Phoenix left as I turned off the computer and returned to the office with his leash hanging from his mouth. Outside, he decorated the Siberian elm and began striding toward Sheriff Posse. I had to hurry to keep up. On the way back we went around the house to inspect the back and planting bed. Because John had been unavailable to help erect a fence, nothing further had been done yet.

"Oh, no!" I shouted when we arrived.

To my horror something had been digging, not just holes but prodigious holes, created with unfettered enthusiasm. The special soil mixture was spread like a black cotton blanket several feet from and surrounding the bed. It wasn't the burrowing of some rock squirrel. It was more like the Holland-Tunnel excavation accomplished by mega-mutant canids. A note to self: Check in the morning to see if this "construction engineer" had left me divot gifts as well. Animals' parasites were an unacceptable addition to my veggie's growth habitat. Then I retrieved a broom and dustpan to sweep up the mess. What a waste. If I saved it, perhaps it could be used elsewhere. Definitely not on the veggies.

Coaching instruction sessions had continually been marked by Moore's increasing absences and undone—or improperly done—exercises, things which I discussed at length with him to further help him understand what they were intended to do and why that was important. But it was to no avail. Today celebrated the fifteenth day of his two-month course. With all the inherent frustration it seemed so much longer than that. His practicum, which was six weeks away, would require him to apply what the *course had taught*, rather than what he had chosen to learn and to feed it back. He had to know the basics before he could go off on his own tangent.

Barbara had kindly volunteered to be Moore's "client" for the two-day, one hour each, phone coaching session. Her "problem" was whether or not to start a business. She'd use my burner phone so he couldn't trace her. I'd set them up on two three-person conference calls, with me listening, which would be recorded and then transcribed. I'd make comments and suggestions by e-mail after each session.

21

Approaching the second month, I was now starting to introduce the subject of marketing. This encompassed how to describe his service, its benefits, and why people with specific problems needed him and his coaching approach. What he provided would be education for the potential client. It would emphasize relationship-building. This month would also cover where to promote himself and how to gain visibility and credibility. This would be interspersed with the professional coaching issues, such as client permission, attraction, dual relationships, referrals, and what the profession deemed illegal or unethical activity. He would be taught how to create a website, how best to attract which media, the need to network online and off-, how to do it, and where.

Brad had begun calling more often. We had to schedule around my teaching sessions with Moore which was sometimes awkward. Brad didn't know whom I was instructing. After his interaction with Moore in the grocery store, he likely would not have understood. Moreover, I had no desire to explain what I was doing and why. Until I was finished with this course, my weekend days were tied up except for evenings.

While Moore and I had had scuffles over various coaching techniques and principles, we had major clashes over dual relationships, particularly dating or having sex with his coaching clients. While he "might" be able to coach friends, family members, or employees because coaching is not the same as counseling, there were some inherent problems in doing that. Specifically, he needed to consider such issues as the dynamics of an already-existing relationship, hidden agendas, and where the power and control lay in it. However, having a sexual relationship was not only considered unethical but also dangerous.

"What's the big deal? If we click, so what?"

"That's the rule because when you're providing a psychological or behavioral service, the client comes to you for your expertise and help because he or she is in need and vulnerable. You are in an influential position to prey upon that vulnerability. There's a power imbalance where you're the one in power."

"Come on. Get serious."

"You could be seen by the female and outsiders as persuading her that if she doesn't do what you want sexually, you won't help her. If anything goes wrong with the relationship, coaching or personal, you're the one responsible because you're the one in control."

"Wait a minute. You can't prohibit me from getting involved with some stone fox. It's none of your damned business or anyone else's."

"If you want to date or have sex with a client, follow up with her *after* she is no longer your client."

"That's not fucking acceptable. I'll do whatever I want."

"Yes, you obviously can but doing so will open you to all kinds of possible criminal or civil liability as well as criticism from fellow coaches and other professionals in the behavioral services. That kind of word always gets out. That wouldn't be good for your professional reputation. Your reputation is the basis of your practice and business."

He didn't respond.

Saturday morning Brad stopped by around 8 A.M. with a roll of chicken wire and recycled steel, high-strength, two-inch by three-inch by six-foot T-posts with metal anchor plates. After we had refilled the planting bed with new soil and amendments, we wrapped the unrolled four-foot-tall poultry netting around the supports which we had placed three feet away from the sides of the planting bed and secured with wire. After an hour, all that was left to do was add a wood-framed wire door at the short end of the fence near the portale. Until then, we wired the enclosure shut.

After a quick brunch, a kale salad with cranberries, walnuts, and smoked salmon, Brad left and I readied myself for Moore's call. I hadn't received any of his assignments for several days. Noon came and went. At one-fifteen he e-mailed me, arguing about networking.

"I can see that networking online with Twitter, LinkedIn, and Facebook could be useful to sell my coaching but it makes no sense to me to network offline. Going to dull networking events, being social with hopes of snagging a client, is not my idea of fun. Besides, you talk about me providing help first before I get anything in return. That sounds like shit. How do I know they'll return my 'good deed'? It sounds like a lot of work with no guarantees."

"Networking isn't about selling. It's about creating relationships which is what marketing is all about. As I've said, selling and marketing aren't the same thing. So, you don't go to these events to 'snag a client,' you go to make yourself visible and credible. This means it's not just about you but about you and the other individuals as a unit. You give and receive. They give and receive."

"Oh really?"

"Being helpful to the other person creates positive feelings of trust, which is the basis of marketing. You don't buy from someone unless you trust them to provide you with what you want. Depending upon what you want from them, they will provide you with some help, although not necessarily at that moment. Your goal is to make these other persons feel comfortable passing your name along because they see your service has value and they trust you."

"It sounds like a lot of work for an unspecified benefit. Why can't I just put ads online and in newspapers and magazines?"

This contentious talking about ads and relationships continued until I could segue into talking about websites. I re-iterated what I had already sent him on them then provided links to examples of simple but elegant sites that were shown to be effective in reaching and enrolling coaching clients."

"I'm not checking them out at this moment."

"That's fine. Feel free to do it at your leisure."

Before we ended the session, he also received links to professional website designers. His assignment was to decide on a name for his website then check with GoDaddy for the availability of that same-name domain. Next, he was to roughly construct the website. It was to be a draft of what his site would finally contain. Specifically, he had to detail all its components with his own—not copied—marketing language. Having done that, he had to explain what each component was designed to do from snaring the reader's attention all the way to getting the reader to respond in some way to his offer of service. We'd talk about creating a relevant e-mail name to go along with his site and developing an e-mail list next time.

Moore's draft website construction showed a complete lack of understanding of what each component was expected to do. We spent an entire weekday evening session revisiting the psychology of marketing and how each component of the website had to flow logically to the next. I had provided him with a schematic of what went where. All he had to do to structure his website was clearly delineate: What the potential client's problem was. Why it needed a solution. What was likely to happen if he or she didn't solve the problem. How a solution could make things so much better. Why he was the *one* to help them find that solution and apply it. Then call upon the potential client to show interest.

His assignment had been to take a premier example of a coaching website, from the ones I had provided, and explain what each sentence did and how it persuasively moved the reader along to involvement at the end. After this grueling project with Moore, I thought my canonization was in order: Saint Kiri.

Brad and I constructed the wood-frame door for the garden area then went to Santa Ana Garden Center to buy individual pots of veggies which we then planted together. Because the garden was being created in the middle of New Mexico's scorching growing season, with the sun's radiation desiccating almost any plant material other than cactus, we covered the planter with shade cloth for the hottest part of the day. Attached by twist-ems to the chicken wire fence at four points, one each per side, it could be removed totally or partially with ease. Phoenix on a short lead sat supervising us, warbling his suggestions and comments, from under the portale.

As I finished watering each plant thoroughly through the chicken wire, I turned the hose on Brad. Phoenix began barking, jumping, wanting to join the fun. Brad snatched the hose from me, and stuffed it down the back of my blouse. Then Phoenix began barking more loudly, sounding annoyed but unsure, as if he couldn't decide if what Brad was doing was attacking his personal human or playing. And if it was playing, why wasn't he invited to join in?

Inside, Brad gave him some more doggy treats from a sealed plastic bag he'd brought with him and we retired to the bedroom. Unfortunately, the door hadn't latched properly. After a few hard bumps, Phoenix bounded in. He knocked us both onto the bed, our soggy clothing still clinging to our bodies. He was cavorting about on the bed, ready to participate in the fun. To put him out or not to, that was the question. When I coaxed him toward the door, he thought it was part of the game. He jumped around in circles. When I raised my hand, he lowered the front of his body, elbows down, paws out, as if he were praying for me to throw something for him to chase. He shivered with religious anticipation.

However, when I grasped his harness and tried to lead him out, he stopped. As his ears drooped, he turned his head and displayed a look of sadness I had never witnessed before. It seemed to suggest a sense of rejection. I looked back at Brad. Raising my eyebrows, I put out my free left hand to the side, palm up, and shrugged.

Brad shook his head and chuckled, "When's his next spa appointment?"

I let go of Phoenix, scratched him under his chin, avoiding his healing wound, and replied, "I'll be sure to make it *soon.*"

It was time for Moore's session. There was a disputacious e-mail awaiting my arrival.

"This marketing stuff is more work than I thought it would be. I see the need to have a website. After all, I expect to see a website whenever I look up some service or product. But why should I create it from scratch? Why can't I copy another website and make a few changes, like pictures, and fit my coaching into it? That would be a whole lot simpler."

I responded, "If you intentionally copied most of another website, that would be illegal. You would be liable for copyright infringement of the website design."

"Big deal."

"What you need to do is figure out what you want on your website to look like, using examples from the ones I've shared with you and others you've found yourself. After you decide on your marketing message, you can have a website designer put it together for you. You don't need to do it all yourself but you do need to have the basics, like your marketing message, ready to be put in place."

"That sounds like a lot of unnecessary work."

"And don't forget about a having novel title that suggests what benefits you offer that will attract people. For example, 'Your Problems Don't Have to Immobilize You by Interfering with Your Job or Life.' That's very basic and needs to be personally enhanced."

"You were going to tell me more about the practicum that's coming up. How does it work?"

"In a minute. First, I want you to tell me what population you generally see your coaching service helping. For example, would you be solving problems regarding work and business or personal issues? Then, you need to decide what specific kinds of issues? For example, relationship? Or financial? You need to go for some specific type of problem and segment of the population so potential clients can more easily find you and identify what you do with their particular problem. You need to clearly define who constitutes your target client base."

"I don't see why I can't address *whatever* problems they have. If I target specific groups of clients, that reduces the number of people who will use my service. That sounds dumb to me."

"The problem with offering a general service to everyone is that it's a shotgun approach. It will be difficult for you to make yourself stand out from the crowd of problem-solving coaches, to get clients to *your* website and identify with *you*."

"I don't see it that way."

"That's your prerogative. As for your practicum, I have asked a friend who has never experienced coaching to be your client. She doesn't know anything about you except that you're my student. You'll speak with her about the problem she wants to solve. You'll coach her over the phone on two successive days, as if it were the first two sessions of her time with you. Under normal coaching circumstances, you wouldn't be doing two sessions in a row with clients. Once a week or every two weeks may be good, depending upon the problem, to allow the client time to process and work on what has occurred in each session."

"If she's cute and sexy, maybe I'll date her."

I thought, "Sure, sweetheart. Barbara would be thrilled, with a hearty 'Hi yo, Silver! Away!'"

The session finished up with more about how to market. He still needed to determine and plan how to reach his audience. We covered the myriad ways, such as through newspaper articles; teleseminars; webinars; seminars; being a guest on a podcast; televised, radio, or on-paper interviews; the long list went on. I tried to impress upon him that he couldn't rely solely on social media if he expected to present himself to a wider audience. His assignment was to write up his marketing plan draft and describe how he was going to implement it, using the list of media outlets. By the time he finished the course, he should be ready to hire a web designer, assuming he had actually done any of the exercises I had provided. That was something about which I had my doubts.

As the temperatures rose, Pet Paradise became even busier. Cancellations became non-existent. For

Phoenix, "spa-ing" would have to be an improvisation at the house. At Walmart an eight-foot by thirty-inch bright blue, yellow, and white children's inflatable pool caught my eye. I knew at first glance how he'd respond. Back at the house Phoenix was inside, standing at the backdoor screen, watching impatiently as I inflated the pool on the ground. When he spied my uncurling the hose, he began pawing at the door. But when the water squirted out of it in a heavy stream, he nearly burst through the dark aluminum mesh. Barking, he pushed and shoved the door, challenging its lock. As soon as the pool was three-quarters full, I opened the door. He shoved through, swinging the door back, sending me landing on my bottom on the brick patio. He made a beeline for his own personal spa. Once he was sloshing in the water, I righted myself and attached his leash to his harness.

He scooped up water with his nose and swished his head in it. Then he rolled onto his back, his legs peddling the air. Flopping on his right side, he pushed himself to circumnavigate the pool, his tail rotating like half-a-rudder. I threw a yellow rubber ball I'd purchased with the pool into the water to him. He looked startled then overjoyed. Suddenly he broke out in a canine song from "days of yore," drawn, no doubt, from when canines first trod upon the new land, which he rendered with a wobbly vibrato. When he finished, he looked at me like a child enraptured with its first ice cream cone. I smiled in return, nodding. We'd do this again.

That night's session started off badly. Moore hadn't e-mailed me his assignment. Ten minutes late, he e-mailed me he said hc wasn't pleased with the way things were going.

"I don't feel I'm any closer to becoming a coach than I was at the start. It all feels like bullshit. A waste of my time and money."

"It might have helped if you had handed in all the exercises and assignments you were given so we could have seen how you were doing. If there were problems, we could have addressed them then and there. However, what might still help is your doing them now. Then for the next few days we could go over them together, in detail, to assist you in regaining that ground."

"It was up to you, dear professor, to make sure I was getting it."

"That's what all the assignments, exercises, and readings were designed to do, provide feedback to both of us so we'd know what you had and *hadn't* gotten."

"I'll let you know." His e-mail responses stopped.

While the practicum taking place looked questionable, I decided to hold off on letting Barbara know. I still did have to determine how to evaluate Moore's participating in the course. Rave reviews were not in his future.

22

The next morning around six-thirty Phoenix was attacking the front door, barking. I looked out the window. My heart fell. Moore's truck was parked against the fence, once again partially obscured by the profusion of silver lace vine. Like the vines entangled on the fence, he was fighting for supremacy. I threw on my sweats, attached Phoenix's leash, opened the door. Phoenix exploded through the opening, teeth bared, screaming dog obscenities at Moore who was walking toward the side of the house. A large crowbar in one hand.

"Get the hell out of here before I sic Phoenix on you and call the police!" I shouted.

He stopped. And for a fraction of a second he looked unsure about what to do. Then he faced me directly, smiled, and sliced the thumb of his free hand across his throat. Phoenix and I began moving toward him. His smile seemed to slip. Then he raised the crowbar over his head, threw his shoulders back, and set his legs wide apart. He was readying himself for the attack. Yet his renewed smile began to sag imperceptibly. It was as if his formerly karate-dislocated knee reminded him that he wasn't against just a snarling dog. A shadow fell across his face and his smile evaporated.

Slowly, with the crowbar on high, he began to move sideways a step or two at a time toward his truck, then he stopped. Phoenix and I followed his lead and moved sideways while simultaneously edging closer. It was particularly at this moment I was glad I'd worked harder on my legs. Minutes clicked by in slow motion as if we were mimicking Neo's fight moves in *The Matrix*. Ten minutes had passed. Looking unsure, he took another two steps. My holding the determined bundle of canine rage at bay was threatening hints of cramping and burning my quads and calves, if it took much longer. This standoff minuet crept along as he continued to take his side steps.

As he reached his truck, still facing us, he removed his right hand from the crowbar to unlatch the door. The moment it was open, he dropped the weapon inside, and climbed in. His face was dark with fury. Engine roaring, as he turned the wheel to leave, he swerved his extended cab within four feet of me. However, he barely missed Phoenix's attack-poised front legs clawing the air. It was only much later that I could chuckle that he had reminded me of the almost-comically unhinged Jack Nicholson in Kubrick's *The Shining*, ax-splintering his way through the bedroom door, venomously calling to his wife, "Here's Johnny!"

I spent the day trying to collect all the assignments I'd given over the last month and three-quarters that Moore had not sent me or had only partially done. I'd be ready even if he weren't. Phoenix was having none of it.

He placed his front paws on the back of my computer chair to rub my head with his jaw, as he made a throaty ruffing sound. The moment I twisted my arm around the chair to pet him, he dropped on to all fours, ran for his cotton rope toy, and deposited it in my lap. His tail swatted the chair. When I didn't throw it immediately, he began to whine and make reversing half-circles. Looking at me to get my attention, he ran a few feet toward the living room. Then when I didn't do his bidding, he came back to whine some more. How frustrating it must have been to be without the words to communicate his precise desires. He was slowly learning how hard it could be to successfully train his human to obey his *every* wish.

Finally finished with Moore's exercises, I went out to do my six-mile run and get some time in at the gym and the dojo. My body felt slack and untoned even though I'd missed only a few days. Back home, just as I concluded my five-minute shower, Brad called to suggest a casual lunch at the Placitas Café, just around the corner from Blades' Bistro. I held the phone to Phoenix's ear and he pulled his jowls into a smile.

Phoenix wanted to join us but much to his disappointment we drove off without him. Surrounded by local art in many media on the café walls and floor, Brad had a portabella burger and iced coffee and I had a taco salad with grilled eggplant and iced tea. While it was a very pleasant repast, my mind kept wandering to tonight's session. Brad excused himself to talk the café's proprietor, John, and returned with a raw beef marrow bone for Phoenix. Brad knew how to please the dogs in his life. And he wasn't doing too badly with this human either.

As soon as we walked in the door, Phoenix's look of dispiritedness vanished. He excitedly followed his nose to the white plastic bag in Brad's hand. Pawing, he tried to grab it away but Brad held it fast until he could deposit it on the kitchen floor. Gleefully, Phoenix became engrossed in gnawing and shoving the meaty femur around the linoleum. If only, I hoped, he wouldn't try to bury it in the sofa cushions or bed.

Six o'clock was rapidly approaching. Given what had happened earlier in my yard, I wondered how Moore was going to be acting. Not that it really mattered. "Dr. Stoddard" was professionally ready for Moore irrespective of his mood and behavior. He signed in at 6 P.M.

"I looked at the assignments when you sent them and I think it would be a total waste of my time to go over them. You obviously have a different take on how I should answer them. I'm not here to please you by telling you what you want to hear. You do it your way and I'll do it mine."

"I've been presenting what you need to know and do in order to become a professional problem-solving coach, but if you don't wish to learn by following what I'm teaching, that's entirely up to you."

"Yes, it is up to me. I've also decided I don't want to spend the time to do the practicum. I think I'm ready. You wouldn't agree with how I'd do it anyway."

"You may be right. But you still have a few more days left in your course. We could continue to work on your marketing and your website. There's more we could cover that you might find useful."

"No. I'm done. Just send me my certificate for taking the course. If this course is supposed to be an example of what good professional education is like, I'm surprised you're still in business. You're a pathetic instructor. And don't expect me to give you a positive review for this pitiful course."

"That's fine."

There was a minute break between e-mails. Moore replied, "So, aren't you going to wish me success or even luck? No. That's exactly what I'd have expected. But I will be a success in spite of you. So long, Professor."

No other e-mails from him appeared. It was done, finally. I exhaled deeply as I slumped in my chair. A feeling of relief like a snow-melt mountain stream circulated throughout my body as I inhaled the invigorating smell of pines. I was free of this schedule. As I lay my head back on the chair, Phoenix walked over to lick my cheek. He had garbage breath from chewing on the bone. But that was okay in the larger scheme of things. In fact, everything was okay now that the course was over. I smiled broadly and said aloud, nodding with self-praise, "I did a good job, irrespective of what my so-called 'student' seemed to think."

It took a moment before excitement bubbled to the surface as I remembered what was before me now that Moore's participation was done: Getting my revenge plan into action. Suddenly, my Caped Crusader-self felt revitalized. I printed Moore's International University of Professional Coaching certificate, on which I stated only that he had attended the two-month training. There was nothing to suggest he had actually completed it, which they usually indicate. I signed the professor's name and slipped it with a label for Moore's address into a Priority Mail envelope for Harry to re-send. He'd supply the new Priority envelope. It was time to take that well-deserved break before starting afresh tomorrow. Phoenix was at the front door, waiting for me.

Early the next morning, after mailing Moore's certificate, I called Barbara to tell her that I wanted to make a direct transfer of a large donation, in Teddy's name, to her non-profit's account. I initially had wanted to write a check from my university's Wells Fargo's account to Barbara for $4,700. But I worried about anyone being able to see that the deposited check was from a local bank, even though it was through the university. I didn't want there to be any confusion or questions about it should anyone inquire.

After creating a super-special letter from "Dr. Stoddard" to CARMA and Barbara, I dropped by her animal shelter. I presented her with the "original" of the letter she would have received by mail as well as two copies of Moore's revelatory self-survey e-mail. One e-mail copy was to be presented to the police and the other kept for showing to the press, which would likely be requested.

"I'm going to create a press release about the letter. If reporters should ask, say very simply it was an out of the blue donation from Dr. Robert Stoddard. No, you had never met him so far as you know. He said he felt obligated to donate the money to rescued animals' care here because this was where Clayton Moore was perpetrating his serial animal abuse."

"How would he have known about me and CARMA?"

"In the letter he says he had read online about your no-kill, non-profit and what it had accomplished over the years. If they ask to see the letter, you can show it to them. However, if they ask you about the envelope, tell them you threw it away. They might ask only because the press release will state that Stoddard was 'killed' in Italy after sending you the note and donation."

Overcome by the transfer amount, she gave me a big hug. When told she didn't have to participate in Moore's practicum after all, she gave me another hug. I shared which Animal Control office to go to and to be sure to ask specifically for Officer Rodriguez. "Do not give it to a fat cop named 'Hardess.'" Grinning slyly, holding the papers to her bosom, she said would follow my directions to a T.

Back home I began writing a press release about the $4,700 windfall for the rescue organization for the *Albuquerque Journal*. It stated: *Dr. Robert Stoddard, PhD, formerly a Boston psychologist, educator, and coach and who had been killed in an auto accident in Milan, Italy, had contacted Barbara Bayer, of the Companion Animal Rescue and Medical Assistance (CARMA) in Corrales, before his death, to donate $4,700 for her animal rescue non-profit.*

In a touching note, he explained that Clayton Moore, of Bernalillo, whom he had instructed, had told him in e-mails that he was a serial animal abuser and had even assaulted a puppy in public at Albertson's in Rio Rancho—a case that had remained unsolved. The $4,700 was Moore's payment for an intensive coaching training course he took with Stoddard online. Stoddard, who was an animal lover and advocate, felt the money could be better used to rescue, treat, care for, and adopt out companion animals where Moore had performed his abuse.

With Stoddard's letter was a copy of an e-mail from Moore to him stating Moore's continuing animal abuse as well as his seeking revenge on a local woman who had filmed his attack at Albertson's. Stoddard asked Ms. Bayer to hand it over to the appropriate authorities.

Feeling vindicated, I mailed it anonymously to the *Journal,* with Barbara's phone number, and e-mailed a copy to Barbara.

When they would run it was an unknown. Reporters would most certainly contact Barbara first to check out Stoddard's letter and Moore's e-mail, to verify the validity of the press release information. If necessary, she could show them the transfer deposit in her bank account which would merely list the university account as having sent it. Maybe my "Animal Abuse Avenger" Superhero suit could be gotten out of mothballs. And maybe there was the slight scent of optimism in the air.

As I took my six-mile run then went to the gym and my karate practice, clouds seemed to be lifting, becoming whiter and fluffier, in a brilliant cerulean-tinged satin sky. Rodriguez would have all he needed to arrest Moore and get him convicted. I would no longer have a threatening stalker to agonize over.

Pulling into my garage, I could hear my cell phone ringing. I had inadvertently left it on the kitchen counter. The remote closed the garage door as I unlocked the kitchen door. Stumbling over a leaping Phoenix, I caught my phone on the fourth ring. It was Barbara.

"I took the e-mail to your Animal Control station and asked for Rodriguez but he wasn't there. The heavy-set guy, Hardess, the one you warned me about, said they didn't know when he'd be back or *if* he would be back. I asked who was taking over Rodriguez's case load. He said those cases were being spread around.

Then he demanded to know why I wanted to know. I didn't know what to do."

"What did you do?"

"I excused myself and left. I wanted to talk to you first."

My mind was reeling. "What you did sounds like the best thing to do for the moment. I don't trust Hardess. Maybe when the article comes out, the *real* police, or Animal Control people, will come by to question you too. They could see Moore's e-mail then. Thanks for trying."

"It's too bad about Rodriguez." She clicked off.

That meant that until the article was published, there was no likelihood of Moore being arrested. So much for my experiencing a panoply of bright blue skies, cobweb-like mare's tails cheerfully scudding across them, with gentle breezes caressing my face. I knew that once the article hit the public, things could change rapidly ... and radically. In the meantime, it was back to having to stay hypervigilant.

Just after I had lathered up in the shower, my cell phone rang again. Phoenix was barking at it. Hastily wrapping a towel around myself, I jogged into the kitchen, leaving a soapy, wet trail in my wake. No sooner had I answered than the caller clicked off. The ID said "Private." That was puzzling. Could it have been Carrie? If so, hopefully she'd call back. I had asked her not to leave any messages just in case Moore got hold of my phone. Perhaps there wasn't a problem, but only a positive update on her new life.

I carried the cell phone into the bathroom so I could finish showering. It wasn't until I was rinsing myself off that I did a palm face. I suddenly realized how stupid it had been to leave the phone in the kitchen. I had let my guard down. I had made a false assumption that all was well. There was no reason to believe that. My cell phone should have been with me when I was running, at the gym, at the dojo, and on my way home. It should be fully charged and on my person at all times.

Shaking my head at having been so careless, I knew not only that I was still possibly Moore's target but also that things would heat up once the article about him in the newspaper came out. He'd be enraged, beside himself. He'd come after me with a fury that was beyond imagination. And while there was no way he could know or even guess I had had something to do with it, he'd automatically project the blame onto me. I was the source of everything that had unjustifiably gone wrong in his world. Another slip up on my part could be lethal. And I hadn't contacted a lawyer yet for my "In case of my death" letter.

Under the portale, Phoenix received a complete brushing. Then with him on a short lead, I tended to my immature garden, devotedly checking for insect pests and any yellowing leaves for removal. As soon as I had watered the plants, I re-filled his pool. He stood up on his hind legs, barking with elation. The moment he was released, he dashed into the water. This time I had brought several bath towels to envelop him in when he finished before he rendered me soggy again. The moment the excess water was captured in the thick terry cloth, I ran fifteen feet from him so he could complete his toilette by spiral-air-drying his fur.

Since I hadn't let Brad know there were no more evening coaching lessons, he called at 8:15 P.M.

"How about that Caramel Frappuccino you promised me weeks ago?"

"Sounds good. Do you mind if I bring Phoenix?"

"Of course not. I'll be by in ten minutes."

Phoenix and I sat outside Starbucks on Rt. 550, just half a block east of Camino del Pueblo. We were at an umbrella-ed table enjoying the slight breeze as Brad used my Starbucks card inside. My now-dry dog was curled around my feet. He sounded as if he were humming his contentment. Brad was getting his *venti* brain freeze; I was getting a tall Caramel Macchiato; and Phoenix was getting a small dish of vanilla yoghurt without the nuts or fruit syrup. We talked for nearly an hour as Brad shared his current engineering projects and I detailed the coaching course I had designed. He was still in the dark about my Marvel Comics Animal Abuse Avenger plan and would remain so. I had no doubt he would have thought I was certifiable—at least a few bricks short of a load—if I had revealed it.

Even though we were feeling relaxed and comfortable as we approached my home, I suggested we all check out the house and property since Moore was occasionally dropping by to vandalize the house and terrorize me. There was nothing to suggest there was a problem. The front door and garage door looked untouched. Windows looked intact. There were no spray-painted warnings on the front and sides of the building. I felt all was well.

But as we turned the corner into the backyard, I gasped and clutched by throat. The chicken wire fence around the raised vegetable bed had been removed, stomped flat, and twisted into a Mobius strip. The young plants had been torn out of their bedding and literally ripped apart. Phoenix's pool had been slashed repeatedly with a knife. On the back door in red paint was the ominous ultimatum: "You're next!"

Brad shouted to the heavens/.

"Son of a bitch! We've got to do something about this bastard before he really hurts you."

"Like what? The police have my reports and pictures of what he has continued to do. They know he's assaulted me ... twice. The cop who was going to take over the case had an accident and isn't available. I don't hold out much hope for a guy named Hardess whom I saw first and who has been dismissive of my claims."

"Okay, we'll have to think of something else." He paused for a moment as he gazed at the destruction, his anger dissipating slightly. Then he shook his head and chuckled humorlessly, "And I was so looking forward to consuming the fruits of our garden labors."

"Yeah," I whispered, as I took in the carnage with tears beginning to stream down my cheeks. "Well, there go my mouthwatering salads ... and my French Provençal ratatouille." Brad put his arm around me.

Phoenix slipped his leash out of my hand to race to his pool where he tried to roll in the now-absent water. His ears back and his eyes open wide, he looked at me as if to ask what happened. Where was his special play pool? Before either of us touched the obliteration, I took several pictures of the planter, pool, and back door with my cell phone for the record.

23

With his jaw set, Brad began poking through the remnants of plants to see if anything were salvageable. What wasn't torn or cut to pieces was wilted with its roots dried out. He gathered them up and angrily shucked them into the garbage receptacle against the back of the house.

"Come stay with me until this is resolved. You can't stay here. It's too dangerous."

"Thanks, but that would be inconvenient for both of us. I have lots to do here to get ready for teaching late-summer classes. However, if you happen to know someone at the Rio Grande Zoo who would lend me a tranquilizer dart gun with a ballistic syringe capable of taking down an elephant, that could help."

"Very funny," Brad nearly chortled. "How about getting a body guard or some kind of security service?"

"To guard my body or the house?"

"Yeah, well, that's a good question. Even with the cameras here, you can't know if anything is going on at the house when you're away. And with Phoenix here alone ..." Brad stopped. He dropped his gaze as his face clouded over. "But, then again," he seemed to be musing out loud, "Moore has attacked you in your car, at UNM, and in Albertson's. What the hell does that mean? Two body guards?"

"Wait a second. We may be going about this the wrong way." Something was occurring to me. "Let's take another tack. What if we found some huge hunk of muscle to scare the crap out of Moore? In 1940's crime films dealing with this situation was easy. You hired some huge, flat-nosed types in ill-fitting suits to threatened jerks like Moore with the prospect of cement booties. Of course, that's not as impressive a threat here in the desert. Still... Do you happen to know any mountains of muscle who'd like to have a little fun pulling off such a masquerade?"

"Well, that's really funny you should ask because actually I do. There's an engineer at the Army Corps of Engineers who might fit the bill. He's huge and intimidating-looking. And he has regaled me with stories about his acting exploits. He might enjoy this new role."

"Tell me about him."

"JoJo's about 6'8" with bulging biceps and thighs, no fat, short black hair, a heavy brow, deep-set, laser-piercing ebony eyes, an aquiline nose, and a permanent five o'clock shadow-like beard. Something like the Hulk, except he has coffee-colored skin instead of green, he's overwhelming, even frightening, when you first encounter him. If you'd like, I'll talk with him. If he's interested, I'll introduce the two of you."

"Great. Go for it. As soon as possible, please."

Two days later, without any discoverable Moore-created mishaps in the interim, Brad brought us all together. JoJo looked like a shrink-wrapped super-pack of meanness about to burst its plastic skin until his face softened into an endearing, toothy smile. When he extended his seven-inch-width hand to me, my hand disappeared in his. Happily, his vice-like grip didn't break any of my hand bones but surely could have without any effort.

"So, I hear you're looking for an actor to play a heavy. That fits me, don't you think?" He glanced down over his massive presence. He laughed easily. "Too often I've been stuck with the 'gentle giant-type' roles. Being a heavy is so much more fun."

"You certainly look as if you can handle yourself and anyone else," I smiled. "Did Brad tell you what I need?" He nodded. "Well, let me go over it to fill in the details. I filmed this guy brutally attacking a puppy at Albertson's. He saw me and has come after me as a result. This psychopath stalks me, has assaulted me, and has tried to kill me by pushing my car into busy traffic on Paseo del Norte.

"I've reported him several times to the police—for all the individual attacks, vandalism, and his overall campaign of terror. Despite all the evidence I've provided, so far nothing of substance has been done. The other day when I wasn't home, he destroyed a vegetable garden Brad and I put in and sliced up my dog's pool. Long story short, he has repeatedly threatened to kill me." I paused to show him the cell phone picture. "What I need you to do is scare the bejesus out of him so he'll stop."

"Okay. What do you want me to say? Or do you want me to improvise?"

"You should say something like you heard about him from your shrink, Dr. Sumner—that's me—whom he's been terrorizing. That he's an animal abuser. You like animals and do *not* like animal abusers. She's been helping you learn impulse control because of your *murderously* violent temper.

"This is his final warning. If he continues to threaten or harm her, or if you hear about another animal attack, you'll 'squash him like the little stink bug that he is. You'll re-arrange his face and remove his balls so he won't be a pretty-boy, drugstore cowboy any longer.' Something along those lines. You get my drift."

JoJo began to laugh, a deep ebullient sound that resonated in his colossal chest before it exploded into the air.

"And he kills animals too? I love animals. What a son of a bitch bastard! I can't wait. This will really be fun. I haven't had a part like this in years. So where can I find this mother-fucker?"

I gave him Moore's home address and when he was likely to be there after work. "But if you think it would be more effective to do it at his place of work, he's an orderly at the UNM Neurosciences Clinic, generally there between 8 A.M. and 5 P.M. on weekdays. Doing it at his place of work would have the added benefit of doing in front of an audience where you can raise your voice so your threats can be overheard. Just not loud enough to bring on security personnel. By the way, if you could do it as soon as possible, that would be great."

JoJo wrapped his meaty arms around me, picking me up in the process, and nearly suffocated me against his giant washboard abs. That was that.

Two days later in the morning Brad called to inform me that JoJo had done the deed.

"Wow. That's great! You two decide when you're available and he can share his Oscar-nominated performance over dinner here. Any time, the sooner the better. Just give me enough notice so I get a few items at Albertson's."

"How about tonight? We were going to go out for a beer but would prefer to enjoy your company. Besides JoJo is eager to entertain you with his acting prowess."

"Works for me."

Albertson's didn't have any of their special seafood cakes—crab, salmon, and lobster—that I bought there whenever they had them and froze them for future use. Unfortunately, I hadn't replenished my stock of them lately. These were four-inch diameter cakes, chuck-full of large pieces of seafood, not mostly soggy bread someone had passed the seafood package over. The plan was to get three of each. JoJo no doubt was a big eater. When I asked the young woman behind the deli counter about where they were, she looked confused. She declared with a tone of misplaced authority, "We've never had those." After re-describing them in case I hadn't been clear, I gave up. There was no point in arguing. Carefully scrutinizing their glass-fronted cases one more time, disappointed, I drove to the Freight House to pick up dinner there.

During a dinner of a dozen of codfish tacos with roasted paprika aioli, avocado, red chili kimchi, and cotija with side salads and a quart of maple bourbon pecan ice cream for dessert, JoJo waxed poetic about how he caught Moore just as he was leaving the clinic and gave him the "full monty." His acting out the interaction was awe-inspiring and worthy of some kind of prestigious award. I laughed until tears ran down my chin and risked totally wetting my pants. JoJo needed a Marvel Superhero white suit and red cape, if only one could locate that much Spandex.

"Bravo!" I applauded. "I only wish I could have been hiding behind a shrub to witness it firsthand. If I could have contained my hilarity, that is. How did he take it?"

"You've heard of the British stiff upper lip. Well, he was trying hard but his upper lip was quivering too much to make it work. He reminded me of a calf unsuccessfully trying to grab hold of its mama's udder. The business about re-arranging his face and cutting off his balls just about did him in. He turned the color of a flounder's underbelly and sank toward the sidewalk as his knees gave way. I suspect he had to change his tighty-whities when he got home."

We all laughed heartily all over again.

We were in the kitchen when my burner cell phone rang. Before I could check it there was the detonation of shattered glass. With one crash after another the front windows exploded. Sharp shards and hard, brittle splinters sprayed the dining and living rooms. I looked for Phoenix. He had already concealed himself under the bedspread in my bedroom. Tiptoeing over the sparkling chips and slivers, I snatched the phone and looked at what the front camera was filming.

"It's Moore!" I shouted and ran for the front door with JoJo and Brad on my heels. Outside Moore was in the process of reloading his 12-gauge shotgun. Phoenix dashed out the door behind us. Snarling, he jumped on Moore, trying to tear out his throat, knocking him off balance. His left front paw was leaving red paw prints and a trail of blood all over Moore's Lone Ranger shirt. Brad seized the shotgun as JoJo tackled him. As I ran for Phoenix, I called the police about the domestic terrorist attack.

Ten minutes later two cruisers, flashing emergency lights and sirens wailing, arrived with cops with their guns drawn. As one put the cuffs on Moore, he talked with Brad and JoJo. The other surveyed the extensive damage. Walking the premises with him, I explained about the already existing reports, replete with photos and videos, I'd filed about Moore's assaults and terrorizing exploits. Furthermore, there were four of us total, including my landlord, John, who could and would testify as witnesses to his crimes over the last several months. He took our names. They hauled Moore into one of their vehicles and departed.

Before us was devastation. Glass particles littered everywhere, inside and out-. While I swept up and vacuumed the debris inside, Brad and JoJo went to Home Depot for measured sheets of plywood to screw in over the two large openings. I rolled up the Native American throw rug in the living room and took it out back to the patio to delicately slip it into a large garbage bag. It would have to be cleaned separately by professionals. Then I remembered Phoenix's paw.

When the police arrived, he had hobbled back into the bedroom. His foot was still bleeding. Between his pads was an embedded piece of glass. Before I used pliers to pull it out, I washed his paw with soap and warm water. Then I applied Neosporin to the resulting gash until I could take him to the emergency animal clinic in Albuquerque. Having his foot cocooned in gauze pads and adhesive tape kept his mouth busy and, hopefully, his mind off his foot's pain.

Brad and JoJo returned and screwed the sheets into place with John's drill which I hadn't as yet returned. I knew John would be oh-so delighted with something new to do for his rental.

JoJo stated grimly, "This is my fault. Apparently, I miscalculated. I thought I'd scared the little shit enough to leave you alone. I never expected reprisal. I should pay for the window replacement."

"No, no. This was my idea. Perhaps I should have known better. I can't let you pay for this."

Brad joined in. "How about we all chip in? I also was part of this game that didn't work out for whatever reason."

"I'll give it some thought. But first how about we finish our coffee now? I'll make a new pot. We can go around the back way to get to the kitchen."

"Sure," they responded together, "we can top off our cups."

JoJo added, "And if there's any more of that delicious ice cream?"

As soon as they left, I called the twenty-four/seven emergency clinic and took Phoenix down. After checking with a magnifier for other glass slivers or microscopic pieces, they re-cleaned his paw with antiseptic, re-bound it, and provided Clavamox. In order for him not to continue to gnaw at the bandage, he received a large Elizabethan collar. When his early burns were being attended to, he had been forced to wear an E-collar. This wouldn't have held pleasant memories for him.

Fortunately, his underjaw was sufficiently healed that the collar wouldn't abrade it. The moment he realized that it would interfere with everything he was going to try to do, from eating and drinking and playing to cuddling, he looked up at me with pleading eyes and began to whine softly.

The next morning as I was re-vacuuming all the floors and front stoop, and sweeping the immediate area of the yard into a dustpan, I saw yesterday's paper stuck in behind the left-hand terra cotta pot of lavender. A quick perusal of it suggested what had likely precipitated Moore's bombardment last night. There was my press release in an article with comments from Barbara, whose shelter was now $4,700 richer, and quotations from Moore's self-confession e-mail.

Moore was arrested, charged with several human and animal crimes, booked, and held. In his hearing he pleaded "not guilty" but wasn't released on bail. He was still a danger to me. Nobody mentioned his ongoing danger to animals which was also extreme. His trial occurred much sooner than anyone imagined, almost immediately, which was a first.

At his trial his jury constantly glared at him. Decked out in his western finery, with his metallic-toe boots, all of which was contrary to the suit and tie his lawyer had begged him to wear, he was viewed as the most arrogant and vilest of creatures, a serial animal abuser, who furthermore had graduated to going after people: The poor, innocent woman who tried to stop him from kicking the puppy, had filmed his actions, and reported him to the authorities. From my seat behind the prosecutor's table, I swear I detected triumphal smiles as the foreperson read the verdict: "Guilty." The jury silently nodded in unison, "Yeah, guilty as hell, you piece of excrement!"

The long-fought game of *Clue* was over. Everyone now knew that Colonel Mustard had done it in the conservatory with the lead pipe. Moore would have several years to think about becoming a problem-solving coach ... or even a drugstore cowboy again ... whenever he was released ... and wherever he decided to go. It wasn't likely to be Bernalillo or anywhere nearby.

24

It took days before the front windows were replaced. Brad and I reconstructed the fenced veggie garden. In another few days Phoenix could be released from his restrictive *Man in the Iron Mask*-like prison. By the time his foot had sufficiently healed, I had gotten him an appointment for a half-day at the doggy spa. Brad and I would take advantage of it.

Sadly, my dreams of being the one who would finally avenge the animal abusers of the world never came to fruition. It had been more wishful thinking ... and more damned hard work ... than I had wanted to believe.

But I *had* avenged Teddy. Maybe I'd evened the score a little.

Perhaps, after all, the current laborious method of trying to create awareness while slowly saving those that one could, and working on legislation and enforcement were the only realistic ways to go—no matter how agonizingly snail-like and frustrating they were. According to the Dalai Lama XIV, "If the goal is noble, whether or not it is realized within our lifetime is largely irrelevant. What we must do therefore is strive and persevere and never give up."

But still ... I really longed for a Marvel Superhero, a caped crusader and savior of animals in a white bodysuit, emblazoned with the golden "AAA" on the chest, with red cape unfurling patriotically in the breeze. Someone ready, willing, and able to work instant, universal animal-protection magic. I suspected JoJo would be perfect for that role.

ABOUT THE AUTHOR

Signe A. Dayhoff, PhD, MA, MEd, is a social psychologist who was graduated from Boston University with post-graduate training in counseling, emotional intelligence, and positive psychology. For thirty-six years she has been a cognitive-behaviorist, coach, and author, specializing in alleviating social anxiety and enhancing social effectiveness. An applied feline behaviorist and rescuer, she is "mom" to twenty-six senior, chronically ill, and disabled cats. She also writes and consults on human-cat relationships and the human-animal bond.

She has taught different areas of psychology at Boston University, University of Massachusetts, and Framingham State College and has done research at Massachusetts Institute of Technology, Scripps Clinic and Research Foundation, and Fairview State Hospital. She is author of eighteen books: twelve of which are self-help and five of which are cat memoirs. This current book is her first novel.

Her cat memoirs include:
- *What Faust the Dancing Cat Taught Me*
- *Faust the Dancing Cat Tackles Strippers, Scammers & Bears*
- *Faust the Dancing Cat Does Vegas*
- *Remarkable Tales of Cats Who Whisper to Humans*
- *How Intrepid the Disabled Kitten Triumphed to Help Others*

Check them out at
http://effectivenessplus.com/books